# NEVER CLOSER

## Margot Shepherd

Umbel Press

## UMBEL PRESS

Copyright © Margot Shepherd 2023

Margot Shepherd has asserted her right under the Copyright, Designs and Patents Act 1988. to be identified as the author of this work.

ISBN: 978 1 7395198 0 3
eISBN 978 1 7395198 1 0

Typeset in Baskerville by riverdesignbooks.com

For Sarah

# 1

# Jo

*5 November 2017*

She knows he isn't coming, but still a tiny thread of hope lingers. As soon as he uttered those words over breakfast – 'I'm going into work for an hour.' – Jo knew.

She wanted to say, 'But it's Sunday and we organised this trip weeks ago.' But she didn't. She just bit her lip.

'I'll meet you at the station,' Rob said, his eyes fixed firmly on a piece of buttered toast.

Jo paces up and down the platform, glances at her watch. A long goods train roars through, wheels rattling against the sleepers. She steps back as the air churns around her. Dust curls from the wagons like steam. She phones him. It rings and rings, then goes to answerphone. 'Where are you?' she says, annoyed with herself for persisting with the pretence. The 11.37 glides into the station, the doors open with a musical *tang-tang*. She hesitates for a moment; she's been looking forward to the exhibition at the British Museum for weeks. Why should she let him ruin it? She steps on board, pushing through a group of bickering teenage girls crowding the doorway. Bags and cases spill into the aisles, a rumble of chatter, the smell of perfume and deodorant mixed with body odour. She squeezes into a seat between a large man and a woman, neither of them making any attempt to give her more room. The doors close with a pneumatic hiss and the train jolts forward. Jo settles back. She loves trains, the *clickety-clack* of the wheels, that sense of moving forward, of going somewhere else. It's part of the excitement of a day out.

She watches the houses backing onto the railway line flit past, peering into the gardens, imagining their inhabitants. Perhaps a family with young children or an elderly couple who lovingly tend their small patch of land. The train stops at a signal beside a garden full of plastic toys: a small slide, a doll's house, a red scooter lying on its side. It didn't seem long ago that her house was cluttered with toys. With first Kate, and now Jessie at university it has become unbearably empty.

Her phone dings. A message from Rob: *Experiment with the fruit flies took longer than I thought.* Anger hums in her veins. She types a message: *Why do you always let me down?* Then deletes it. Instead, she folds the rage inside her body, puts her phone in her pocket and smooths the rayon crêpe of the dress Zoe had given her yesterday.

Still grieving for her mum, Jo had sought some comfort from her friend since none was forthcoming from Rob. Visiting Zoe's shop was like travelling back in time: the Utility wardrobe with open doors revealing a rack of 1940s' and 1950s' dresses, the shelves displaying handbags and gloves, the old wireless playing The Andrews Sisters singing 'Shoo Shoo Baby' on a low volume. The only clue to the shop's modernity was the veneered strip flooring and the ceiling lights gleaming on the clothes and furnishings.

Zoe had just had a windfall. She'd been contacted by a young woman who'd found boxes of vintage clothes when clearing her grandmother's house. Zoe had bought the lot. There were dresses and coats, shoes and hats. Proudly showing these to Jo, Zoe had removed a dry-cleaner's wrapper to reveal a red and grey dress with cap sleeves, buttons to the waist, and a gathered skirt.

'It's lovely.' Jo ran her fingers over the bodice. 'Early 1940s?'

'I think so. It would suit you.' Zoe held it in front of Jo. 'Why don't you try it on?'

Jo hesitated. If she tried it on, she would be tempted to buy it and then Rob would be annoyed. He hated her vintage clothes. But she didn't want to offend Zoe. At that moment, she decided, Zoe's friendship was more important. She slipped into the changing room and pulled the dress over her head. The rayon crêpe slid over her body. It was always the same when she wore vintage clothing – the feeling that she was slipping into someone else's skin, someone who exuded confidence. In front of the shop's full-length mirror, she half-turned to examine the back and smiled. It was a good fit except for the length. Just a little too long. Always her problem.

'It was clearly made for you,' Zoe said. 'It's yours.'

'I don't think I could afford it …'

'It's a gift.'

Jo frowned. It was too generous. The dress could have sold for £70 or more. 'Will you let me help in the shop today, as a thank you?'

By the end of the day, they had sorted through all the clothes and there was just one item left, wrapped in black tissue paper, at the bottom of a box. Jo had an immense feeling of well-being and calm. She wasn't sure if it was the shop, the dress or just being with Zoe. Maybe it was all of them: a magic combination. 'All these wonderful clothes. It feels like Christmas,' she said.

Zoe grinned. 'Do you want to unwrap the last item?'

Jo nodded. 'What do you think it is?'

'My guess, it's a handbag.'

Jo reached into the box, unwrapped the paper and revealed a brown lizard-skin handbag in almost perfect condition.

'Wow,' Zoe said. 'That's worth a lot. I feel guilty now. I should have paid the granddaughter more.'

The brass clip opened with a satisfying *click*. Inside, nestled in a tan suede lining, was an old exercise book. A corner had been torn off and there was crease down the middle. *Diary of Alice Lawrence, 1940–1942* was written in large letters across the centre. The pages were narrow-lined and the edges wrinkled as if at some point it had been carried in the rain. Jo flipped through it, intermittently reading a few sentences. The writing was small, the letters slanting to the right and words squashed together as if the writer had tried to fit as much as she could on a line. It was mostly written in faded, dark-blue ink with the occasional entry in pencil. 'Was the grandmother called Alice?'

'I don't think the granddaughter ever said. She told me she's very old – 95, I think, and now in a care home. I could tell she's extremely fond of her.'

'I would love to read this.'

'Take it. Tell me if it's interesting.'

Now Jo pulls the diary from her bag where it has been ever since she left Zoe's shop. She opens the first page.

### Wednesday, 18 December 1940

I've decided to keep a diary about my work as a technical assistant at the Dunn School of Pathology. I got the idea from Dr Heatley, my boss, who I often see writing his journal. Peter ridiculed me when I told him.

He's been annoying me since the moment I woke him up, urging him to get out of bed, get dressed, eat his breakfast. Mum had already left for the early shift at the Steel Press Factory. She expects me to make sure he goes to school because she worries he'll play truant. How fair is that when he's the lucky one? He gets to go to school and doesn't even like it. I left for work without him; he was going to make me late. But as I wheeled my bike from behind the privy into the alley, I heard the back door slam and he shouted for me to wait.

As we cycled, we heard the throaty growl of a Queen Mary transporter before we saw it lumbering towards us, the bed of the trailer laden with the burnt-out wreck of an aeroplane with a black cross on the fuselage. Peter of course punched the air: 'Another one down.' But I didn't feel any gladness. I could imagine the horror of it, the plane spiralling to the ground in a ball of flames. What would the pilot's last thoughts have been? Did he think of his family? Mum says I have too much imagination, because I read so many novels. But I think a bit more imagination would do Peter good. He says that when he's old enough, he'll join the RAF. I hope the war is over before he's 18. We might argue and get annoyed with each other, but I still love him and couldn't bear it, if he was killed.

After Peter turned off towards his school, I was overtaken by a truck of soldiers in their khaki uniforms, which made me think about Dad and whether he'll make it back to Oxford for Christmas Day.

I still want to pinch myself when I arrive for work, even though it's three weeks since I started. It's such a fine building, although its elegance is rather spoilt by the piles of sandbags around it. It looks like a house for the landed gentry rather than a building housing offices and laboratories.

My day started in the incubation room. Before I opened the door, I tied on my silk facemask and prepared myself for being enveloped in a blanket of heat. The room is heated to a temperature which is optimal for the growth of the mould, *penicillin notatum*, but not for the poor assistants who must spend hours emptying the vessels of their precious harvest. Dr Heatley made our facemasks from parachute silk on his landlady's sewing machine. He is the master of invention in the lab. There is nothing he can't do!

Every available space in the incubation room is filled with shelving, from floor to head height, stacked with an assortment of vessels: biscuit tins, bedpans and pie dishes, which have been growing the mould on a sugary broth for the last five days. Dr Heatley has been experimenting with different types of vessels, trying to find the best container for cultivating penicillin. He is having some special ceramic pots made, which will eventually replace all the tins and dishes.

I'm one of 6 technical assistants, all female, 16 or 17 years old. We do the same jobs. Most of it is mundane but it pays well: 15 shillings per week, which will increase to £1 after I've been working for a month. Ruth was working with me today. She knows all the gossip. 'I heard Dr Chain arguing with Professor Florey in the corridor earlier,' she said in a muffled voice. 'He was complaining about inadequate equipment. He resents the money that's been spent on Dr Heatley's pots, when he has such limited resources for his own work.'

It's so silly. They're both working on the same project. Dr Heatley works on generating penicillin. Dr Chain is trying to isolate the antibacterial element.

It's a strange job, growing mould, but I enjoy the friendship of the other girls and the feeling of a purpose, doing a job that might eventually cure sick people. When friends first asked me about my new job, I explained that I grow mould and harvest the substance it produces. But it didn't sound like I was contributing to the war effort. So now I say I'm working on a new drug that might cure gas gangrene. Peter keeps giving me pieces of bread encrusted with mould – 'As a donation to the lab'. The joke is wearing thin now, but I take it lightly. We need as much humour as we can muster when the news is so grim: another city bombed; another ship sunk. There never seems to be any good news.

Jo brushes the buttons on her dress with her fingertips. How strange to read the diary of the young woman who once wore it. She has a peculiar sensation as if she is being drawn into another life, while at the same time, she is a little uncomfortable. What would Alice think if she knew, when she wrote her diary, that seventy-seven years later a stranger would read it?

She phones Zoe who answers after two rings. 'I've just been reading the diary.'

'Is it interesting?'

'It's fascinating. Alice was one of the technicians involved in the development of penicillin.'

'Does that make her famous?'

'No, not at all. There were a number of them, all young women. The production of penicillin was clearly very laborious. They did all the donkey work.'

'Typical. They did all the hard work, and the men got all the glory.' Zoe pauses. 'Are you on the train?'

'Alone,' Jo says.

There's silence at the end of the phone. Finally Zoe says, 'You have a good time. And come and tell me all about it next week.'

The train is slowing to a halt, people are standing, pulling bags and cases from the overhead racks. The doors open and they crowd from the train. Jo steps onto the platform and is suddenly overwhelmed by a sense of foreboding; it hits her like a blow to her chest and she gasps for breath. Something is very wrong. Jessie? Kate? Rob? She needs to find somewhere quiet to phone them to set her mind at rest. The cavernous space of the main concourse is filled with a cacophony of sound: shouts and laughter, the Tannoy announcing the next departing train, a whistle blowing, a train rumbling onto a platform, brakes squealing. She navigates her way through the crowd; a man on his phone is so preoccupied that he heads straight towards her. She takes quick, evasive action and heads to the bookshop, an oasis of calm. With deep unease like a dark shadow circling, she pulls her phone out and glancing at the screen sees two missed calls from the same number and an answerphone message, all within the last few minutes. The area code is Oxford. Jessie? She knows immediately something terrible has happened.

She dials her answerphone. The message says, 'I'm calling from the John Radcliffe Hospital. We have you as the emergency contact for Jessica Collins. We need you to call us urgently.' Her hand trembles as she rings the number back and, as she waits for a response, she leans against a bookcase and thinks she's going to be sick.

Finally, someone answers.

# 2

# Alice

**24 December 1940**

As Alice wheels her bicycle to the Dunn's bicycle shed, a van swings into the car park, tyres crunching the snow. The driver door opens and Dr Heatley unfolds his thin body from the front seat. She remembers then that he was travelling to Stoke-on-Trent yesterday evening to collect his specially designed ceramic containers. He must have driven back overnight. He stretches. 'Good morning, Alice.'

Alice loves the way he speaks to her, as if she's someone important rather than being a lowly assistant. 'Good morning, sir.'

'Alice, please don't call me sir.'

'Sorry, s—' She just manages to stop herself from saying it. Her cheeks burn.

He laughs and she can't help smiling. He opens the back doors of the van and reveals several hundred vessels piled to the roof, packed with straw. 'Aren't they wonderful?' he says. 'Now we'll be able to produce enough penicillin to treat our first patient.' He rubs his hands together, as if he's just won a prize in the Pools.

His enthusiasm is catching and she nods in agreement. He has such belief in this project, and yet they still have to prove it works in humans. All they've managed to show so far is that it cures bacterial infections in mice.

Alice fetches a trolley and helps him unload as many pots as will fit. They are strange containers, like a cross between a bedpan and a shallow hot water bottle with a narrow spout. They look much more professional than the bizarre utensils they are currently using to culture the mould.

As soon as she enters the building her glasses steam up. It takes a moment for them to clear before she can wheel the trolley to the autoclave room for sterilisation. She tries to be careful, these vessels are precious, but no matter how slowly she walks they still clatter against each other.

A shout in a German accent from the end of the corridor startles her and she stops abruptly. 'Can you keep the noise down?' Dr Chain glares at her, his hair awry as if he has been running his hands through it in exasperation. Even his black moustache appears menacing. Alice stares back, determined not to let him think she's afraid. She waits for another outburst, but instead, he turns on his heel and clumps towards the stairs. He's known for being rather temperamental which everyone puts down to his European origins. She hasn't told her mum that Dr Chain is a German Jew. She will only go on about how he should be interned, and they will argue again. 'They are not our enemies,' Alice said to her in their last quarrel. 'They came here to escape the Nazis and then we lock them up.' Her mother's narrow-mindedness never stops being a huge disappointment.

She tries to move the vessels so they aren't touching and pushes the trolley forward again. But they still knock together and she is on edge, expecting another outburst. She breathes a sigh of relief when she's finally inside the autoclave room. Before unloading them, she runs to the laboratory to enlist more help. Megan and Ruth are at the bench preparing culture medium. Alice is out of breath, as she pants, 'Dr Heatley's here with the new pots.' They both look up surprised.

Ruth follows Alice out of the room. 'I can't believe he drove all night in that snow. I thought he'd stay in Stoke and travel back today.'

Alice unloads her trolley and makes her way back to the van. She meets Ruth and Megan coming towards her with full loads. 'Watch out for Dr Chain. He's not happy about the noise,' Alice says.

Ruth grimaces. 'It's just his way of objecting to the money that's been spent on these.'

Once all the pots are safely unloaded Alice goes to the incubation room. Her first job is to remove the broth from the containers so the penicillin can be isolated from it. She pushes a suction bulb onto a glass pipette and removes the lid on a biscuit tin revealing a fluffy green-and-blue blanket of mycelium floating on a bed of liquid. Gold droplets dot the surface. She squeezes the suction bulb and slips the pipette underneath the mould. As she slowly releases the pressure on the bulb, a yellow liquid fills the glass. She expels it into a one-gallon bottle and repeats this until all the liquid has been removed. It has always intrigued her that the fresh medium she fills the vessels with is colourless, but as the mould grows it secretes substances, including penicillin, turning it yellow. When she was first shown how to collect the culture medium, she asked Dr Heatley if penicillin was yellow. He said, 'The mould discharges lots of substances into the medium, not just penicillin. When we purify it, the colour disappears, as you will see.'

She works systematically, along one set of shelves, and when all the bottles are filled, she takes them out of the room.

It's so refreshing in the cool corridor, but the comfortable temperature doesn't last long because her destination is the cold room, where the bottles will be stored until the penicillin can be extracted. She unloads them as quickly as possible and is soon wishing she was back in the incubation room. Being too warm is preferable to the cold.

Her next job is to clear the shelves of all the old culture vessels. She had assumed they would be thrown away, but Dr Heatley is adamant that they may still be useful, so they too must be washed and sterilised before being stacked in the storage room. She has no idea where she will find space for them – it's already packed full of rubber piping, glass tubing and bottles of every shape and size, which may also have a purpose one day.

Once the new vessels are sterilised, she helps Ruth and Megan fill them with culture medium. They spray them with spores and stack them on the now-empty shelves and leave them to incubate. They will be ready to harvest when she returns from her three-day Christmas break, when the whole process of collecting the medium, sterilisation of the pots and reseeding with the spores will be repeated.

Everyone's mood is lighter than usual. Alice supposes it's partly because they are all looking forward to Christmas and have been told they can finish work early. But she suspects it's also because of Dr Heatley's optimism that these pots are going to make all the difference to the production of penicillin.

She finally finishes at five, only an hour earlier than the normal end of her working day. She finds Dr Heatley in the laboratory writing up his notebook.

'I'm leaving now. Have a good Christmas,' she says.

'It won't be different from any other day, Alice. I will be working as usual.'

She is surprised and a little sad for him. She had imagined he would be spending it with his family. But he doesn't seem unhappy. His work seems to be his life. And for a moment Alice envies him this: to have such a purpose.

As she leaves the building, the path to the bicycle shed sparkles with frost. The puddles are like glass. The sky is clear and, although she's grateful for the extra light, it's a sure invitation to the German bombers. But maybe they are all heading home for Christmas too.

On her cycle ride, all she can think about is whether her dad is back. Yesterday, after tea, her mum asked if she would put the Christmas decorations up. It felt a bit like tempting fate, and Alice said she would rather wait until her dad was home. For once her mum didn't argue, she just nodded. It was a rare moment of understanding between them.

Alice decides to assume her dad won't be back and then she won't be disappointed. But when she opens the back door, there he is sitting by the fire with a cup of tea, as if he'd never been away. 'There's my girl,' he says as he stands up and opens his arms. She runs to him and bursts into tears. 'You're making my shirt wet,' he says and laughs, but she can see his eyes are glistening.

She hangs her coat on a hook in the tiny space at the bottom of the stairs. Her mum calls, 'Tea's ready', and chivvies them all to sit down. The tiredness that had been surging through her mind and body on her journey home disappears. It's so lovely to have tea together, all of them sitting round the table.

'So what's it like? What sort of gun do you have? Do you have to practise bayoneting dummies?' Peter says, the questions he's been eager to ask tumbling out one after another.

'If you don't mind, Peter,' her dad says, 'I'd rather not talk about it. I just want to enjoy being home.'

Alice is glad because, like her dad, she wants to pretend for the next few days that there is no war. Peter looks disappointed. The war is all he ever wants to talk about.

'Are we going to your mother's house for dinner tomorrow?' her dad says, looking at Alice's mum.

'She's been preparing Christmas food all week,' her mum says.

Alice beams. 'It will be just like a normal Christmas.'

Her dad smiles at her. 'I've been thinking about your gran's food for days.' And Alice understands why. Despite the rations, her gran's house always seems to be one of plenty. Alice's Aunt Vivien still lives there and, as a teacher with a good wage, they don't have to penny-pinch like her mum does.

Alice sees the expression on her mum's face harden. She wants to say to her, 'Don't spoil it. Don't take what he said the wrong way.'

'It's because Gran doesn't work,' she says quickly. 'And because she has a garden full of fruit and vegetables which she can store for the winter, not just an apron of concrete like in our yard.' Her mum's face softens and Alice feels the tension seep away. She needs to savour the next few days, imprint them in her memory, because who knows what her world will look like in a year's time.

~

Three days later, Alice sits in bed and, despite wearing her coat, is still feeling cold. Even Peter has gone to bed, and he doesn't feel the cold like she does.

Her dad has gone and the house seems achingly empty without him. How she wishes he hadn't signed up, that he'd waited until he was called up. She had been bewildered when he told her. 'But why?' she asked.

'To do my duty,' he said.

Her mum was cross because he would earn even less than in in his job at the Cowley factory, building Tiger Moth planes. But when he was home for Christmas, she realised that the truth of it is, he wanted to escape. She thinks about her friend Margaret's parents and sees how contented they seem in each other's company. Margaret says there is barely ever a harsh word spoken. Before he joined up, her parents were arguing constantly. Not over Christmas though. There were no rows, but she could sense a distance between them.

There is a wedding photograph of them on the parlour mantlepiece, looking so happy. When did it go wrong between them? The photograph shows her mum was a very pretty woman with a tiny waist. Not anymore. Her hair is a frizz from too many cheap perms, she has lost her figure and she smokes so much her fingers are brown. She has become a sour woman. Perhaps that's why her parents don't dance anymore. She used to love watching them. They would push the sofa back in the parlour and turn on the wireless dance music. It's a long time since that happened. The last argument Alice remembers, was her mother complaining that her dad was always going to the pub. His retort was that she never wanted to go dancing or the cinema and he had to get his fun somewhere.

She rubs her hands together to warm them and reads what she has just written in her diary.

### Sunday, 29 December 1940

We were a quiet family this evening. Dad's departure has left us all unsettled. For the few days he was home we pretended there was no war. We didn't even listen to the news. Every day with him was precious.

But reality hit home today. Mum is back at work, but Peter and I went with Dad to the station. On the newspaper stand outside the station entrance the headlines were grim. London had been bombed yet again. The station was packed with servicemen, the air was thick with fog and smoke. And that's how my brain felt – befuddled. I knew it wouldn't help Dad if I cried. But it was so hard to keep my feelings in check. We were surrounded by men saying farewell to their loved ones for what might be the last time. Peter's face was white, and I could see he was struggling as much as I was. Dad shook his hand and told him to look after Mum and me. Peter nodded but said nothing, as if speaking would unleash his tears. Dad hugged me tight and said, 'I'm so proud of what you're doing', then turned and boarded the train without a backward glance. We looked for him in the carriage, but it was a sea of men in that strange dim blue light they use for blackout. Peter took hold of my hand as we left the station. It was if the clock had turned back six years and it was such a comfort. He was completely lost in his thoughts and then, as if he suddenly realised what he'd done, he withdrew it.

Ever since she left the station Alice has held herself together, as if she's wearing a coat that is too tight. Finally, the stitching gives way and she starts to cry gentle tears at first, which gradually escalate into great heaving sobs. She buries her head in her pillow to muffle the sound. The last thing she needs is her mother saying, 'Pull yourself together, girl.' She considers such emotion a weakness. But Alice releases the barricade which has held back the thought she has been trying to suppress – she might never see her dad again.

# 3

# Jo

*5 November 2017*

In the taxi, Jo's breathing is ragged. She feels numb. There are no tears. She can't get a grip on her thoughts, which keep sliding away from her as her mind imagines the scene at the hospital. What if it's too late when she arrives? What if …? Don't think about it. Think about what needs to be done. She picks up her phone and dials Rob's number. It goes to answerphone, and she leaves a message. 'Rob, Jessie has suspected meningitis. The John Radcliffe Hospital phoned me and told me to get there as soon as I can. She's desperately ill. Please come as soon as you get this. I'm on my way there now.'

As soon as she ends the call she worries about him driving. Thank goodness she doesn't have to drive; she wouldn't cope with the stress of it. But then if she was driving, at least she would have to concentrate, instead of allowing all these terrible images of Jessie to spin through her head.

She phones Kate, pleading mentally that she will answer. It rings three times and when she hears her voice, Jo manages to splutter, 'Jessie's in hospital,' before tears pour down her face. It takes her several minutes before she manages to explain coherently what has happened.

'I'll get the next train,' Kate says. 'I don't know how long it will take. Four hours probably. I'm sure it'll be okay, Mum. She's in good hands. It's a very good hospital.'

*Ever positive, always optimistic Kate*, Jo thinks.

Jo can see the taxi driver eyeing her in his rear-view mirror. He will be listening and she hates that she's been airing all her personal information to a stranger.

She watches the streets flash by and every time they stop at traffic lights or are stuck at a junction, she wants to swear at the other drivers, to scream with frustration. Once they're on the M40 the journey becomes familiar. It was only a month ago that she was driving Jessie to Oxford, the backseat down, the car brimming with boxes and cases, shoes and coats stuffed into every crevice, her duvet and pillows squashed to their tiniest size. When Jessie had shown her everything she was taking, Jo was sure it would never fit in her car. But she had filled every nook, unpacking and repacking to make it all fit. Just when she thought she'd finished, Jessie appeared with her guitar, bought for her sixteenth birthday, played for about six months and then abandoned like many of her fads. Jo knew it would sit in the corner of her college room gathering dust and would never be touched. But she just raised her eyebrows, sighed with frustration and didn't say a word because she knew Jessie was nervous and the slightest knock would result in an explosion.

Rob kept out of the way and left her to it. Since there was only room for two in the car, he was not coming with them. She always packed the car now. She had taken over the job from him years ago. When he did it, he took hours; everything had to fit neatly together as if he was doing a jigsaw puzzle and when of course it never did, he would begin their journey in a foul temper.

Jo feels sick again and is so thirsty her tongue is sticking to the roof of her mouth. She finds her water bottle in her bag and guzzles down half of it. She asks the driver if he can lower the window a little. Cool air blows on her face and eases her nausea. She pushes herself into the corner of the seat and allows herself to think about Jessie's illness.

She'd been meticulous about her children's vaccinations; she liked to think she was an informed parent and knew all the benefits outweighed the risks. Both had the meningitis vaccine as teenagers, and she was relieved it had been available. She was well aware it was a high-risk time when people moved away from their homes to new environments where they were exposed to bacteria and viruses. If Jessie had meningitis, then it was most likely to be viral and viral meningitis was less life-threatening than the bacterial form. But the nurse she'd spoken to had said Jessie was extremely ill and she should get to the hospital as soon as possible.

The taxi swings into the dropping-off point for visitors. Jo's hands shake as she pays the driver. Once she's outside the vehicle she freezes. Moving forward seems to be the hardest thing she's ever done. There are a multitude of signs, but none say 'ICU'. She turns to the reception desk but there is a long queue. 'Oh no,' she says turning away. 'Where is it?'

A man with a hospital name badge asks, 'Are you okay. Can I help?'

She swallows and forces back her tears. 'The Adult ICU?' she manages to say. He walks part of the way with her, then shows her the signs to look for. She follows them through a labyrinth of corridors. In her hurry she takes a wrong turning and her heart pounds. She runs back, retracing her steps to find the right route until at last, she arrives at the closed doors of the ICU. A sign by the door instructs her to turn off her phone and to *Please use the hand sanitiser.*

She powers off her mobile, squirts antibacterial gel onto her hands then presses the bell. The intercom crackles to life. She explains who she is, and the door swings open. The intensive care unit is exactly as she'd imagined it on her journey from all the films and TV dramas she's seen. At the nurses' station she explains again that she is Jessie's mother and one of the nurses stands. 'I'll show you where she is.' She leads her to a single side room with a large glass window. Jessie is lying so still, like those marble effigies in churches.

The nurse is speaking but her words are like a distant background noise. Jo turns to her. 'I'm sorry, what did you say?'

'As a precaution, you have to wear a surgical mask. In case she's still infectious.' The nurse points to a box of masks on the wall by the door. 'Once she's had antibiotics for twenty-four hours you won't need to wear one anymore.'

Jo thanks her, then pushes the door open.

Jessie is hooked up to two drips and a ventilator and is surrounded by monitors. Everything in the room seems to be blue. There are blue curtains, blue flooring, even a blue blanket on the bed. As she steps across the floor tiles the sheer effort of getting herself to Jessie's bedside is like walking through thigh-deep water.

A nurse in royal-blue scrubs, apron and gloves, as well as a mask, is adjusting the drip. He turns when he sees Jo. 'You must be Jessie's mother,' he says in an Irish brogue.

Jo nods. She wishes she could see his face properly to read in his expression what Jessie's chances are.

She wants to take her daughter's hand, feel the warmth of it, but she must be satisfied with sitting beside her. She takes a deep breath. Jessie is alive. There is hope. 'Hello, my lovely,' she says and wonders if Jessie can hear her.

As if he has just read Jo's mind, the nurse says, 'She's sedated.'

Jessie has painted her nails dark pink, to match the streaks in her hair. She has experimented with lots of colours in the last year, but this dusky pink is her favourite. Her hair looks matted and greasy, and Jo wants to brush it away from her face, rest her hand on her forehead, an action she must have performed hundreds of times when she was feverish as a child.

'How's she doing?' she says. 'Has it been confirmed yet?'

The nurse hesitates.

'That it's meningitis,' Jo says.

'We don't know yet if the cause is viral or bacterial, but the severity suggests bacterial. We've started her on antibiotics. That's routine in these cases. If it's bacterial, she has the best chance if they're started immediately.'

'I don't understand. She's had all the vaccinations.'

The nurse turns away to check the drip again.

'What are her chances of recovery?'

'I'll get the doctor.' The nurse walks out of the room, his rubber clogs flapping against his feet.

Jo slumps into a vinyl upholstered armchair beside the bed. As a mother her instinct is to care for Jessie. But how can she help her? She has to relinquish her role and leave it to the medics now. Maybe Jessie can hear her, maybe speaking to her is something she can do. So she talks to her about anything that comes into her frazzled mind: her frantic journey, seeing Zoe yesterday, her new dress.

'Mrs Collins?'

Jo looks up startled. The doctor is standing at the end of the bed, young, bespectacled, a stethoscope around her neck. No white coat, no mask. She rearranges her serious face to a solicitous smile that says it all. 'I understand you've been asking the nurse about Jessie's prognosis.'

Jo stands and walks towards her. She wants to be able see her eyes clearly, to understand whether she's telling her the truth.

'I'll be completely frank. She's not responding as well as we hoped to the antibiotic, which is not a good sign. Antibiotic resistance is a growing problem in meningococcal meningitis. We've just started her on a different antibiotic, but it's too early to say whether she's responding better.' She pushes her glasses up her nose. 'The nurse said that Jessie had had the meningitis vaccinations. Unfortunately, it doesn't cover all strains of bacterial meningitis. It doesn't cover meningitis B which is more common in very young children. But teenagers can get it as well.'

Jo's mind is racing. Should she have known this? Is this something a good parent would know about? She remembers reading something about babies getting a new meningitis vaccination. 'Are babies vaccinated against it?'

'It was introduced in 2015.'

'So why only babies; why not teenagers?'

'I think eventually they will be vaccinated as well.'

Jo wants to shout. Eventually? That's no good. Why wasn't it available for Jessie? She scratches the red patch of eczema on her hand, then hides it quickly behind her back.

'Are you on your own?' the doctor says.

'My husband is on his way.'

'Good,' she says. 'We'll keep you informed and if there's anything you want to ask, don't hesitate.' She looks as if she's going to say more but instead she turns and leaves the room.

Jo collapses into the chair. Antibiotic resistance doesn't

sound good. 'Did you hear that, Jessie? You have to fight this. You've never let anything beat you.' Tears gather in her eyes. No, she won't cry, she has to be strong. She inhales deeply, her breathing jerky, her heart racing.

She searches in her bag for her phone to check if there are any messages from Rob. Then remembers she's turned it off. She'll have to leave the unit if she wants to check it and she knows she can't leave Jessie now. She has a mother's irrational fear that if she's not by Jessie's side, she will deteriorate. 'Hurry up, Rob,' she says out loud, 'I need you.' She can't cope with this alone.

The Irish nurse appears again in the doorway. 'Would you like a cup of tea?' he says. Jo could hug him.

'I would love one, thank you. I'm really thirsty.'

'It's the adrenaline,' he says.

He reappears minutes later at the door and signals to her to come into the corridor. He hands her a green cup of dark-brown tea. 'There's a room for visitors with a kitchenette,' he says. 'Just turn right and you'll see it ahead of you. The toilets are next to it.'

'Thank you,' Jo says.

The tea is very strong and sweet. She drinks it quickly. The nurse hovers beside her and takes the empty cup. Once Jo's back by Jessie's bedside she scrutinises the monitors and the bed chart, trying to read whether Jessie has a future: oxygen levels stable, heart rate 130, temperature 40 degrees. They don't look good. She remembers all the times she watched Jessie sleeping when she was a child, peering into her room to check all was well before she went to bed. Curled in a foetal position, thumb in her mouth with her other hand clutching the velveteen ear of her beloved Dumpy. And all through her childhood, her teenage years, she was hurtling towards this, like the lines written about her life coming to a full stop. Is this what the Fates decided after her birth? Was this how long they'd made her thread of existence?

The ventilator wheezes, the monitor beeps, in the corridor trolley wheels rumble and voices murmur. She sits, stunned, her brain unable to face this new reality. The waiting is hard. She should be used to it though: waiting for fractious baby Jessie to fall asleep, waiting up when teenage Jessie was out for the evening, unable to sleep until she knew she was safely home. Worrying when she was late. Always worrying about her safety. But that's the bargain Jo had made when she became a parent. In return for all the precious moments she must live with fear. A fear that she'd tried to ignore, to hope the gods were on her side. Then one day, they're weren't.

She sees Rob in the corridor with a nurse, putting on his mask. At last, there might be some reprieve from her pain. He could at least share it. 'Oh, Rob,' she says standing and when he wraps his arms around her, she clings to him.

He turns to Jessie. 'My poor girl,' he says. Jo hopes Jessie can hear because she would be amused by his words. 'Hey, Dad, are you feeling okay?' she would say. But Jessie can't hear, may never hear anything they say again. Jo releases a sob and Rob holds her tighter. He is crying quiet tears, which must be pooling in his mask, like hers. He releases Jo, reaches into his pocket for a tissue and wipes his eyes. 'What have they told you?'

She relays to Rob as best she can what the doctor said. There is fear in his eyes, and the confusion that she must have exhibited when the doctor explained the prognosis. A nurse with ginger hair, who she hasn't seen before, bustles in pushing a small stainless-steel trolley rattling with tubes, syringes and swabs, followed closely by a different doctor with the sleeves of his shirt rolled up to above the elbow.

'We're going to do a lumbar puncture,' the nurse says. 'To confirm the infection is bacterial. Would you mind leaving the room? Relatives often find this distressing to watch.'

Jo can sense that Rob is about to argue so she takes his arm and steers him through the door. She removes her mask and throws it in the clinical waste bin. 'When was the last time you had a drink?'

'Hours ago. As soon as I saw your message. I ran to the car and just drove.'

Jo follows the nurse's direction to the visitors' room. She's grateful for the chance to do something useful, even if it's only making Rob a hot drink. There's a sofa and two chairs, a sink and small worktop at one end and beneath the work-top, a fridge. The room smells of body odour and coffee. A middle-aged woman and man are seated on the sofa; the man is asleep. The woman looks shattered; her skin reminds Jo of plants that have been kept in the dark. She has deep purple shadows under eyes which are bewildered, as if she can't believe what is happening. The two chairs are occupied by teenage boys, the couple's children, she assumes.

Jo fills the kettle and removes a mug from the drainer. It's stained brown and she's tempted to rewash it, but the woman might have washed it and she doesn't want to offend her. She spoons instant coffee from a jar and looks in the fridge for some milk. There is none.

'Sorry, love,' the woman says. 'I used the last of it.'

'Black is fine,' Rob says.

A bag of sugar spills a trail of crystals along the worktop.

Although Rob doesn't take sugar, he looks like he needs some energy, so she stirs in a spoonful.

'Here,' one of the boys says to them standing up from his chair, 'You look like you need this more than me.'

'Thank you,' Jo says. 'You sit down,' she says to Rob and once he's settled, she hands him the cup of coffee then perches on the arm. She thinks about Kate on the train. All those people staring as she tries to hold her tears in check. It is already one-thirty. Hopefully she'll be here soon. She stands, unable to relax. She needs to be back in the room by Jessie's side.

'I'm going to see if they've finished,' she says. Rob looks crushed, his body sags in the middle and he slouches forward.

She rushes back to Jessie's room. The medics are just leaving. More solicitous smiles. 'How long before you get the results?' she asks the red-haired nurse.

'We get some within a few hours but the full results take forty-eight hours,' she says.

Jo must look aghast because the nurse puts her freckled hand on her arm. 'It doesn't make any difference to the treatment. It just helps if we can confirm it.'

Jo puts on another mask and slips into the chair by Jessie's side. She's lying in a slightly different position and her gown is bunched up on one side. At least she didn't have to feel the pain of the lumbar puncture.

Rob appears in the doorway. His colour has returned but he still looks dazed. *That must be what I look like*, she thinks. *As if I've slipped into a horrible dream. In a moment I'm going to wake up and none of this will be true.*

He drops into the armchair on the opposite side of the bed. 'Anything from Kate?'

'I can't turn on my phone to check.'

'I'll call her. I expect she's frantic too.' He pulls his phone out of his pocket and she watches his disappearing back. He was never any help when Kate and Jessie were ill, always avoiding the sick room. She aches to talk to her mum, to hear her calming voice. Grief rears up and hits her like a gut-punch. Oh, Mum, how can I do this without you? You were the one person I could always rely on to give me support.

Half an hour later and he's still not back. What is he doing? She needs the toilet and can't delay going until he returns. Anxiety is crushing her bladder. In the bathroom she catches sight of herself in the mirror: her face bloodless, her hair awry. She grips the edge of the sink feeling unsteady. Black spots smudge her vision. Her heart hammers in her ears. The ICU staff have enough to deal with, they don't need her unconscious on the bathroom floor to add to their workload. She focuses on her breathing and her heart slows.

When she returns to Jessie's room, Rob is back. 'Kate will be here in half an hour,' he says. 'Her friend Daisy is driving her.'

'Thank goodness for that. I couldn't bear the thought of her on the train. I'm afraid I got a taxi. I couldn't think what else to do. It cost rather a lot.'

'It doesn't matter,' Rob says. 'All that matters is that Jessie gets better.' He flops back into the chair, his long legs sprawling untidily across the floor.

But now Jo finds she's worrying about Kate hurtling down the motorway towards them. Images of Daisy's car weaving in out of lorries and white vans, Daisy's foot hard on the accelerator. She wishes she didn't know now. Surely the gods couldn't do that to her.

Kate's arrival is heralded by the red-haired nurse, who reminds her that only two people at a time should be by Jessie's bedside. The nurse is so apologetic about this that Jo can only say, 'I understand.' Kate is outside the room, face blotched red. Jo holds her. It is such a comfort to have her here, safe. 'You go in. Where's Daisy?'

'She's parking the car. She dropped me at the entrance. I just wanted to be here as soon as I could be. It seemed to take forever.'

Jo watches through the window as Rob stands and hugs her. Jo can hear them murmuring, but has no idea what they are saying. She glances at her watch. It's taken Kate less than three hours to drive from York. What speed were they were doing? She shudders and as she glances down the corridor, she sees Daisy hurrying towards her. 'Jo, I'm so sorry.'

'Thank you, for driving Kate.'

Daisy shrugs her shoulders as if to say, 'What else would I do?'

Jo shows her where the kitchenette is so she can make a drink.

'When did you last eat?' Daisy says. Jo can't imagine eating anything. She looks at her watch. It's mid-afternoon.

'Breakfast, I suppose.'

'I'll get a selection of sandwiches and stuff,' Daisy says.

Jo hovers outside Jessie's room, hoping Rob will come out and she can go back in. A senior nurse appears beside her. 'I'm sorry we have to be restrictive on visitors,' she says.

'But as it's a single room, it's okay for you to go in as well.'

Kate is talking to Jessie, telling her about the journey from York and how worried she is about her. Like Jo, she needs to communicate with her, even though she's sedated. 'Do you remember when you fell off the swing in the park? There was so much blood, I thought you were going to die. And I thought Mum was never going to forgive me if anything happened to you. Because I was supposed to be looking after you. But you were fine. And you're going to be fine this time too.'

Kate and Jessie hadn't been close as teenagers. They'd had to establish themselves as separate identities, separate from their parents, separate from each other. That need was especially strong in Jessie. But there was a bond cemented in childhood that would always be there.

When Daisy arrives back, she waves through the corridor window and shows them a bulging carrier bag. As if to try to tempt them, she pulls out, one by one, packs of sandwiches, bags of crisps, chocolate bars and bottles of juice. Rob stands and leaves the room. Kate hesitates, but Jo encourages her to go and eat. She will stay.

Ten minutes later Kate is back. She rests her hand lightly on Jo's shoulder. 'You must eat too. To keep your strength up.' Kate pauses. 'Daisy is leaving shortly.'

Jo is not in the least bit hungry, but she will try to keep Kate happy and show her appreciation to Daisy. In the visitors' room, Daisy is washing some dirty mugs. 'The sandwiches and drinks are in the fridge,' she says. Jo takes a bite of an egg sandwich. But it's like eating cardboard. Daisy offers her a bottle of orange juice and that at least tastes sweet. She gives up on the sandwich and puts it back in the fridge, hoping Daisy isn't offended.

In Jessie's room she collapses back into the chair and watches her daughter, searching for some positive sign, however tiny, that she is winning the battle against her unseen enemy. When Rob returns, he walks over to the window and stares at the darkening sky. His phone rings. 'I must have forgotten to turn it off,' he says looking at the screen. 'It's my Ph.D. student,' he murmurs and leaves the room.

It's late evening, she's tired and a dragging ache threads through her stomach. She rubs her hand across it trying to relieve the tension and remembers when her skin stretched and her belly swelled, her hands cradling the weight of it: Kate had arrived early, but not Jessie. Her due date came and went, but Jessie held on, stubborn even then, determined not to be evicted from her watery world. Jo barely slept at night, unable to find a comfortable position and from the endless trips to the bathroom. The gynaecologist had placed a cold stethoscope on her swollen belly. 'Baby's a bit too comfortable in there,' she said. 'All sounds healthy, but for your sake we might try a bit of encouragement in a week's time, if she's still holding on.'

But even that threat had no effect. Jessie remained and grew some more. Jo walked and walked, despite the discomfort, to encourage her child to be born. But Jessie always did things her way, hated to be told what to do, fought against the boundaries in a way Kate never had.

'She's a fighter,' she says, not realising she had spoken out loud until the Irish nurse writing notes on the bed chart replied: 'She is.'

# 4

# Alice

The laboratory hums with quiet chatter. All the technical assistants and technicians have gathered to hear Dr Heatley's announcement. Alice guesses what he's going to say: she's heard the rumours. He strides into the room and the babble subsides. The smile on his face reveals his message is good news. Alice listens, eyes focused on him.

'I thought you would all like to hear that Professor Florey has started treating our first patient,' he says. 'He's a policeman: PC Alexander. He was scratched by a rose thorn in his garden and the wound became septic. The bacteria spread to his eyes and scalp. His left eye was so badly infected it had to be removed.'

Alice grimaces. No-one speaks.

'Then his lungs and shoulder became infected. The bacteria were slowly destroying his organs and he was in great pain.' He pauses and swallows. A shadow crosses his face. 'He was oozing pus.'

*Poor man*, Alice thinks.

Dr Heatley continues. 'Yesterday he was started on penicillin – an injection every three hours.'

'Is it working?' George, the chief technician shouts out. This is what they all want to know.

Dr Heatley nods. 'Today, within twenty-four hours of

being treated, he's much better. His scalp has stopped discharging pus, his temperature is down and his appetite has returned.'

Alice feels a surge of excitement. This is what all their work has been for. Are they on the cusp of something momentous? She watches Dr Heatley. 'All our—' He falters. He is normally so calm and cool. It is as if he's struggling to contain his elation. He's always believed penicillin has the potential to be a life-saver and at last he has his proof. He stares beyond them all to the back of the laboratory. 'All our hard work has finally paid off,' he says. As soon as he stops talking everyone else starts and the noise level rises and rises.

He claps his hands and waits until the chattering gradually quietens. 'I know you're all excited, but I need you to get back to work. We need to make a lot more penicillin.'

Slowly the group disperses. Things have moved rapidly since Dr Heatley's ceramic pots arrived. As he predicted they have increased the production of penicillin and two weeks ago, Professor Florey decided they had enough to start testing in humans. There had been a discussion about people in the laboratory volunteering to test its safety. Dr Heatley said they could test it on him. Alice was horrified, but he said, 'Someone has to be the first.' But Professor Florey said he couldn't risk it. It could do permanent damage and he would never forgive himself. He wondered if perhaps they could test it on someone who didn't have long to live and with that thought he had set off for the Infirmary to find a suitable volunteer.

She heard later that a lady dying of cancer had volunteered to have the first dose of penicillin. Professor Florey said she was glad to do something that might help save people's lives. Alice hoped God recognised what an amazing sacrifice she was making. She found it hard to concentrate all day; there was less chatter than normal, and she could see that everyone was on tenterhooks like her, hoping the penicillin injection didn't cause this lady any more pain than she was already in. Later that day the professor came back rather disgruntled because within two hours the lady had developed a fever. She recovered quickly, but it meant that either the batch of penicillin or the distilled water that had been used to dissolve the penicillin powder contained some contaminants.

Dr Heatley spent the next day purifying it and when they injected her again there were no side effects. Professor Florey said he was confident that penicillin was not toxic to humans, at least in small doses, and the next step was to find a patient with a bacterial infection unresponsive to any other drug. This was the real test. Would it cure people? And now it seems the question has been answered.

Alice wanders back to the bench where, before the announcement, she was weighing out penicillin into glass vials.

As Alice pushes a rubber bung into a vial, Dr Heatley pulls up a bench stool and sits beside her.

'Did you cycle today?' he says.

Alice puts down her spatula. 'I did.'

'I wonder if you could run an errand for me. Do you remember me telling you that Dr Chain has shown that penicillin given to mice can be found intact in their urine?'

'Yes,' Alice says, wondering what this has to do with cycling to work.

'Professor Florey asked the nursing staff looking after PC Alexander to collect all his urine. We want to extract the penicillin from it. We can't afford to waste any. Every bit is precious. Can you cycle to the John Radcliffe Infirmary, pick up a bottle of what he produced overnight and bring it back to the laboratory?'

Alice wonders what she can use to cover it. What will people think if they see a bottle of urine sloshing about in her bicycle basket?

But Dr Heatley has already thought about this. 'Don't worry. It will be disguised in a brown paper bag.'

'Do you want me to go now?' Alice says.

'You can leave what you're doing. Megan will finish this job. I would like you to help me with the extraction apparatus when you return.'

The cycle ride is just what she needs. She's been feeling disgruntled all morning. Dr Heatley's news lifted her mood for a moment, but as soon as she sat at the bench the black cloud returned. Yesterday evening, desperate to get away from her mother's constant sniping, Alice had gone to Margaret's house, a short walk from Alice's home. They had talked about everything from film stars to wireless shows and their favourite music.

'I love Bing Crosby and Frank Sinatra,' Margaret said. 'They're both dreamy.' They were lying on their fronts, on Margaret's bed, with their heads propped up on their hands.

'I heard an American band on the wireless last week. Glenn Miller and his orchestra,' Alice said. 'I've never heard anything quite like it. My feet were tapping and my body was swaying. Let's go to a dance, Margaret. It would be such fun.'

'I'll have to ask my parents. I think they will say I should wait until I've finished my exams. Can you wait that long?'

'I suppose so. Show me what you're learning.'

Margaret clambered off the bed and took her shorthand textbook from her desk. Alice stared at all the lines and loops, circles and hooks. The strange squiggles represented consonants and vowels and some whole words: a dot on the line meant 'the' and a dot above the line meant a hard 'a'.

'It's like another language,' Alice said.

'It's a challenge but I have to learn if I'm going to be a secretary.'

*I'm sure I could learn it, if I was given a chance*, Alice thought. She bowed her head and said quietly, 'You're so lucky to be able to go to college.'

A spark of anger was ignited: her envy of Margaret attending college, her anger with her parents for taking her out of school, then at her Aunt Vivien for persuading her she could be a teacher like her, giving her a dream that was unrealistic. She was even cross with her dad for not winning the battle with her mum, for being too soft and wanting an easy life. The teachers were probably glad to see her gone. One teacher put on her school report, 'Alice needs to learn to listen and not ask too many questions'.

By the time she reaches the Infirmary her temper has cooled. As she has never been to the Infirmary before, her focus is on following Dr Heatley's directions to the ward where PC Alexander is being cared for. Alice explains her mission to a nurse, who bustles off to find the sister. As Alice waits, she admires the nurses in their uniforms with their starched caps and aprons, scurrying from one bed to another. The ward smells of a strange mix of disinfectant and the scent of flowers brought in by patients' relatives. She loves that it is so ordered that the floors are squeaky-clean and the beds neat and tidy. She's just picturing herself in the uniform when the sister arrives with a large bottle in a brown paper bag.

~

Back at the Dunn, she takes her precious cargo to the cold room, as Dr Heatley instructed, then tells him it's been safely delivered.

'Thank you, Alice,' he says. 'I must do some repairs to the extraction system before I can isolate the penicillin from it. Could you help me now?'

This system is a very precious piece of equipment, which Dr Heatley fashioned out of glass tubes, pumps, gallon bottles and copper cooling coils. It means working in the cold room, where all the extractions take place. But this is more than compensated for by having Dr Heatley for company. Some of the tubing has become blocked and she helps him take it apart to clean.

Her work is routine, but if she tries to learn something new every day, it keeps her day interesting.

'Do you mind if I ask some questions?'

'Of course not.'

'Why does mould make something that kills bacteria?'

'It's a defence mechanism,' he says. 'Moulds are just trying to survive. Like we are. So when they're invaded by bacteria, they produce a chemical which destroys the bacteria. It's a kind of chemical warfare.'

Alice had assumed it was just chance that the mould happened to produce something that killed bacteria. But it makes perfect sense now.

'Will penicillin cure all bacterial infections?'

'We're growing many different types of bacteria in Petri dishes and testing them with penicillin to answer that question. I'll show you when we've finished this job.'

When they stop for a dinner break, he shows her a Petri dish streaked with thousands of white dots of the diphtheria bacillus. In the centre there is a symmetrical island of clear agar, where a drop of penicillin has destroyed all the surrounding bacteria.

'How does penicillin kill them?'

'If you look at the plate under the microscope, you can see it destroys the bacterial cell wall. I think that the reason it doesn't kill some types of bacteria is because they have much tougher cell walls.'

'So you need a different way to kill them?'

'Yes,' he replies. 'And in time I think we will find other chemicals that work, perhaps from different moulds.'

He pauses. 'Alice, I'm pleased you want to understand what you're doing. It will make you a better technician. But I don't have time to answer any more questions. If you can be patient, I will find the time later.'

But Alice is puzzled and she can't wait. 'Why doesn't penicillin damage the cells in the patients who are treated with it?'

He places a glass cover over the dish and lays it on the bench. 'Because bacteria have rigid walls, which have a very different composition to those of the cells in our bodies.'

Alice stares at her feet. A hot flush rises from her chest. She's sure if she'd stayed on at school, she would have known that.

Dr Heatley is quiet for a moment then says, 'Shall I lend you a book about bacteria?'

During the tea break the topic of conversation is inevitably about Dr Heatley's momentous announcement. That they are working on a powerful new drug has dawned on everyone. Before, it had just been a hope. Now, it's a reality.

'What will you do if the Germans invade?' Ruth says to Dr Heatley. 'We wouldn't want our discovery to fall into enemy hands.'

'I think we should carry razor blades to slash our wrists,' George says

Alice shakes her head. She doesn't believe he would do it. It's all talk. Male bravado. 'I couldn't do it,' she says. 'I'm not brave enough.'

'What if you knew you were going to die anyway?' Megan says.

'Perhaps,' Alice says. 'But I don't think you can ever really know if you have enough courage until you're faced with that situation.'

Dr Heatley has been listening but not passing comment. 'We would have to destroy all our work,' he says. 'But we wouldn't want to lose the strain of mould, *penicillin notatum*, as it would be key to starting production of penicillin again, once it was safe to do so.'

'How could we hide it from the Germans?' Alice says.

'Ah,' he says. 'We could rub spores of the mould into our coats, which could lie dormant for years.'

'That's ingenious!' Alice can't help smiling at the image of them all covering their coats in mould.


At the end of her working day when Alice is about to go home Megan tells her Dr Heatley wants to see her in his office. She thought he'd forgotten their earlier conversation.

He's sitting at his desk when Alice enters. He picks up a

small maroon hardback, scuffed and a little faded. She notices the title in gold lettering on the spine: *Microbiology applied to Nursing*. He opens it at the Contents page and points to two chapters on bacteria. 'Read these. I think they'll help you. I'm sure there will be some things you don't understand, and I don't mind if you want to ask more questions.'

'When would you like it back?' she says.

'You can keep it,' he says.

'Thank you,' she says. How kind the man is. How generous. Alice is sure it's not one of his books. It's far too basic. He has clearly gone to some trouble to find a book that is the right level for her. She is more in awe of him than ever. As she walks to the cycle shed, she decides she will read the whole book and show Dr Heatley she is not stupid.

As her mum is working a late shift, Alice cycles to her gran's house for tea. The house is only two streets away from home and Alice usually visits several times each week. Peter is already there when she arrives.

Two days ago, they'd had a big argument and they aren't speaking. She discovered he'd been reading her diary. She keeps it in an old biscuit tin under her bed with a few other precious items: her old teddy bear, now very threadbare; a hair ribbon that she wore for Maypole dancing; a few photos of Peter and her as children; and birthday cards that are too beautiful to discard. Everything is in a very precise order. So when she opened the tin and found everything in the wrong place, she knew why. He denied it, but she could see from his face he was lying. She's always been able to read his thoughts. Sharing a bedroom and sometimes a bed when they were younger must have engendered a connection between their two brains.

It bothers Alice that they continually rub each other up the wrong way when they used to be inseparable. In the Infants and the Juniors, they always walked to and from school together. She watched out for him in the playground, not because her mum drummed it into her that as his big sister she had to take care of him, but because she loved him. Alice had learned to stand up for herself at school and other kids soon learned they would have her to contend with if they hurt her little brother.

Her relationship with Peter changed when she went to senior school, and he had to fend for himself. She'd never forget leaving the house for her first day. Peter looked bereft, as if she'd deliberately deserted him. For the next few days without her to protect him, he came home from school covered in bruises. Her mum wanted to speak to his teacher, but her dad said it was time he fended for himself. She'd made him too soft. All the softness soon disappeared. That was when the bond between them changed. It was like a guillotine came down and sliced the cord that bound them. They stopped laughing together. Now he laughs *at* her instead.

It was made worse by the bedroom divider. When Peter and Alice shared the room, they would often whisper to each other in bed until they fell asleep. Knowing he was only a few feet away gave her a feeling of blissful contentment and there were times when he would climb into her bed, and they slept curled together. She doesn't remember if it was her mum or dad who decided it was no longer appropriate for them to share, but remembers her dad putting up the wooden divider that cut the room and the only window in half. She likes her privacy now, but she also likes that she can hear Peter shuffling about on the other side of the thin wall.

Alice and Peter always seem to get on when they are at their gran's house, so she's hoping he'll apologise for reading her diary and they can at least be on speaking terms again. The house is always spotless and there's a quietness about it as if the old-fashioned heavy furniture and the smell of polish somehow relaxes them. Or maybe it's the old clock in the hall, which ticks quietly in the background chiming every hour. The rhythm of it must get into her blood and calm her. It is always a place of refuge when the atmosphere at home is poisonous.

At the tea table, she talks through her day with her gran and Aunt Vivien. When she tells them all the questions she'd asked Dr Heatley, Gran laughs. 'When you were a child, you used to drive your mother mad. You were always asking "Why?"'

'You needed to learn,' Vivien says. Her aunt had taught her to read before she went to school, borrowing books from the infant school where she teaches. When Alice got stuck on a word, she had to wait until her dad came home from work to tell her what it said. Her mum was always too busy. She remembers being so greedy for words that once she tried to read his newspaper before he'd read it and he was furious with the crumpled mess she'd made of it. She was forbidden then to touch it, but still she would try to grab a page before it was rolled up into firelighters or torn into squares for the privy. She read any words she could find, on the back of cereal packets, on tin labels ...

Vivien rests her elbows on the table. 'I knew I had to try to persuade the headmaster to take you early.' Alice has heard this story many times. Auntie Vivien loves telling it and Alice loves hearing it.

Peter groans and Alice kicks him under the table. 'Ow,' he says loudly and Gran frowns at Alice.

'The headmaster had *The Times* on his desk,' Vivienne says. 'He picked it up and asked you what words you recognised, expecting you to read a few simple ones. Instead, you read out loud the first paragraph of the main article.' Her aunt always imitates his look of amazement at this point, eyes wide, mouth open. Alice thinks she exaggerates, but she had started school a few weeks later. She remembers the pleasure she'd felt at her desperate need to learn being finally fulfilled.

'Your behaviour at home improved dramatically,' Vivien says.

'You were the naughty one,' Peter says, trying to look adorable. 'Not like me. I was an angel.' Vivien and Gran laugh. But Alice doesn't. Peter is just repeating her mother's words: how Peter looked like an angel with his blonde hair and blue eyes, how he barely cried as a baby, whereas Alice was difficult, always having tantrums when she couldn't get her own way.

'Well, that's changed,' she says. 'I don't read other people's diaries, unlike you.'

Peter coloured and the tablecloth suddenly seemed very interesting. Vivien looked at him quizzically. 'Is this true?'

Peter pushes a pile of crumbs into a neat pile. 'I'm sorry.'

It was all Alice wanted him to say. And she forgives him because she hates to have a rift between them. She breaks the silence that descends on the room by producing the book that Dr Heatley has given her and showing them the chapters she's going to read.

While the book is passed round the table and examined, Alice thinks about how once there were no books in her house, except for a bible which her mum kept locked away. But now there is a row of books on her bedroom bookshelf. Some are school prizes, but most are gifts from Vivien. Alice has read them so many times they are dog-eared and their pages are falling out. They're like old friends. Her favourite used to be *The Secret Garden*, but then *The Mill on the Floss* took its place, perhaps because she identifies with Maggie Tulliver. But she doesn't like the ending, so she's made up her own whereby Maggie and Tom live happily ever after. Now she has another book to treasure.

# 5

# JO

Jo wakes to the sound of a clattering metal trolley, followed by the squeak of shoes on the linoleum. For a moment she isn't sure where she is and then reality hits like a blast of cold air. Her heart rate quickens as she scrutinises Jessie for any change. She is still surrounded by beeping machines and blinking lights, cannulas snaking out of both arms to the intravenous drips. But the bed chart reports her temperature has come down to 37.4 degrees; the monitor shows her heart rate is 80, oxygen levels are good. These are positive signs. Her anxiety level drops a notch.

It's still dark outside. She stares at the clock and is surprised that she has slept for nearly five hours. Kate is slumped sideways in the chair on the other side of the bed, her long hair veiling her face. Jo stands and stretches. Her neck aches and she has pins and needles in one arm. She leans over to Jessie and holds her hand. It's warm, but there is no response, no flexing of the fingers.

'Good morning,' she says quietly, not wanting to disturb Kate, but needing to communicate with Jessie. 'We're still here, willing you to get better. We're not going anywhere.' She wonders what time Rob will arrive. He found a B&B to check in to on the first night. He needed a bolt hole. Somewhere he could have a shower and crash out when the need took him. But Jo and Kate have remained by Jessie's side for the last three nights. If Rob appears in Jessie's room, his visits are fleeting. When the doctor appears, he never seems to be around, so she absorbs whatever news she is given, alone or with Kate.

A chair creaks and she glances across the bed. Kate is awake and has that look of concern which has been a regular feature since she was a small child. She remembers 3-year-old Kate putting her arm round a distressed child of the same age at playgroup and being quite astonished that one so young could be compassionate. 'You okay, Mum?' she says.

'Yes. Apart from some aches and pains. I'm going to get a coffee. Do you want one?'

Kate shakes her head. 'I'll get something later.'

The kitchenette is empty and Jo is relieved she doesn't have to make conversation with other worried relatives. She tips three teaspoons of instant into a mug and pours on the boiling water. Someone has put a new carton of milk in the fridge. These little things are what she needs now to help smooth her day.

She returns to Jessie's room to find Kate slumped sideways again, snoring lightly. It's a sign of just how tired they are that they can sleep in these uncomfortable chairs. For the first time she senses a change in Jessie; the doctor was more optimistic yesterday evening, but Jo could tell she didn't want to raise their expectations. She won't sleep anymore. Perhaps she can manage to read Alice's diary in the night-time lighting. Alice's work with penicillin has flitted through her mind several times in the last few days. Thanks to Florey, Heatley and Chain, and the girls like Alice, Jessie has a chance to recover from her infection.

**Saturday, 22 February 1941**

PC Alexander's condition has stabilised, but we have no more penicillin to give him, so we are all hoping that he has turned a corner and will continue to improve. The small amount of penicillin we have managed to produce over the last week has been reserved for Arthur Jones, a 15-year-old, who developed septicaemia following an operation to put a pin in his femur. He's the same age as Peter and that made me think how distraught I would be if it was Peter that was ill. We have enough penicillin to treat him for five days. Will it be enough?

No news from Dad. Mum says that no news is good news. They tell you soon enough when there is bad.

**Friday, 28 February 1941**

Arthur Jones seems to have recovered. Not so PC Alexander. His condition is deteriorating again, and we still haven't made enough penicillin to give him more. We can't make it fast enough. Professor Florey has been trying to find drug companies to help with its production. But none of them are interested. Dr Heatley says we have to prove it's effective before they will help, but we need more penicillin to be able to do that. He says the professor is going to try America next. There are many more drug companies in the USA than in Britain. Apparently, Professor Florey is held in very high regard there. I hope he has some success. I so admire his determination. Despite all the setbacks, Professor Florey and Dr Heatley just keep going. If there's a problem, they always find a way round it. They really believe that penicillin will be a life-saving drug one day.

~

Jo stops reading; an alarm is sounding somewhere in the unit and immediately her body is filled with a cold wash of panic. A nurse and doctor run past the room. For a moment she'd been lost in Alice's life and able to forget her new world, filled with people teetering on the edge of death. She glances at Jessie and then at her monitor, which bleeps reassuringly. Kate is awake again but looking very drowsy. Jo wanders over to the window. The sun is rising, revealing a pale-blue sky that is clear of clouds. The coffee has kicked in and Jo has an overwhelming urge be outside, to sense the wind on her skin, to feel the earth under her feet. For the last three days she has become unmoored. As if she has somehow slipped through the fabric of her reality into another one, where nothing makes sense and there is no structure to guide her.

Goodness knows how many more days she's going to be here. The pressure in her head has been building and building, and her head is going to explode if she doesn't get outside to fill her lungs with fresh air. But can she leave Jessie? What if something happens while she's out? A turn for the worse. She would never forgive herself.

The Irish nurse, who is always cheerful, advances into the room. He checks the monitors and replaces one of the drips. 'Her temperature's down,' Jo says.

'It is. She's doing grand.'

'When do you think they will wean her off the sedation?' Jo asks.

'The doctor will be in later. You need to talk to her.'

'I was thinking I might go for a short walk, but I don't want to go if …' She trails off, unable to complete the sentence.

'I don't think the doctor will be here for at least an hour, so now is probably a good time to go. It's a good idea. You need to take care of yourselves. When Jessie comes round, she's going to need a lot of support.' The nurse smiles and Jo watches as he pads out of the room, still unsure what she should do. The nurse's words echo in her head: 'When she comes round'. Usually, the doctors and nurses are careful in their choice of words when she asks about Jessie's progress. Until today. Dare she be optimistic?

'Go, Mum,' Kate says. 'I'll phone you if the doctor appears.'

'I won't go far. I need to get out of here for ten minutes.'

Jo trails through the corridors looking for the exit signs. It feels like an escape, as if she's running away, and the guilt almost makes her turn back. She passes very few people, most are hospital staff: a porter wheeling a gurney, a cleaner mopping the floor. Near the entrance the M&S, where they've been buying their food supplies, is shuttered.

The automatic doors swing apart and she steps outside. After the warmth of the unit, the cold air in her lungs is like a hard smack and she breathes again and again until she feels dizzy. Her brain jolts into life. She tips her head back so the sun bathes her face and closes her eyes. She can understand why pagan religions worshipped the sun.

She walks with no idea where she's heading. As her feet hit the pavement the events of the last three days run through her mind. All the signs are positive, although Jessie is not out of the woods yet. The doctor has given her some material to read about the possible side effects of meningitis. To prepare them. They range from hearing loss to brain damage, loss of fingers and even limbs. Some survivors lose their sight, or their kidneys fail so they require dialysis for the rest of their lives.

She lets her feet take her away from the hospital into a narrow street with high walls on either side. Trees overhang the pavement and there are few houses. The ground is littered with leaves and her feet crunch acorns and beech nuts. The road is quiet. It's easy to imagine she's in a village, not a busy city.

Her hands are cold and she jams her fingers into her coat pockets. She thought she would be able to just focus on walking, but memories of Jessie as a young child crowd her head. She has always been the tough one of her two girls. A bit of a tomboy, Jo's mum said. And Jessie had loved that description. She was an outdoors girl, constantly dirty from playing in the garden, building camps and climbing trees. Jo remembers once, on a visit to her parents, they had gone to a stately home with a farm and an adventure playground. There had been a huge climbing net, which Rob had gone up with Kate. Jessie wanted to climb it too but was far too young, so Jo had persuaded her that watching the cows being milked was much more exciting. One minute Jessie was there beside her, then Jo had turned to tell her something and she'd gone. She remembers the same gut-churning moment of fear as when the hospital had telephoned to tell her Jessie had meningitis. Back then she'd had a terrible dread that someone had snatched her. Thank goodness Jessie had been wearing a scarlet coat so was easy to spot running towards the playground. By the time Jo reached the climbing net, Jessie was halfway up. Despite her fear of heights, Jo was behind her on the net in less than a minute. Nothing else mattered but Jessie's safety.

She notices a church ahead of her: grey stone with a rectangular tower. She's not religious, but there is something about the old building which draws her to it. After the clinical surroundings of the last few days, it feels like an antidote, a stepping back in time to a simpler life. A creaking gate opens onto a narrow, paved path, leading her past gravestones, some sunken, some leaning precariously, all mottled with lichen. The porch has all the usual church notices about services, dates of a lunch club for seniors, details about a women's group. The wooden door looks ancient. It is studded with huge black nail heads and the iron hinges span half the door. She turns the ringed door handle. But the door won't open. How disappointing. She tries again, but this time she pushes hard and it gives way. Inside her feet tapping on the tiled floor seem an intrusion in the emptiness.

The aisle between the pews is wide and the roof is supported by fat round columns. At the far end a Norman arch is decorated with a ladder pattern patched with faded crimson paint – Jacob's ladder to heaven perhaps. The sunlight sneaking through the windows turns the old wooden pews a honey gold. Jo slides into one. She wonders how many people have worshipped here over the years. How many people has it brought comfort to? The quiet in the building calms her. As if over hundreds of years, all those kindred spirits who have sought consolation in this ancient place have left an imprint. At this moment she wishes she had a belief. How it would sustain her.

The intensity of the sunlight increases and colours appear on the pew in front of her: red, green and blue. In the wall to her right a stained-glass window is creating a light show. She turns to admire it. An angel holds a staff in one hand and from the other hand, a fish dangles. His huge wings are the colour of lush grass and behind him there is a purple path. Beneath it, a small brass plaque reveals this is the angel, Raphael.

Her phone bleats. In the silence of the church the sound is offensive. She pulls the phone out of her pocket. A message from Kate.

*Where are you?*

*Has something happened?* she types.

*The doctor is withdrawing the sedative.*

She hurries out of the church and once she's on the pavement, she breaks into a run: a jog at first, her legs pump up and down faster and faster until she's sprinting. As she crosses the road her feet slip on a soggy mass of leaves and she almost falls. 'Hey, slow down,' a man shouts, but she doesn't stop. She keeps hurtling towards the hospital.

When she bursts through the main entrance, her lungs are on fire as she gasps for air. The route through the maze of corridors seems to have imprinted itself into her subconscious and within moments she sees the ICU with the door open and a man exiting. She dodges through the gap, knocking his arm. She tries to say, 'Sorry,' but the only sound she emits is a breathy wheeze.

Two nurses and the doctor are standing by Jessie's bed. Kate is hovering in the doorway alone, her fist pressed against her lips as if she's trying to stop herself from crying. When she sees Jo, Kate flings both arms around her.

'Where's Dad?' Jo whispers. Kate shrugs. 'He was here when they withdrew the sedation. They wanted to wait for you, but he insisted. Then he disappeared.'

The doctor motions to Jo. 'Can you come and talk to Jessie? She needs a familiar face. It will be less frightening for her.'

Jo moves over to Jessie's side. The endotracheal tube is still in position and she can hear the ventilator rhythmically pushing oxygen into Jessie's lungs. Jo's chest is still heaving from her sprint and her heart is thudding.

The doctor says, 'Jessie, can you open your eyes?'

Come on Jessie, open them. There's a stillness in the room as if everyone has been immobilised in an invisible web. The doctor repeats her question, louder this time. Jo squeezes Jessie's hand and her eyelids flutter open. 'You're in hospital, but you are going to be fine,' she says. There's a confused look in Jessie's eyes and for a moment Jo thinks Jessie doesn't know her and a dreadful thought flits through her mind, that the meningitis has damaged her brain.

'Jessie, I'm Dr Page. Can you hear me?'

Jo notices that the doctor has turned the volume up on her voice. Jessie frowns as if she's trying to make sense of the words. After what seems like minutes, Jessie makes a barely perceptible dip of her head.

'You have a tube in your throat that is helping you breathe,' Dr Page says. 'I know it's a little uncomfortable, but we want to work out if you can manage without it. Can you squeeze your mum's hand?'

Jo feels a light pressure on her hand. She glances at the doctor. 'It's very weak, but it is a response.'

'Jessie, we're going to disconnect the ventilator now,' the doctor says. She removes the connection and the machine is turned off. 'Can you take a breath in for me and then breathe out?'

Jo reaches her hand towards Kate, who moves beside her. What if Jessie doesn't breathe? Her heart is pounding again, and she is holding her breath as if she can't breathe unless Jessie does. Kate grips her hand. Then Jessie takes a spontaneous breath in, as if she's been underwater for a long time. And she breathes out. There is a visible movement as the tension in the room dissipates. Jo glances at Kate and smiles.

'If she can breathe for thirty minutes, we will remove the tube,' the doctor says. 'Can you talk to her? She's going to be confused and I think she has some hearing loss, so keep your voice quite loud.'

'Hey, Jessie,' Jo says. 'We've been really worried about you. Kate is here. And Dad. You've been in hospital for three days. You had meningitis and were very sick, but you're so much better now.' She glances at the doctor again, feeling rather self-conscious in front of all the clinical staff. The doctor nods at her, as if to say, 'Keep talking'. Jessie's eyes flick open again and she holds Jo's hand tight, just as she did as a young child when she was frightened.

'You're doing really well,' Jo says. 'Do you remember when you were learning to climb, and you kept falling off the climbing wall? You didn't give up, you just kept having another go until you reached the top. You were so determined. Don't give up now. You don't need that ventilator anymore – you can breathe without it.' And as she gazes at the rise and fall of Jessie's chest something she hadn't dared contemplate during the last few days settles on her shoulders like a light shawl: hope.

# 6

# Alice

**18 March 1941**

Alice is dreaming she's cycling to work, but all the roads are blocked by the army and she's late. No matter which way she goes she never gets any closer. The siren wail cuts across her dream journey and she is instantly awake, heart racing. Throwing off the bed covers she runs through Peter's room. He's already on his way down the stairs. The stupid boy has left his gas mask on the bedpost. She grabs it and slings it round her neck with her own. Her mum, face pale with tiredness, appears in her bedroom doorway. 'Not again,' she says. There have been alerts nearly every night for the last week. It's not been like this since last autumn. Sometimes they're short, and they are no sooner up and out of the door when the *All Clear* sounds. But last night it didn't sound until nearly six o'clock.

Alice is at the bottom of the stairs in seconds, pulling on her coat and slipping on her shoes. She dashes out of the front door, and heads to her gran's where her dad installed an Anderson shelter before he joined up. As they rush into the garden, her gran and aunt are just emerging from the back door. 'She insisted on getting dressed,' Vivien says, pursing her lips.

The shelter is fitted out with two bunk beds and a camp bed, which Peter sleeps on. Alice's gran and mum have the bottom bunks, Vivien and Alice have the top ones. 'I won't sleep,' her gran insists as Vivien tucks her into the bed which is always made up with sheets and blankets ready for these events. When her aunt stays overnight at her friend Pat's house, Alice and her mum have to coax her gran into the shelter. She hates going in there; says it makes her claustrophobic.

Within minutes her gran is snoring, and Alice can imagine her aunt smiling. She can hear planes overhead and then the sound of the *ack-ack* guns reverberate across the night. She hopes Margaret is safe in her shelter and wonders if her aunt worries about Pat, who lives alone.

Alice stares into the darkness with fear coiling around her stomach. How can she possibly sleep? The guns pound again and the earth seems to shake. She hears Vivien's voice, quiet and reassuring, asking if she's awake.

'Yes,' whispers Alice.

'How's PC Alexander?'

Alice doesn't reply, then Vivien's voice cuts through the silence. 'What happened, Alice?'

'We ran out of penicillin. No matter how hard we tried, we couldn't make enough. His condition deteriorated and he died. We really thought we'd cured him. We thought, at last some good news. But in the end, we failed.'

She cries quietly, but her aunt must have heard because she says, 'Give me your hand.' Alice stretches her arm across the narrow gap between the bunks until she finds Vivien's hand. Just that touch and her nearness soothe her.

She hadn't told anyone all the details before. Her mum is exhausted every day and usually comes home from the factory with a headache from the noise of the riveting machine. And she probably wouldn't be interested.

Then Vivien whispers, 'But if you'd had enough penicillin, would he have been saved?'

'I think so.'

'You just have to make more and then next time you will be successful.'

Alice smiles at that. If she could see what they have to do to produce the tiniest amount of penicillin – they need so much to treat one person.

When the *All Clear* sounds four hours later Alice trudges home with Peter and her mum. A thick fog has descended and the smell of cordite hangs in the air. In her room she peers round the blackout curtain. There are no signs of any fires, so perhaps Oxford has been spared again. How long can their luck last? Yesterday, Bristol had been heavily bombed. She thinks about all the poor souls who lost their lives and makes a resolution to be more patient with Peter when he's being irritating.

She's so tired she thinks she'll sleep instantly. But sleep doesn't come and as her mind turns over the night's events, she thinks about her dad and the letter that arrived yesterday. It had been lying unopened on the kitchen table when she arrived home from work. Her mum was busy preparing tea and said she'd been waiting for Peter and Alice to come home so they could read it together. Alice ripped it open, desperate to read its contents just as Peter came in. 'Can you read it aloud so we can all hear his news,' her mother said. And she stopped what she was doing and stood quietly as Alice read it out.

Alice sits up and reaches for the diary and a torch on her bedside table. The letter is in a paper pocket she'd made in her diary after her last entry. She slides it out and rereads it.

*My Dear Family,*

*I feel like I have landed on the moon, this place is so alien. Sand and rock, dust and flies. Boiling hot in the day and freezing cold at night. But the nights are spectacular. I can lie for hours and stare at the sky brilliant with pinpricks of light. The stars look much more intense than at home and so many more are visible. And the sunrises are not like at home where there is a gradual lightening. Here there is an explosion of colour.*

*Alice, I was so impressed at Christmas by your journal that I bought an exercise book before I left England to try to record this strange life: the black days and the fear interspersed with moments when I am glad to still be alive.*

*There is little I can tell you about the fighting as it will all be censored, but there are days of inactivity when we are all bored and then days in battle when every part of my body seems alert, as if I have fire running though my veins. Afterwards I'm exhausted with the noise of it still in my head.*

*The dust storms are a nightmare as you think there is no enemy in sight and then they loom out of nowhere. Buried men from our troop today. The padre said some prayers, but it didn't seem right that the poor sods are buried in this strange land.*

*My mechanical skills are much appreciated, as we are forever having to fix up the tanks and trucks.*

*It's strange how I hated being told what to do at work and now that everything is orders and we have to obey, there is no arguing and I just accept it. Maybe it's because it's for a common goal, fighting for King and country, not to line some factory boss's pockets.*

*I hope you are all well. We don't hear much news, but*

*occasionally it filters through about the devastation that is being reaped on Britain by the air raids, and it makes us even more determined to defeat the Axis.*

    *Love Dad*

After Alice had read it, she went outside with Peter, and they looked at the stars. It was a clear night for once. Just standing there and thinking that thousands of miles away her dad could be watching the same stars gave her such a strange feeling. Peter said he felt it too. They stood there until they started to feel cold, then went in.

Alice smiles when she remembers her mum saying they were both bonkers. She'd asked if she could keep the letter and her mum had shrugged and said, 'You might as well, since you'll be the one writing back to him.' It's always Alice that writes. Her mum says as she's the one who's clever with words, she should write a letter from the whole family. When she first said this, Alice asked why they couldn't all write their own letters, and her mother muttered something about the cost of postage. Sometimes she asks what Alice has written, but never wants to read it. But at least that means she can say things her mother might not approve of.

Since she can't sleep, she decides to write to her dad. It will feel like they're having a conversation, even though she might have to wait a month or more until a reply arrives. By the time she's finished writing all the stress of the night has evaporated and when she lies back down in bed, sleep finally overtakes her.

# 7

# Jo

**13 December 2017**

Jo stands in Jessie's bedroom and stares out at the front garden. The flowerbeds are bare, except for the perennials withered by frost and the leafless stems of the shrub roses. The days are haemorrhaging light. It will be the shortest day in just over a week, and then she tells herself it can only get better: gradually the days will lengthen again and she can look forward. But still the darkness that encroaches on her day creeps inside her head. She summoned all her reserves to stay strong at the hospital, but now she is coming undone.

The street is busy with early morning traffic. A group of secondary school girls josh each other as they dawdle on the pavement. Did their parents ever think, as their daughters breezed out of the house that morning, that they might never see them alive again? Of course not, because how could they survive if they were so strung up with fear? Life goes on. They put one foot in front of the other and they are safe. What else can they do? They would go mad. They read the papers and see a tragic story of a family who have lost a son, or a daughter and think, poor souls, and then continue with their life never considering it could be them. For that is unthinkable. They would be paralysed by anxiety. Their brain shuts it out.

Jo twists away from the window and picks up her duster.

The room is strangely empty despite Jessie being home as most of her belongings are still in Oxford. She starts with the dressing table, usually a clutter of make-up, hair clips and scrunchies. All that remains is the hexagonal Moorish jewellery box Jessie had bought in Andalusia: a holiday with her school friends just before they all started university. That seems such a long time ago now. She dusts the top of the picture frames on the walls: an enlarged photograph of Jessie on a zipwire; a collage of photographs of her friends; a poster she'd bought of Half Dome on the family holiday to America. Jessie's desk is equally tidy, just an old notebook, a pot full of pens and a paperweight with a flower trapped inside, suspended forever in glass. Jo runs her duster along the edge of the shelves crammed with books from Philip Pullman to an Advanced Physics textbook.

'What are you doing, Mum?' Kate stands in the doorway frowning. 'You hate cleaning. And you did Jessie's room last week. I can't believe it needs doing again.'

'I know. It doesn't make any sense, but it makes me feel better.'

'Like a penance? It's not your fault she got ill.'

'Mums are supposed to protect their children.'

'We're adults now and you can't protect us from everything.' Kate wanders over to the window and stares out for a moment. 'Can I do something to help?'

'Can you persuade Jessie to have some breakfast? She managed some of that quick porridge yesterday. You just add milk and put it in the microwave for two minutes.'

'Okay,' Kate says.

Jo starts on the bed. She carefully folds the memory quilt her mother had made for Jessie from scraps of her outgrown clothes. Jessie had debated whether to take it to Oxford but in the end, she'd left it behind. Jo used to love telling Jessie a story about each piece of fabric, not just what item of clothing it was from, but an escapade when she was wearing it. She pulls the sheets from Jessie's bed and puts on clean ones.

She hadn't realised how difficult it was going to be to pull Jessie through the next stage. Although the doctors had warned her that many patients suffered from depression, they had assured her there was no evidence of any brain damage. But Jo worries the doctors are wrong. Jessie seems to be a different person. Before her illness it was always obvious when Jessie was in the house. She had something to say about everything. Now she barely says a word. Jo had voiced her anxiety to Rob yesterday, wondering whether she should contact the consultant. She'd told them, when they left, that they should phone her if they had any concerns.

'For god's sake,' Rob had exploded. 'Will you stop fussing.'

Of course, he's not the one picking up the pieces. Jo is back to being a full-time mum.

Jessie says she can't concentrate. She listens to audiobooks, watches animated films on TV – all her favourites she watched as a child – as if she has regressed. Perhaps she has, to a safe place that was her childhood. Jo wonders whether she needs some counselling.

The other side effect is the terrible nightmares. In all of them Jessie is about to die when she wakes screaming. She describes how she was being buried alive in a deep hole or was drowning in the sea while Jo stood and watched on the beach, seemingly unconcerned. The worst was when an enormous lizard-like creature was sitting on her chest eating her alive, starting with her face.

On her first night home, Jessie climbed into bed with Jo and Rob in the early hours of the morning petrified. It took Jo almost an hour to calm her, curling round her as if she was a young child again, until Jessie flung her away and returned to her own bed. This was repeated night after night. After the first occurrence Rob moved onto the sofa in the living room and slept there, claiming he needed a good night's sleep when he was working.

Jessie has no appetite and no energy. It's as if she has used so much energy fighting the infection, she has exhausted all her stores. She would stay in bed all the time if she could, but Jo is determined that Jessie tries to engage in the rhythms of a normal day. Fortunately, Jessie's stubbornness and deter-mination have melted, so she allows Jo to cajole her to get up and lie on the sofa with her duvet and pillow. But this lack of pushback is also worrying. Jo ordered her some light fiction. The books arrived two days ago but remain unopened. Jessie says she can't focus, the words just move around.

A shout from the living room interrupts Jo's thoughts. She's immediately alert and running down the stairs. 'Why are you being so horrible?' Kate yells. Before Jo can enter the room Kate storms out.

'What's happened now?' Jo says.

'I made her some breakfast, like you asked. Not a word of thanks, but I let that go. She took one spoonful, spat it out and said, "I can't eat it, it's disgusting".'

'That's the first time since we've been back that Jessie has been difficult, argumentative … more like her old self,' Jo says. It's strange that she's actually pleased Jessie is being awkward. 'It's time for you to go back to York. You've been a star and I really appreciate all the help you've given me. I don't know how I would have coped at the hospital without you by my side.'

'It was just as well I was there. Dad was weird. I never realised he had such a phobia about illness. But he shouldn't have gone back to work as soon as Jessie was off the ventilator. That wasn't fair on you.'

Jo shrugs. She's not getting into a discussion with Kate about Rob. 'It's time for you to get on with your own life.' Term has finished, but Jo knows Kate is missing her friends in their shared house. If she goes now at least she can have ten days with them before she's home again for Christmas. 'I'll pay for your ticket,' Jo says, in case Kate is worrying about the cost.

'Thank you.' Kate hesitates. 'But what about you, Mum? What's happening about your job?'

For the last eight years Jo has been working part-time as a data-entry clerk in a school office; a job which fitted neatly around being a mother and running a house. They've given her unpaid leave for as long as she needs it.

'I'm going to hand in my notice. It's clear Jessie's recovery is going to be slow.'

'But I thought you enjoyed it.'

'I do.' She loves the chit-chat with the other admin staff and the school kids dropping by. 'But I'd already resolved to move on before Jessie was ill. I want to retrain, to do something that will challenge my brain.' What she doesn't say is that taking that step is hard. As if there is an invisible barrier holding her back.

'Good for you,' Kate says, but she has a puzzled look as if it's never occurred to her that her mum might have an ambition to do more in her working life.

'When do you want to leave?' Jo says.

'I think I'll go now. Would you take me to the station? It will only take me a few minutes to pack.'

It's a sudden decision, but Jo feels it's the right one. Kate dashes up the stairs and Jo glances anxiously through the open living-room door. They have only been home for a week, and Jessie hasn't been left on her own yet. But it's only a 10-minute drive to the station. Jessie will be fine.

In the kitchen Jo pulls two cereal bars from the cupboard, a banana from the fruit bowl and a bottle of orange juice from the fridge. By the time she's found a small carrier bag to put them in, Kate is in the hall with a rucksack on one shoulder and a look of immense relief on her face. Jo hands her the bag. 'To keep you going,' she says. She picks up the car keys and pokes her head round the living-room door. Jessie is lying on the sofa feigning sleep.

'Jessie,' Jo says loudly. Jessie's eyes flick open. 'I'm just taking Kate to the station. I won't be long.' There's a distinct look of alarm on Jessie's face, but Jo doesn't wait for a reply. The front door is open, and Kate is already on the doorstep. Jo closes and locks the door.

When Jo arrives home the first thing she always sees hanging on the wall is the print of Eric Ravilious's *Newt Pond*. She stands for a moment and lets the muted colours, the reflected trees in the pond, soothe her anxiousness.

The sound of the TV reverberates through the house; Jessie is watching *Finding Nemo*. Despite the grey day the light is off and the TV is throwing neon images across the room. Jo hears a faint giggle, the first she's heard since Jessie became ill. Like the sun burning off cloud on a grey day, it lifts her mood. She pokes her head round the door and waves to Jessie to let her know she's back.

In the kitchen she makes herself a cup of coffee and turns on the radio. There's a news item about the Spice Girls' reunion concert and her mind spools back to the day she'd first met Rob.

It was the first term of her second year of university, and she was at a party in a house rented by her friend, Amy, and four other students. Amy, like Jo, had a northern working-class background, but unlike Jo, felt at home living in the south of England. In her first year Jo berated herself many times for choosing a southern university full of middle-class students. Why hadn't she chosen Sheffield or Leeds? What was she thinking? She'd been seduced by the sea and thought it would be exciting to go somewhere completely different. Jo had helped Amy and her housemates set up the disco lights and clear the living room of furniture to create a dance floor. Jo didn't like parties, but she loved dancing; it released all her pent-up frustrations and with a belly full of alcohol to obliterate all her inhibitions, she intended to have a good time.

She was dancing with Amy and there were so many people there was barely room to move when 'Wannabe' belted out from the speakers. And she and Amy were the Spice Girls on that dance floor, swinging their hips, leaping up and down, flinging their arms. They knew all the words. She was rather drunk by then. Girl power, that's what it was about. She knew the song was aimed at young teenagers, but she didn't care. In her lurex top glittering under the lights, she could be a Spice Girl too. She wonders now what happened to the feeling that, as a woman, she could have power just like the men.

She saw Rob leaning against the wall watching her. He looked different from the other lads. 'Well turned out,' her mother would have said. His T-shirt was ironed, his hair well cut. He smiled and she smiled back. He covered his ears with his hands and screwed up his nose. Then 'Wonderwall' was playing and everyone was singing along. Jo sang the words she knew and ad-libbed the rest. The energy of the crowd flowed into her, and she wanted that force to last for ever. She'd never felt so alive. Rob's eyes seemed to follow her as if he was mesmerised. And at that moment she felt as if she held a power over him.

'Can I join you?' he said in a public-school voice.

She pushed her hair away from her damp face and laughed. 'You're not a Spice Girls fan then?'

He gestured with his hand. 'This is more my style.'

'I'll dance to anything,' she said.

She separated from Amy and danced with him. The music was so loud it was impossible to have a conversation. She couldn't stop smiling and kept thinking, *I must look an idiot*, but she didn't care. He seemed to be studying her face in a way that she would have found embarrassing if she wasn't so sloshed. He towered above her, even though she was wearing three-inch heels. His dark hair, parted in the middle, kept flopping forwards onto his forehead whenever he looked down.

When the song finished, he said, 'Shall we get another drink?' She followed him to the next room where a table was crowded with bottles of cheap wine, cans of beer and a giant bucket of punch. She'd tried the punch when she arrived. It tasted like neat alcohol with bits of orange floating in it. She pointed at the bucket. 'That's lethal.'

'I'm sticking to beer,' he said.

'That's wise. Perhaps I'll have beer too. The wine's pretty awful.'

He poured lager into two plastic cups. It was ghastly stuff, not what she called beer, but she was thirsty from the dancing, so she downed it quickly. He suggested they sat on the stairs where it was quieter. There was more light there and she could see his features clearly: grey eyes and pale skin, a long thin nose. She leaned back against the balustrades. He seemed familiar. Had their paths crossed before? 'Have I seen you somewhere?'

'Molecular Biology lectures,' he said.

She had no memory of him there, but he must have registered somewhere in her subconscious. She always sat at the front away from the cocky ones at the back, who chatted and disturbed her concentration. She imagined that was where he would sit. He had that air of confidence that she'd encountered before in students with a public-school education. They talked about the course, which lecturers they liked and which were boring, which modules they'd enjoyed and which they'd hated.

'Have you thought about what you want to do after university?' she said.

'A Ph.D.,' he said. 'And you?'

'I want to be a clinical biochemist. It's what I've wanted to do ever since I was 13.'

'It seems a very young age to be fixed on such a definite career.'

'I was ill, and the doctors didn't know what was wrong with me. I had loads of visits to hospital for blood tests. The phlebotomist told me what would happen to my blood samples. I was a curious kid and asked to see the lab where they were processed. I was fascinated that they could work out what was wrong with someone from their blood. She gave me a guided tour and I knew immediately that was what I wanted to do.'

'Like a vocation,' he said and sniggered. She wasn't sure then that she liked him. He was a bit high and mighty with his snobby voice.

'Where are you from?' he said.

'Barnsley.'

'Ah,' he said. 'That explains the accent.'

'Where are you from?' she said.

'Woking.'

'Ah, that explains the accent,' she said.

He laughed, his face softened and she decided to give him a second chance. She told him she was proud of her accent, her heritage, that her grandad had been a miner, that she'd been with her mum on a protest march to support the strikers. He'd listened attentively and seemed genuinely interested. He'd walked her home and outside her student house they'd swapped phone numbers. He turned to go, then turned back and pressed his mouth against hers. She felt a longing rush through her body, quite unlike anything she'd ever experienced before. He rested his forehead on hers and she closed her eyes, wanting him to never leave. But he said in a tender voice, 'I'll ring you tomorrow', and left. She stood and watched him until he was out of sight.

Jo turns off the radio. She feels the familiar pang of regret that the career she'd dreamt of had never come to fruition due to Kate's birth in her final year at university, followed by Jessie's arrival two years later. Time had flown by and

Rob persuaded her she'd left it too long and anyway, she had a family to look after. But once Jessie has recovered she has no more excuses, except her lack of confidence, to retrain and build herself a career.

She wanders into the living room. The film has finished, and Jessie has earbuds in, listening to something on her phone. That's all she uses her phone for now – to listen to stories or music. She has stopped communicating with her friends. This is also quite out of character. Before her illness, Jessie was constantly messaging them.

'Jessie,' Jo says loudly, standing in front of her.

Jessie pulls out the earbuds and frowns.

'Your friend Ellie phoned me.' Jo has had several chats with Ellie, who she can't thank enough for phoning for the ambulance when she realised how sick Jessie was. 'She said she's been trying to contact you.'

Jessie rubs the edge of her duvet between her finger and thumb, a throwback to her childhood. 'I just don't feel like talking to people. I can only understand what you say because you talk slowly and loudly and look at me when you're speaking.'

'You could just message her; say thank you.' Jo doesn't say it but Ellie's quick action probably saved Jessie's life.

'I just can't focus. Even writing messages.' She buries herself under the duvet so only her head is visible.

Jo frowns. Is this lack of ability to focus something to worry about? More evidence that there is some sort of brain damage? 'I've given her a brief update. I've thanked her many times. She understands you're still unwell.'

'Thanks.'

Jo's mobile phone rings. She looks at who's calling and

when she sees it's Rob's mother, she recoils. What does she want? She lets it ring six times then decides she should answer it.

'Hello, Jo. It's Caroline. I'm just ringing to see how Jessie is. I haven't heard from Rob since she left the hospital.' She pauses. 'I left him a few messages, but I guess he's very busy at work. I was wondering about coming over, to visit her.'

Oh no. That's the last thing Jessie needs. Jo runs her hand through her hair and tries hard to be pleasant. 'I'm sorry, but she really isn't ready to receive visitors yet. But I'll tell her you called.'

'Oh, that's a shame, I was so looking forward to seeing her,' she says. 'I've been very worried.' There's a noise in the background, a hiss of a barista, a clink of china. She had assumed Caroline was ringing from home, but she's clearly in a coffee shop. Is she nearby? Had she hoped to just drop in, then thought better of it and phoned?

'I'm sure you have. I'll let you know as soon as she can have visitors. Sorry, I've got to go. Jessie is calling me. Bye.'

Jessie is frowning. 'I wasn't calling you.'

Jo is beginning to think Jessie has selective hearing. 'You could hear me?' she says.

'You speak very loudly on the phone, especially when you're stressed.'

Jo scratches her hand. The patch of eczema that started as a small island on her hand is now a vast country. It stretches up her arm and down her side. If she has anything tight next to her skin it erupts into red sores that itch. 'It was Caroline. She wanted to come and see you.'

Jessie pulls the duvet over her head and groans. Jessie and Kate have always called their grandparents by their first names. Caroline had visibly shuddered once when 3-year-old Kate had mistakenly called her 'Grandma'.

Jo feels terrible for lying, but swears she has developed antibodies to Caroline. She has never taken such a dislike to anyone before. She supposes it all began when she first met her. It must have been three months after she'd been going out with Rob that he told her his parents were coming to visit and asked if she would join them for a meal.

'I'd rather not,' she said. If he was posh, she guessed his parents would be even posher. But after considerable pressure from Rob, she agreed. He had fussed about what she should wear – jeans wouldn't be suitable. This made her even more anxious. Eating out with her parents meant the Beefeater or the Carvery. Her dad was a meat-and-two-veg man. And in Brighton, she rarely ate out as money was tight. So when she arrived at the hotel restaurant for lunch she nearly turned round and walked out again. It was bad enough that she had to meet his parents, but the place was dripping money: plush carpets, obsequious staff, thick white-linen tablecloths and silver cutlery. His parents were already at the table, studying the menu, both with a glass of red wine in their hands. They stood to greet them. Rob's mother embraced him and his father shook his hand. Jo was astonished to hear Rob call his parents by their first names.

His mother turned to her. 'You must be Jo,' she said, drowning Jo in the scent of her perfume. When she looked as if she was going embrace her too, Jo held out her hand. She wasn't comfortable with such intimacy with someone she'd never met before.

Caroline was immaculate: wavy, blonde hair, not a lock out of place, lashings of make-up and glossy lipstick. A black dress, gold necklace and matching earrings, a large diamond ring. His father, in suit and tie, shook her hand. 'David,' he said. 'It's good to meet you at last,' as if Rob had been hiding her away from them for a very long time. She wondered if they'd asked to meet her before and Rob had declined. The waiter helped her into her seat, and she stared at the menu wondering how on earth she was going to eat anything. The prices were mind-blowing. She wasn't sure what many of the things on the menu were, so for a starter she opted for the something that she'd heard of: soup. Her throat had constricted, swallowing anything was going to be hard. When the main course arrived, swimming in a rich creamy sauce, she was overwhelmed with nausea. The conversation floated above her head as if she was sitting at the bottom of the sea. Rob was interrogated about his marks for his coursework and there was much talk about Rob's brother's success in a City bank. *Poor Rob*, she thought, *always being measured against Justin.* Being an only child had some advantages, although her parents never put pressure on her. When she did try to answer questions aimed at her, what she said came out sounding ridiculous. Afterwards, she went to the ladies and as she came out Rob and his parents were in the hotel foyer. She heard his mother say, 'She's very pretty but a bit gauche.' Caroline didn't look the least bit embarrassed when she realised Jo must have heard her. She just smiled as if she had just said that Jo was delightful. Rob blushed, although Jo wasn't sure if it was embarrassment of her or for her.

He drove her back to her student house. They barely spoke. As he pulled the car up outside, she said, 'That wasn't very nice of your mum', and instead of apologising he said, 'Well, you barely said a word and hardly ate anything.'

'I did try. I just felt so uncomfortable. I've never eaten out in a place like that before. My background is very different from yours.'

'Well, you're not going to succeed in life unless you try harder. You didn't exactly impress them.'

'I didn't know that I was being interviewed for the position of Rob's girlfriend. As I clearly didn't come up to scratch, you'd better find someone they consider more suitable.' And she flung open the car door and slammed it behind her. The car moved off at speed, kicking up a trail of dust.

He phoned a week later when she was on her way to a practical. 'I'm sorry,' he said. 'That was unforgiveable of me.' She didn't respond and there had been a long silence. 'Jo,' he said, 'are you still there?'

'Yes,' she said.

'I miss you,' he said.

Caroline's cutting remarks and criticisms have been a constant part of her married life, whether it's the food she cooks or her mid-twentieth-century furniture, found in junk shops and renovated, or her textiles from the same period. When Jessie or Kate behaved badly, it was because Jo wasn't strict enough with them. And whenever Jo mentions Caroline's comments to Rob, he always accuses her of being oversensitive. Caroline reminds Jo of the bullies she encountered at school. Once they'd detected her vulnerability on their radar, they picked her out for their cruelty.

'I'm glad you put her off,' Jessie says. 'I can't face seeing anyone.'

'Was I rude?'

Jessie shakes her head.

The letter flap in the front door rattles, followed by a

thump. Jo retrieves the mail: two letters, a magazine and large envelope with her name and address written by hand. Intrigued she checks the postmark: Oxford. Must be something for Jessie, perhaps from a friend. She wanders into the kitchen, slits it open and tips out the contents. Alice's diary flops onto the counter. There is a handwritten note on NHS paper.

*One of the cleaners found this and, assuming it was important, put it in my desk drawer. I've been on sick leave for four weeks and when I returned to work today, I found it. I remember talking to you about the diary – it seemed important to you. I guess it must have been lost at some point. We would love to hear how Jessie is faring. She was a popular patient.*
*Elaine Walsh, Adult Intensive Care Unit Matron*

Jo had assumed she would never get it back. She wasn't sure when it had disappeared, probably when Jessie was moved from her isolation room in ICU to the ward. She'd asked the nurses if they'd seen it. No-one had and everyone had been so busy, she didn't pursue it. She'd felt something significant had been lost, but Jessie was getting better and nothing else mattered. Somehow it didn't seem appropriate that she should mourn its loss when her daughter had almost died. So she had put it to the back of her mind.

To have the diary returned is like a being given a special gift and it makes her realise how much she values it. She hasn't told Jessie about the diary, or its loss, and she ponders why. Did she feel guilty for taking an interest in Alice when her daughter was so ill?

Jo sits in an armchair in the living room. Jessie has her earbuds in again and has the shut-in look which means, 'Don't talk to me'. Jo flips through the diary until she reaches the last page she'd read. She's about to immerse herself in Alice's world when Jessie pulls out her earbuds and asks, 'What are you reading?'

'It's a diary written by a young woman in the early 1940s. She worked on the development of penicillin.'

Jessie pushes the duvet halfway down her body and sits up. 'Where did it come from?'

'I found it in a handbag in Zoe's shop. I had it with me when you were in hospital. I thought I'd lost it, but it just arrived in the post with a note from Matron.'

'Will you read it to me?'

'I've read some of it. Do you want me to go back to the beginning?'

'No, it's okay. Just read where you're up to. But you need to speak loudly into my cloth ears.'

Jo pulls her chair close to Jessie and faces her so she can see her lips. 'You need a bit of background first. Alice is a year younger than you and lives with her parents and younger brother Peter. Her mum works in a factory making armaments and her dad is in the army overseas. Her best friend is Margaret and her gran and Aunt Vivien live nearby.'

'Okay,' Jessie says.

### Saturday, 29 March 1941

This afternoon Margaret went with me to help choose some material and a pattern for the new dress I want to make. Now I'm earning, I can make my own clothes and choose material and colours that Mum would never select. She likes dull colours that make her blend in like camouflage: browns and dark blues. She's like a sparrow, whereas I love vibrant colours.

We're planning to attend a dance at the Carfax Assembly Rooms in four weeks. I chose the pattern immediately – a tea dress with a V-neck and cap sleeves. It has a full skirt, cinched at the waist, and four buttons on the bodice. Choosing the material was more difficult. The haberdasher, Mrs Foster, was very patient. As she rolled out one bolt after another, she said there were rumours that clothes and fabric would be rationed soon, and I was lucky there was still a good choice. But none was what I was looking for. I wanted something with a dash of red in it. Margaret wandered off to look at knitting patterns.

I was about to suggest we try a different shop, when Mrs Foster said she had some new fabric just come in that she hadn't unwrapped yet. She disappeared into the back room and I heard a rustling of paper. She reappeared with a bolt of rayon crêpe with a pattern of a scarlet rose, and grey hatching on a white background. It was beautiful and I knew at once that it was exactly right. I felt so lucky. Who knows when I'll be able to buy such lovely material again. Mrs Foster measured out the yardage specified in the pattern then cut with her large scissors; the *kerch-kerch* sound of the scissors made me want to rush home and start making it. As she was wrapping it, I chose some buttons to match the colour of the rose in the fabric. Margaret wandered back, with a cardigan pattern and five balls of powder-blue wool. I've never taken to knitting like

Gran and Vivien, whose clicking needles are a constant background noise at Gran's in the evening. Perhaps it's because Mum doesn't knit.

## Sunday, 6 April 1941

Today I spent a very happy afternoon making a start on my dress. Mum and Peter had gone to Gran's, so I had the house to myself. I cleared the table and gave it a good scrub. Then I cut the amount of fabric I needed for the bodice, folded it in half and laid it out. I removed the tissue-paper pieces from the pattern packet and cut carefully along the dotted lines for my size. After I ironed the pieces with a cool iron to remove all the creases, I arranged them on the fabric with the centre back of the bodice along the fold and all the other shapes in the same direction, but with the least wastage. I love that part of dressmaking. It's like doing a puzzle. Once they'd been pinned in place, I took a deep breath and cut. I was really careful not to make any slip-ups. When I first started dressmaking, I was always in a hurry. But I soon learned that was a mistake. I have to be patient and check and double-check everything. So I took it slowly. I really wanted this dress to be a success. I pinned the pieces for the bodice together then stitched them with a tacking stitch. I had asked Mum if I could use her sewing machine and she said, 'As long as you put it away after you've finished using it and don't leave any mess'. I know she really misses the time when she earned money by making clothes for neighbours and relatives. She's really bitter about having to give it up to work at the factory.

I haven't used the Singer for a while, but I remembered instantly how to wind the cotton onto the bobbin, how to pass the cotton from the reel through the hooks and levers until I could thread the needle. I did a trial run on a scrap of material, making sure the stitches were even. I love the rhythm of the Singer, the clatter of the needle as it bobs up and down, the rattle of the bobbin. A garment can take shape so quickly. Perhaps that's why I prefer sewing to knitting.

'She has so much energy,' Jessie says. 'I like Alice – she reminds me of the old me.' She slumps her head on the pillow. 'But I can't imagine ever being like that again. I don't have the energy to do anything. I can't even read.'

'Shall I read some more?' Jo says.

'No, I'm tired now. I want to sleep.'

Although Jo is pleased Jessie is interested in the diary she is glad to have a moment to think about what she has just read. She is certain the dress Alice described is the one Zoe had given her: the material and the style are unmistakeably the same. That Alice had made the dress herself makes it very special and this link through time makes Jo feel deeply connected to Alice. It is as if the past is seeping into the present.

But where is the dress? She remembers wearing it when she went to the hospital. Once Jessie was off the ventilator Kate had gone home with Rob to collect a change of clothes for Jo. But Jo has no recollection of seeing the dress since she came home. That thought sends her pulse racing.

# 8

# Alice

**26 April 1941**

Alice slips on her finished dress and stares at her reflection in her gran's full-length wardrobe mirror. She's never worn red before; it seems such a bold colour, but she's pleased with the fit and the style compliments her figure. She rushes down the stairs, eager to show off the professional job she's made of the garment. At the dance tonight she'll be able to hold her head up high. She might not be pretty like Margaret, but she will look well-dressed.

It's late afternoon, and her gran and Vivien are sitting in the garden with a cup of tea, having a rest after planting potatoes. Although most of the garden is now given over to vegetables and the Andersen shelter, her gran still has a few flowers which she grows in a border by the house wall. Alice can hear the bees dipping in and out of the forget-me-nots.

She twirls round in front of them, letting the skirt swirl and swing.

'You look lovely, dear,' Gran says. 'That colour looks good on you. And your dressmaking skills are quite equal to your mother's now.'

'Don't tell her that.'

'How grown-up you look,' Vivien says. 'Shall I curl your hair now?' As they walk to the back door she whispers, 'Do you want to borrow some make-up?'

'I heard. Don't go overboard,' Gran says.

Alice follows her aunt upstairs to her bedroom. She sits at the dressing table and watches in the mirror as Vivien takes the length of hair that is always flopping in front of her face and rolls it up around her fingers to the top of her head. She pins it in place, then repeats this on the other side, this time rolling it to just below her side parting. 'There,' she says, 'two rolls. The curls will take a bit longer. You are in luck because I managed to get some setting lotion.' Vivien divides the rest of Alice's hair into four sections, combs through the lotion, then wraps each length around a rag strip tying the ends together near the top of her head.

Alice giggles. She looks very strange. Peter will laugh out loud if he sees her like this.

'Leave those in as long as you can. I'll give you a scarf to wear on your way home.' Vivien smiles at Alice. 'Now, that make-up.'

She shows Alice how to apply face make-up, then lipstick. Although Alice appreciates all the effort she's going to, she's not sure she likes the effect. Her face looks like a doll's rather than a real person's.

'Here,' Vivien says, handing her the powder compact she has just used. 'You can have this to keep. I have another. Now, what about stockings?' And she pulls from a drawer an unopened packet of silk stockings.

'Where did you get these?' Alice asks.

'They were a gift.'

'I can't take them. I might ruin them,' she says, even though she really wants them. She'd been planning to wear leg make-up and paint a line to look like a seam, but to wear real silk stockings would be the final finishing touch.

Vivien shrugs. 'Please,' she says.

It is early evening when Alice walks home with the scarf over her head and the dress over one arm to prevent it getting creased. When she opens the back door, the house is quiet. Peter and her mum must be out. What a relief. Her mum is not going to approve of the make-up or the hairstyle. If she can just get out of the house before her mum is back, there won't be an argument.

She lays her dress on the bed and removes the stockings from their packet. They are so fine and soft, she's terrified of snagging them. She carefully rolls them up her legs, then pulls the dress over her head. Lastly, she removes the rags and combs her hair with her fingers. She rushes to her mum's room to look at herself in her mirror. *Not bad*, she thinks, although her waves will be short-lived. Her hair is so straight, it resists all attempts to curl it.

The back door slams shut. There's a clattering up the stairs, the creak of Peter's bedsprings. 'What are you doing, Alice? It stinks in here.'

She stands in the doorway to his room. 'What do you think?' she says. He's lying on his bed with a book he's been reading for the past week about building model aircraft. He glances up. 'You look amazing.'

'Do you think anyone will dance with me?' she asks and waits for his usual derogatory remark.

Instead, he says, 'I would.'

She is so taken aback she wants to hug him. 'Thank you.' She wishes they could push back the sofa in the parlour like Dad used to and dance to some music on the wireless.

Another time perhaps. 'I'd better get going. Margaret will be waiting for me.'

She rushes down the stairs, bubbling with excitement, and grabs her coat from the passage, her feet dancing into the kitchen. She stops abruptly as if her feet have glued themselves to the floor. Her mum is standing by the sink, her back to Alice. When did she come in? Alice expects her to turn round; she would have heard her coming down the stairs, must be able to smell the setting lotion. But her mum doesn't move, like a spider waiting to spring. Alice rushes towards the back door, 'I'm off now,' she says, hoping to just slip out.

But before she reaches the door, her mum turns and stares at her with eyes like flints. 'Not with that muck on your face. Take it off. You look like a tart.'

Her words obliterate all Alice's joy. And in its place anger flares. How dare she talk to her like that. 'No,' Alice says.

Her mother steps in front of the back door barring her exit.

Now rage is boiling inside Alice. She glares at her. 'What are you going to do? Lock me in?'

A hard, stinging slap smacks across her cheek.

'Don't you ever speak to me like that again. Who do you think you are?'

But Alice is already walking away, out of the kitchen, through the passage and parlour and out of the front door.

'Ha,' she says out loud. 'That'll show you.'

As she steps onto the pavement, she hears her mother yell, 'Don't bother to come back. I don't want you in my house if you can't respect me.'

Alice walks quickly to the corner of Winter Street, her coat over her arm. Margaret is waiting, looking very pretty in a baby-blue dress that matches her eyes.

Margaret stares at her. 'Alice your dress is wonderful. You're so clever. But your face …' She stops, her mouth wide open. 'She hit you again.'

Alice nods. 'Does it look bad?'

'It looks rather sore.'

'All because I'm wearing make-up. I'll be eighteen in seven months – the age mum was married. I earn a good wage, most of which I give to her, and yet she treats me like a child.' She takes the compact out of her bag and powders over the raw skin. 'Let's hope the lights aren't too bright and that it's faded a bit by the time we get there.' She glances over her shoulder just in case her mother is coming after her. But the street is empty, except for two girls playing hopscotch on the pavement.

They walk to London Road and catch the bus to the Carfax. 'You're so lucky to have such mild-mannered parents who have never hit you, barely ever raise their voices to you.' She stares out of the window. 'Mum hasn't hit me since I started working and I thought she saw me as grown-up now, not a child that she could bully.'

Margaret reaches out for Alice's hand, but is quiet, as if she can't think what to say.

By the time they reach the dance hall Alice is too excited to think about the unpleasantness of the argument. She puts it out of her mind, determined it isn't going to spoil the evening.

They leave their coats in the cloakroom and push their way through the crowds to the bar. They both buy a lemonade and stand at the edge of the hall. There's a band at one end and about a dozen couples circling the dance floor. The floor throbs and Alice's feet tap, itching to dance. Her dad had taught her when she was a young child. She would stand on his feet so she could learn the steps as he waltzed and spun her round the room.

Within a few minutes Margaret is asked for a dance and Alice watches as she is whirled away by a tall man who resembles Cary Grant. She's the worst friend to go out with, because all the boys make a beeline for her. But kindness runs in Margaret's veins. *She puts me to shame*, Alice thinks. *My blood is laced with bad humour.*

She'd been worried that with so many young men called up there might not be many left to dance with, but there are plenty of servicemen in their uniforms. The band is playing one of her favourites, 'Oh Johnny', and she tells herself that she's happy to watch and listen. She really doesn't mind if she doesn't dance. After all, who wants to dance with a girl who wears glasses? But then a young soldier appears in front of her. His cheeks are speckled with small spots, but he has beautiful brown eyes, splintered with green. He stares at his feet as he speaks to her, his face flushed with embarrassment. She isn't sure if he is asking her to dance but says, 'Yes', in the hope that he is. He looks up and seems surprised. Alice offers him her hand, and he leads her to the dance floor just as the band start playing another foxtrot.

'Hello, I'm Frank,' he says.

'Hello, Frank. I'm Alice.' She smiles and he grins. He visibly relaxes and his blush fades. And as they move around the floor Alice can't believe her luck. He's such a good dancer.

As the music changes to a waltz Alice says, 'Where did you learn?'

'My mum,' he says. 'She first taught me when I was very small.'

'Did you used to stand on her feet?'

'How did you know that?'

Alice laughs. 'That was how my dad taught me.' She feels an immediate affinity with him, the way they move well together. At first, it seems strange being in such close proximity to a man she doesn't know, but he doesn't hold her too close, as if he's aware too of this strangeness. His skin has a nice smell: coal-tar soap mixed with a slight salty odour. From time to time she sees Margaret with her dance partner. She's not having such a good time. He might be good-looking, but he's clumsy, and once she hears Margaret cry out in pain when he treads on her toes.

The evening flies by and when it's time to leave, Frank says, 'Can I walk you home?'

'My friend's father is meeting us,' Alice says. In fact, he is only meeting them from the bus, but Alice and Margaret have had it drummed into them by Margaret's parents that they must not leave the dance hall with any of the men they dance with.

'Will you write to me?' Frank says. 'I leave England next week for who knows where.'

'I would love to. Tell me where to send my letters.' She takes a pencil and a piece of paper out of her bag and writes her address.

His face seems to light up and she suddenly has an urge to say, 'Yes, you can walk me home', because that would give her more time with him. But Margaret is waiting for her and looking anxious.

'I had a lovely evening. Thank you,' Alice says.

He kisses her mouth lightly as they say goodbye, and Alice feels something melt inside her. As she walks away, her feet are still dancing.

Outside the dance hall the enchantment evaporates as her mother's unpleasantness comes flooding back. She decides she isn't going home and hopes her gran doesn't mind her moving in with her and Vivien. Although they might be in bed, she knows where they keep a spare key.

When they alight from the bus, Margaret's father is waiting for them. He's a lot older than Alice's dad and was wounded in the last war. He walks with a limp and she can see that sometimes he's in pain. Margaret says he has terrible nightmares. On the way he asks her about her work with penicillin and says, 'How marvellous it will be if gas gangrene can be cured.'

Alice feels a little proud of her small contribution to its production.

'You don't have to walk me all the way home,' she says. 'I'm staying at Gran's tonight.' It will be a shorter walk for him, just round the corner from his house.

Margaret bites her bottom lip, but says nothing.

They say goodbye outside her gran's, and she makes her way to the back door. She's just about to remove the key from behind a loose brick when the door opens and Vivien appears.

'How did you know?' Alice says once they're in the kitchen and she's shut the cold night air out.

'Peter,' Vivien whispers. 'Try to be quiet, so we don't wake your gran. He came over and told me what had happened. He was worried. I told him that I thought you would come here after the dance and sent him home. I'm afraid you'll have to share a bed with me.' She puts the kettle on, and they sit in the kitchen, with a cup of tea. 'I'm sorry. It was probably my fault lending you the make-up,' she says. 'Your mother doesn't seem to realise you're almost a woman.'

'She hit me,' Alice says.

Her aunt frowns. 'I'm sorry she did that.' She pauses. 'Did you have a good time?'

'It was wonderful. I will be dancing all night in my sleep.'

'Well, don't kick me,' Vivien says.

The next morning Vivien persuades Alice to walk home with her before church.

'I'm not staying if she treats me like a child,' Alice says.

'I don't mind you sharing my bed for one night, but that is all. I put up with sharing a bed with your mother until she got married. Did you know that? I rather like having the bed to myself now.'

Alice wonders what that would be like, never having her own room or her own bed. 'Mum once told me how liberated she felt when she first got married, having her own house, some space of her own.'

'Your mother married young to escape home.'

'Why did she want to leave so badly?'

'There was a lot of friction between your gran and her.'

'A bit like with me,' Alice says.

'Exactly. You are like two enemies constantly sizing each other up.'

'I rarely win though and it's even harder without Dad to take my side.'

As they approach the back door, Vivien says, 'I'll go in first, see if I can talk her round. You go and get ready for church.'

The fishing rod is missing from Peter's room and Alice is glad as it means he hasn't waited to make sure she comes home. Her aunt had clearly reassured him.

Alice listens to her mum and aunt talking downstairs.

Vivien's voice is calm and measured, her mum's voice is angry and shouty. Then suddenly the argument ends and there is silence.

Although her mum and Vivien argue a lot, they always make up in the end. And she, Alice, has been the cause of many of the fights. She remembers the first time she realised she couldn't see properly. It wasn't long after she started at the high school. At junior school she'd always sat at the front of the class, and never had a problem reading the blackboard. At the high school they sat alphabetically, and she was at the back of the room. With horror she discovered that the teachers' writing was a white blur. The teacher sent her home with a note for her parents that said she needed glasses. As usual, her mum was too busy to look at it and asked Alice to read it out as she scrubbed the sink with Vim.

'Does she think we're made of money?' her mum said. 'She'll just have to let you sit at the front.'

But Alice had talked to her aunt, who was furious with her sister. She took Alice to the pharmacist the following Saturday to buy some glasses. That day was a revelation. All the fuzzy shapes became distinct. The trees were no longer covered in green blobs but individual leaves. She could even read the sign below the Co-op clock on Windmill Road: THE CO-OP WAY. SAVE AS YOU PAY.

Because Vivien hadn't discussed it with her sister first, there'd been a big row at her gran's house.

'We don't need your charity,' her mum yelled. 'She's my daughter, not yours and I'll decide whether she needs glasses.'

'Her teacher says she needs them. I think she's in a better position to judge than you,' Vivien said. 'I'm just trying to help. I know money's tight and you're too proud to ask for help.'

'It's your fault she needs glasses in the first place, because you encourage her to read too much.' And her mother walked out of the house shutting the back door with a loud crash.

Once her dad found out, he was cross, because if her mum had just taken her to get some glasses, Vivien wouldn't have had to get involved.

'Thank goodness for Vivien,' he said. So then her mum didn't speak to her dad or her aunt. It all blew over a few days later. Alice had realised a long time ago that her mum and aunt were tightly bound. She wonders if she and Peter will be like that when they're older.

'Are you ready?' Vivien calls up the stairs.

They walk to church together, her aunt between Alice and her mum, providing a buffer zone. Her gran is waiting inside, and Alice slips into the pew beside her. Vivien and her mum sit behind.

Alice enjoys the ritual of going to church. She loves the singing and the coming together of her community. And on a sunny day, the glow of the stained-glass windows lifts her spirits. She's sure her aunt isn't religious, not like her mum, but Vivien once said that as a teacher, it was important she was seen at church. And there are usually some of her pupils at the service who want to say 'hello'.

She misses Peter's presence even more than usual. He stopped attending church a year ago, says he doesn't believe in God. Her mum says it's just a phase; he's learned some nonsense from the other boys at school and he'll come back to it in good time. Alice has her doubts. In some ways she understands his loss of faith. Even she finds it difficult to marry a benevolent god with all the terrible things that are happening now. It's the only time he has stood up to their mum. He is much more biddable than she is. But it probably helped that their dad said he didn't have to go. He says that both Peter and Alice should make up their own minds about what they believe and not let other people decide for them.

The only time her dad goes to church is for weddings (his own of course) and funerals. Her mum nags him to go, but she's never going to win that battle. Before he joined up, he said if he was working all week, Sunday was a day for him to do what he wanted. Mostly he went fishing and when Peter stopped going to church, he went with him. Alice used to be jealous of the time they had together, so once she missed church and went with them when the weather was warm. Peter was furious that Alice was muscling in on his time with their dad, but she just got bored. There was very little conversation, the only sound was the swish of the line. Whenever she tried to talk to them, she was told to be quiet – she would disturb the fish. And for Alice, sitting quietly is impossible unless she has a book to read.

After the service Alice and her mum walk home in silence. What is only a five-minute walk seems to take an hour. Peter is in the kitchen eating a thick slice of bread and dripping. He grins when he sees her. Throughout dinner he talks constantly about who he'd met at the river and how many fish he'd almost caught. Alice listens, asks questions and laughs at his jokes, but her mum is quiet. It is clear there isn't going to be an apology. *What will happen the next time I wear make-up?* she thinks. *Is she going to explode again? And is it about the make-up anyway or is she jealous of me having a good time?*

If only she could move out, live somewhere else. But how could she afford it? When she was younger, she assumed she would stay at home until she got married and have a family of her own – like her mum had done. But Alice can't imagine getting married. She wants a career like Vivien and to achieve something with her life.

# 9

# Alice

*17 May 1941*

The sun is warm on Alice's back as she cycles to the Infirmary. The world seems to be bursting with life: flowers in profusion in the college gardens, the cherry trees in the streets cascading blossom to the pavements and fresh green leaves unfurling. Dr Heatley had asked for a volunteer to take some penicillin to the hospital and Alice offered immediately. Ever since her first visit, she's taken every opportunity to go there. An idea had planted itself in her brain at that visit and she can't dislodge it. It's not just the order and cleanliness that fascinates her, it's that the doctors and nurses are doing work that is so valuable. What could be more meaningful than spending your life trying to cure sick people? Of course, in a small way that is what she is doing at the Dunn. But anyone could do what she does. Some days it's like being on a factory line.

Today she is taking penicillin for a 4-year-old boy, Johnny Cox. Alice has been to the children's ward before. The sister is formidable. The nurses scuttle around to do her bidding and even the doctors seem in awe of her. *It is rare*, Alice thinks, *to find an occupation where a woman has such high regard*. The sister is younger than Vivien and her mum, and yet she holds so much power. Alice yearns to be someone like her, someone who can command respect. So the idea of becoming a nurse grows a little more. She tries to reason with herself. There's a lot of drudgery, especially for the junior nurses, and she would hate all the orders. But she could swallow that if she knew that eventually she could be a sister. And she would get an education. She'd heard the nurses talking about all the exams they had to sit and although they complained, she envied them that opportunity.

When she enters the ward, the sister is full of smiles. 'Ah, good. More penicillin. Just look at him. He is so much better.'

Alice watches Johnny sitting on his bed talking to the nurses as he plays with some toys. He is such an endearing fellow and she can see many of the nurses are fond of him.

When he was first treated, he had a bacterial infection in his eyes, lungs and liver. The doctors said he had only days to live – penicillin was their last hope. He has been given the antibiotic intravenously for four days and has made a remarkable recovery. And there it is again, that nagging idea in her head – how rewarding it must be to nurse someone back to health. She desperately wants to speak to one of the nurses now, to ask them more about their training and to find out if she has a chance of being accepted into a nursing school, or whether she's just fooling herself and the idea is just fantasy.

The nurses are usually too busy to speak to her, but today a junior nurse approaches Alice as she watches Johnny. It's immediately clear that the nurse wants someone to moan to.

'I'm in trouble with Sister for not cleaning out the bed-pans properly,' she says. 'It's the worst job. They all go in the steamer, but I'm supposed to wash them by hand as well. But I didn't have time.'

Alice listens, but says nothing. She is on the sister's side in this argument. The nurse was being sloppy. And if she was the sister, she would have been furious with her too. Cleanliness is so important. She knows that from her laboratory work at the Dunn.

'She's a tyrant,' the nurse says.

'Why did you want to be a nurse?' Alice says.

'I thought it would be all about saving lives, but to be honest, most of it is sheer hard work. There are times when I think I'll give it up, but then something amazing happens and I change my mind.'

'Like Johnny Cox's recovery?' Alice says.

But before the nurse can answer the sister sails towards them. 'If you chatted less, nurse, you might get your work done.'

'It's my fault,' Alice says. 'I was quizzing her because I'm thinking about training as a nurse.'

The severe frown on the sister's face dissolves. 'Nursing is very demanding and there are some who come into it who aren't prepared for that.' She glares at the junior nurse who scurries away.

'The training is challenging too,' she continues. 'There are lots of exams to pass.'

Alice says, 'I wouldn't mind if I could learn again like at school. And I'm not afraid of hard work.'

'Then you will make a good nurse. Ask Professor Florey to give you a reference.' And she turns and breezes away.


On her cycle ride back to the lab, Alice makes up her mind. She will apply. What does she have to lose? She will talk it through with Vivien, who always gives her good advice, but she is determined now that this is where her future lies.

She only works a half day on Saturdays and as it is almost

twelve o'clock when she returns to the Dunn, Dr Heatley says she can go home. As usual, on a Saturday, she heads to her gran's house for dinner. When she steps into the kitchen, the windows are steamy with condensation from the pans of boiling vegetables. Her gran removes a pie from the Rayburn oven and the earthy smell of cooked kidneys fills the room. Alice tries not to look disappointed. It's not a meal she likes, and she hopes there is some meat in the pie, however small, to help her to swallow the offal.

'Wash your hands and sit down,' her gran says as if she's still a child. Alice glances at Vivien who is draining the potatoes, and they exchange smiles. Peter is already at the table. 'That smells amazing,' he says as Gran places the pie on the table and serves it on to plates. Tiny bits of fatty beef pool in the rich gravy. No-one complains – they are lucky to have any meat at all. The conversation over dinner is dominated by Alice. But not about her nursing plans. She has a feeling her mother will do all she can to stop her applying, so for now she will have to keep it secret from everyone except Vivien. So instead, she talks about the miraculous recovery of Johnny Cox.

'Poor little mite,' her gran says. 'I do hope you're right and this peni-what's-it cures him. It didn't work with that policeman, did it.'

'We just didn't have enough penicillin to give him,' Alice says. 'But the professor has cured several people now who weren't as sick, so they needed less drug.'

'So, he's proved it works,' Vivien says.

Alice nods. 'Although Johnny Cox was very sick, like PC Alexander, the professor has gambled on having enough of the antibiotic to cure him.'

'I do hope he's successful.' Vivien says. 'It must be hard deciding who to treat when you make so little of it.'

'His poor mother,' her gran says. There's a tremor in her voice and Alice looks up alarmed. Tears well up in her gran's eyes and Vivien reaches across the table and takes her hand. Peter stares at his plate.

'I think I'll have a little lie down,' her gran says before she stands and leaves the room.

Alice stares quizzically at Vivien who just shakes her head.

She remembers then that Vivien had once told Peter and her that her gran had a son who died of typhoid fever when he was three years old.

'I feel terrible. I shouldn't have mentioned Johnny Cox,' Alice says.

'Most days it wouldn't have mattered, but today would have been my brother's birthday. But you didn't know that. It's not something we talk about,' Vivien says.

Peter runs his finger round the rim of his water glass. 'What was his name?'

'Edward,' Vivien says. 'Although your gran calls him Teddy when she talks about him. I never knew him, but I often think about what life would be like if he'd lived.'

For a moment the ghost of Uncle Teddy hangs in the room. Alice wonders if penicillin would have cured him and all the children that died from bacterial infections in the past. If only they could scale up their production so many children's lives could be saved.

She breaks the silence. 'I'll wash up.' She stacks the plates, carries them into the kitchen then fills the bowl with hot water. Vivien clatters more crockery beside her and picks up a tea towel. Alice slides the plates into the soapy water.

Through the window she sees Peter has slipped into the garden. This is a perfect opportunity to speak to her aunt alone. 'I've been thinking about this for a while, but when I was at the Infirmary today, I made my mind up – I would like to be a nurse.'

'It's a hard job and it will take four years to train,' Vivien says.

Alice rinses a plate and stacks it in the drainer. 'I know, but I'll never be more than a technician in my current job. I've learned such a lot and I'll miss Dr Heatley and the other girls, but I want a career … Like you.'

'You'll have to wait until you're eighteen.'

'That seems an age away.'

'It's only six months.' Vivien removes the wet plate and wipes it dry. 'You'll be paid a lot less than you are now while you're training.'

'I don't care about that.'

'Yes, but your mum will,' Vivien says, putting the dry plates in the cupboard.

Alice stops washing and scowls. Fury builds inside her. It seems to start in the bottom of her stomach and rise through her throat. 'If she knew, she would try to stop me, wouldn't she?'

Vivien doesn't reply.

Alice clatters more crockery into the sink. 'It would be nice, for once, if she cared about me and what I want. Instead, all she cares about is how much money I contribute to the family.'

'I think your gran would like her plates to stay intact.'

'Please don't say anything to anyone else in the family, not even Peter. I don't want them to know until I've been offered a place at nursing school.'

'I won't. I promise. And I will try to help in whatever way I can. It's a very brave decision.'

Alice sighs. What would she do without Vivien? 'I'm going to tell Dad when I next write to him. I think he'll approve.'

'Have you heard from him?'

'No, not for ages. I feel like I hold my breath between his letters.'

'What about the young man you met at the dance?'

'Frank wrote such a funny letter, illustrated with sketches and cartoons. At first, when he described the heat and dust, I thought he must be in North Africa. But he mentioned liquorice growing by the river and drew a cartoon of a plant dotted with Liquorice Allsorts. Then he drew a bible with "Old Testament" written on it. And later, quite randomly, he said where the T and E rivers meet. I knew he was giving me a clue to his location. It took me a moment to work it out but then I remembered drawing a map of the Tigris and Euphrates in RE at school and knew he must be in Iraq.'

'I'm amazed the censors didn't spot that,' Vivien says.

Alice nods excitedly. 'He said that he often thinks about the dance and what good dancing partners we were, and beside that he drew a cartoon of him stepping on my toes in his army boots that made me laugh out loud.' Remembering it all again makes her smile. She loved getting his letter.

'What an interesting letter.'

'It's hard to think how I can entertain him in my reply. He asked if I would send him a photograph. Do you think Pat would take one of me?'

Vivien's friend Pat is a keen photographer. She even develops the photographs herself in a dark room in the basement of her house. When Pat joins them on family occasions, she takes snapshots of them when they are unaware, so the photographs never look posed.

'I may have one that's suitable. I have a box full of photos in my bedroom that she's given me. I'll look now.'

Alice tips the water out of the bowl and cleans the sink. No-one has ever asked for a photograph of her before. And as she thinks about Frank, she aches to see him again. *Let him come home on leave soon*, she thinks.

She watches Peter through the window. He is already hard at work, earthing up the potatoes. He says his favourite part of gardening is eating what they've grown. He eats like a horse. He's growing so fast; he's taller than her now and keeps tripping up as if he hasn't got used to how big his feet are. She likes to help with the garden whenever she can. They often work side by side in companionable silence, like they used to when they were children. It's such an escape from their yard where nothing blooms but weeds that get in the cracks of the concrete.

Her aunt seems to be taking a long time, so she wanders upstairs. Her bedroom door is ajar. On the bed is an old sweet tin, the lid discarded, and beside it three photographs. But her aunt is not there. She can hear Vivien's voice in the adjacent room: her gran's bedroom. Impatient to see what photographs she has found, Alice sits on the bed and picks up the pictures. There is one of Alice sitting among butter-cups, leaning back on her hands and laughing. That must have been last year when Vivien and Pat had taken Peter and Alice for a picnic at the top of Boar's Hill. There's another where she is also seated, but appears more pensive, with a book on her knee and the river in the background. The last one is in gran's garden, where she is wearing trousers that

Peter had grown out of, spade in hand. She looks happy, but she couldn't possibly let Frank see her looking such a mess and in trousers. She only ever wears them for gardening. Her mum complains when she sees her in them and has made her promise she will never wear them anywhere else. Lots of women are wearing trousers now. They are so much more practical for many of the jobs they are doing, including her mum, who still refuses to wear such things. But if she can escape to nursing school, she won't have to worry about what her mum thinks anymore.

She glances at the tin which is half full of black-and-white images. She itches to see all the other photographs. She never imagined her aunt had so many. As she starts to go through them, she sees they are nearly all of Vivien. Then she sees one of Vivien and Pat in profile, foreheads together in a pose that is unsettling. Pat must have set the camera on a tripod with a timer. Surely, they wouldn't have let anyone else take that shot. A photograph of a man and a woman showing such adoration would be uncomfortable to look at, but this is her aunt and her best friend.

'What are you doing?' Vivien says, her voice angry and loud – a voice Alice has never heard before. 'I never gave you permission to look at those.'

Alice drops the photograph in the box and moves away from the bed, heat rising up her neck and face. 'I'm sorry. I didn't think—'

Vivien picks up the three images of Alice. 'Here,' she says her voice softening. 'Would one of these be suitable?'

'Yes, thank you. I'd like the one taken on the picnic.' As she leaves the room she glances back. Vivien is putting the lid back on the tin and pushing it under her bed.

It's late afternoon when she walks home with Peter. She mulls over in her mind the strange photograph of Vivien and Pat. Peter is chatty – he's always in a good mood when he's spent the day in their gran's garden – and Alice soon lets the image slide from her mind. When they arrive home their mother is on the old paint-splattered stepladder cleaning the kitchen window. 'Did you have a good day?' she says.

'Gran sent you a loaf of bread she baked this morning,' Alice says.

'I've been working hard,' Peter says. 'And now I'm starving.'

There's an opened letter on the kitchen table. Alice knows at once from the writing that it's from her dad. She picks it up and starts reading.

'Can you read it to me?' her mum says. 'I only had time to glance at it.'

Alice exhales loudly. She was looking forward to reading the letter alone in her bedroom. Why is her mother always too busy to read anything? Peter starts hacking at the loaf of bread. 'And me,' he says. She starts reading again, this time out loud.

*Sunday, 6 April 1940*
*My Dear Family*

*Thank you, Alice, for your letters. They keep me going. They remind me why I'm here and tether me to reality, for I am living a strange life. I saw a mirage today. It was the strangest thing. I was absolutely convinced it was a large pool of water. I wanted so much to find it, but I knew it wasn't real, just something to do with light and the heat in the desert. I am weary of the sand and long for trees and lakes. When I can't sleep at night, I imagine I'm by the river at home, fishing. It always calms me.*

*I had a bit of surprise yesterday when I found a snake beneath the truck. I backed away and waited until it slithered away. I think it was some kind of viper. We have learned to respect the wildlife here. Not only the snakes, but the scorpions too.*

*I have lost all sense of time, I'm never sure what date it is. The day is defined by sunrise and sunset, but otherwise time is fluid. It extends and contracts. The one day that is distinct is Sunday when, if he can, the padre sets up an altar on the back of a truck. You will be surprised when I say that I look forward to these services. I want the normality it gives us. We sing hymns and pray to God to help us in our battles. There is an assumption, of course, that he is on our side. If I'm honest I don't believe any of it, but I have to have something to hang on to.*

*I have been writing in my journal. When my mind is in turmoil from the horrors I've seen, it helps to write things down. Next week I have five days' leave and plan to visit Cairo and Luxor, places I never imagined I would see. At least something positive has come out of this dreadful war. I will write and tell you all about it.*

*Love Dad*

The letter has taken over a month to arrive so by now he will already have had his leave and will be back fighting again. Did his trip lift his spirits? She really hopes it did. It sounds like he needed to get away. She wants desperately to hug him. And her worries about his safety flood her mind. She holds in her tears and swallows hard.

# 10

# Jo

*25 December 2017*

Jo gathers up the scraps of wrapping paper dotting the carpet and stuffs them into an empty cardboard box. 'I hope you're impressed, Mum,' she says in an imaginary conversation she's been having with her mum all morning. In the corner of the room the small Christmas tree looks empty now all the presents piled beneath it have gone. Jessie had managed to decorate the tree over the course of a week, with red and silver baubles and tiny lights. Even hanging a few ornaments had exhausted her, but she'd managed a few every day and seemed quite pleased with her efforts when it was finished.

Jessie usually loves Christmas, but this year Jo noticed that when she opened her presents, she seemed bored and indifferent. Kate had tried to inject some excitement, taking an interest in everything Jessie opened and showing Jessie all her gifts. But Jessie's mood has been black for the last few days.

Once the carpet is clear of paper and pieces of Sellotape, Jo takes the box out of the room. It would usually be her mum clearing up, unable to bear the mess, and Jo would help, feeling guilty. Her mum was always tidying. Not that her mum's house was ever *untidy*. When Jo was a child, as soon as she unwrapped a present, the paper would be whisked away before it even fell to the floor. Jo's untidiness used to exasperate her mum when she lived at home. Her dad was always sticking up for her: 'Leave her be. Children are messy. She'll grow out of it.' But she never has. She tries hard not to be, knowing how much it irritates Rob, but it's an uphill struggle.

Today her mum is like a ghostly presence sitting on her shoulder. Her first thought when she woke was that this year, for the first time ever, her mother would not be with her on Christmas Day. She has been trying to push this thought away, not wanting to spoil the day for Jessie and Kate. But it's hard.

Returning, Jo stands for a moment and regards her family. Jessie is curled in the corner of the sofa, her eyes fixed on the ceiling. Kate is sitting on the floor in front of Jessie, flicking through the pages of a book, all her other presents neatly piled beside her. Rob is engrossed with his iPad. There is a quietness in the room. Each member of the family seems lost in their own thoughts and yet there is a connectedness, as if an invisible strand holds them all together. It is so different from the Christmases when Kate and Jessie were children and the house overflowed with their energy. But calm is what they all need after the events of the last seven weeks.

Jessie uncurls her legs and sits up straight. The skin between her eyebrows is pulled into two deep furrows. 'Would you have celebrated Christmas if I'd died?' she says. Her words are like a bomb exploding the peace in the room. Jo feels as if all the air has been sucked out and she can't breathe. Kate turns and gazes at Jessie, her expression not one of sympathy, but irritation.

Rob's face contorts in anger. 'What a thing to say, Jessie.'

'Well, would you?' she says.

'No. How could we possibly have celebrated?' Jo says.

'But you would have got used to me not being here … eventually.'

'That's enough,' Rob says standing. 'I will *not* listen to this kind of talk.'

But Jessie ignores him. 'Grandma died, but we're still celebrating.'

Jo sits beside her and tries to take her hand. But Jessie snatches it away scowling.

'I could never adjust to you not being in my life,' Jo says. 'Part of me would always be missing.' And the fear she'd had in the hospital that they might lose her hits her again like a physical pain in her stomach.

Kate lays her head on Jessie's lap, but Jessie is not interested in being comforted. 'You're squashing me,' she says, pushing Kate away. Rob leaves the room and after a few minutes, Jo can hear him filling the kettle in the kitchen.

'Why do you always spoil everything?' Kate says.

'Sorry, sister, for getting ill and ruining your life.'

This behaviour reminds Jo of Jessie when she was a young teenager; a phase she went through when there was no reasoning with her. Jo doesn't have the energy to deal with it. Not today.

'I'm going to finish getting lunch ready,' she says, glancing at Kate.

Kate stands. 'I'll come and help.'

Rob is disappearing up the stairs with a mug in his hand. He leaves behind him a strong smell of coffee. Jo knows he will disappear to Kate's old bedroom. He started sleeping there after Kate left and refuses to move out until Jessie's nightmares stop. Kate is sleeping on an airbed in Jessie's room. Jo thought Jessie would make a fuss about sharing, but her lack of protest and the absence of nightmares since Kate has been home suggests she is comforted by her presence.

~

Later Jo carries a bottle of Sancerre, Rob's favourite, into the dining room. Kate has laid the table and decorated it with holly cut from the garden tied with red ribbon. Beside each place setting are the crackers Jo has made. She started making them when they didn't have much money and now it's a family tradition. She personalises each cracker with a small gift. It's always hard trying to find something small for Rob that won't irritate him. He hates waste. This year she bought him a USB stick and for the girls a bracelet each from Zoe's shop: Jessie's is made of alternating large and small Bakelite orange beads; Kate's is also Bakelite, but the beads are oval jade. She'd bought them the day before that terrible phone call, spotted them in the shop and knew they would be perfect.

When the children were small, they used to draw pictures to put inside each cracker. One year Jessie had drawn lots of fruit flies for Rob, which he loved. Jo had framed it for him and he put it on his desk at work. It's years since she's been to his office, and she wonders if it's still there. Last year, Jo had transcribed a favourite poem for each of them. Kate's is still pinned to the cork noticeboard in her bedroom among photos and invitations.

This year Jo decided to do something that remembered her mum, who was a wonderful cook. She wasn't a physically affectionate person; she showed her regard for people through the food she prepared. And her mum loved cooking at Christmas. After the funeral, Jo had taken a few possessions that had sentimental value: her rings, a necklace her dad had bought her, her apron and an old, tattered notebook in which her mother had stuck or written instructions for cakes and puddings. It was splattered in places with a smear of grease, a splash of red, a spot encrusted with sugar. She was looking through it when planning the Christmas food and had the idea of photographing and printing one of her mum's recipes for each cracker: the chocolate brownies that Jessie loved; the sticky toffee pudding that Kate adored; the fruitcake that her mum always made for Rob when they stayed, because she knew how much he enjoyed it. Rob would never make the cake, but he would understand its symbolism. She didn't tell them. She wanted it to be a surprise. As usual, Kate had taken charge of Jo's cracker so hers would be a surprise too.

Back in the kitchen steam wafts from the sink. Kate is draining the Brussels sprouts.

'The table looks beautiful, Kate,' Jo says. 'Don't let Jessie spoil today. She's frightened.'

'I know,' Kate says. 'But why did she have to say that today? It could have waited until tomorrow.'

'Have you ever known Jessie not say what she's thinking? Let's get the food on the table. It's all ready.'

Jo opens the oven and releases a blast of hot air. The fat in the meat tray is sizzling and spitting and she eases it out slowly. The smell of the rosemary-and-sage seasoning that she has rubbed into the skin fills the kitchen. She lifts the turkey onto a spiked carving platter, and now there is a sweet aroma from the stuffing. Her mum's favourite: apricot and hazelnut. She carries it to the table and lays it on Rob's placemat with the carving knife and fork. Kate transfers the roast potatoes and parsnips, now golden brown, into a serving dish. The pudding is simmering gently. It is one of her mum's, made in the summer before she went into the hospice. She knew she would never live to eat it but had made it for Jo – her last act of love. Jo had wept a few tears when she had placed it in the pan two hours ago.

Kate calls Jessie and Rob to come and sit down. Jessie shuffles to the table and slouches in her chair. Before they start eating, they go round the table clockwise pulling their crackers, starting with Rob. He seems pleased with his gift and even smiles at the recipe. 'I'll give this to you, Kate,' he says. 'Then you can make it for me whenever I come and visit.'

'No chance,' Kate says and laughs. She pulls her cracker next. 'The bracelet is lovely, Mum; my favourite colour. Can I make the pudding tomorrow? Gran always made it when we visited.'

'If we've got the ingredients, but if not, we can buy them when the shops reopen.'

Rob groans. 'Not *more* mess in the kitchen.'

'I'm not as bad as Jessie,' Kate says.

'Hey, it's my turn,' Jessie says.

'Okay, sis. Sorry for the delay.'

Jo watches them pull Jessie's cracker. She desperately wants Jessie to engage in the festivities, for it to be as normal a Christmas as possible. So when Jessie smiles at the recipe, slips the bracelet onto her arm and says, 'Thank you, Mum,' Jo relaxes. It's going to be okay.

In her cracker, Jo finds a silver marcasite brooch in the shape of a leaf, and a sheet of writing paper on which Kate has transcribed the third sonnet of Seamus Heaney's *Clearances* that starts 'When all the others were away at mass …' Jo bites her lip as her mum's ghostly presence appears again, sleeves rolled up, peeling potatoes in her house in Barnsley.

'I didn't mean to upset you,' Kate says.

'The poem is perfect,' Jo says. 'And the brooch is beautiful. It looks rather expensive.'

'It was a bit of a find in a charity shop.'

Rob pours everyone a glass of wine and Jo raises hers and says, 'To Mum and Gran'. Everyone echoes her, even Jessie.

Jo pins the brooch to her blouse and smiles. Rob carves the turkey and hands everyone a plate of meat. Serving dishes are handed round, there is a clatter of cutlery on plates, and while everyone focuses on eating, conversation stops.

After a few minutes Kate says, 'The recipes are a lovely idea. I especially like that they're in Gran's writing and you can see the smudges and food stains. I'd quite like to copy the whole book.'

'She used to guard her recipes jealously, like they were secrets,' Jo says. 'She only shared them with people she was very close to. But I know she would have loved to share them with you.'

'It's a way of remembering her,' Kate says. 'Every time I bake one of her cakes, I will think of her.'

'She doted on you and Jessie. It's strange – she was never a touchy-feely person when I was a child, but with you two, that changed.'

'Maybe she mellowed as she got older,' Kate says.

Jo has no recollection of her mother ever cuddling her as a child. She was just not a physical person. Once Jo had visited a friend's house after school and had been astonished with how often her friend's mother had touched her daughter: first, an embrace after she and Jo had walked in through the back door; then a stray hair she'd smoothed away from her face; and later, while they had been sitting at the kitchen table talking, she'd laid a hand on her arm. She envied her friend so much it had rattled around in her head for weeks afterwards. Why wasn't her mother like that? Did she not love her? Of course her mother did, she just showed it in different ways. But she was determined that her children would have the physical love that was missing in her life. It was interesting that when her mother saw Jo's behaviour with her children, she seemed to emulate her. And a closeness developed with her mother that had never been present in her childhood. She was never like her friends' mothers, but they would hug when they met and sometimes, when they sat together on the sofa, Jo would drop her head onto her mother's shoulder, and instead of her mother rebuffing her, she seemed content, as if this had always happened between them.

Jessie is quiet. She has only eaten a few mouthfuls; her knife and fork are abandoned on her plate and she is staring at the tablecloth. 'Sorry, I can't eat much. If you don't mind, I'll skip pudding. I need a nap.'

Jo knows that Jessie is fully aware of the significance of the pudding, and for the first time since she has been home from the hospital, a flash of anger at Jessie's selfishness blazes through her. She stops eating for a moment. Then she rearranges her face into a smile, picks up her knife and fork from her plate and takes a mouthful of turkey. Kate opens her mouth as if she's about to say something, but stops when Jo shakes her head.

Rob stares at his wineglass.

The stairs creak. Jessie's bedroom door clicks shut.

When they've all finished eating, Jo gathers up the plates and carries them to the kitchen. She is filled with an over-whelming desire to drop them all onto the floor. To let them smash to smithereens. She grips them tightly in case the angry part of her brain overrides the level-headed part. Rob appears beside her with a serving dish in each hand, which he dumps beside the plates.

'Was it deliberate, because she's in such a bad mood today?' Jo says.

'Don't overreact,' he says. 'It's only a pudding.' After he's gone, she stands at the kitchen sink and breathes deeply, trying to release the fury bubbling under her skin. Now she wishes she had dropped the plates. To feel the shock of it. And to jolt him out of his selfishness.

She brings the Christmas pudding to the table and flames it with brandy, while Kate takes a photo with her smartphone. There's a small amount of wine left in the bottle which Rob pours into his glass. The pudding is delicious as always and will be a hard act to follow in future years. She'll never come up to scratch, so perhaps she'll just buy one next year. 'Sorry, Mum,' she says in her head again. 'I know you won't approve.'

After lunch Jo leaves all the dirty pans and plates – she can't face loading up the dishwasher. It won't all fit anyway; the greasy oven trays will have to be hand-washed. Kate stays in the dining room to message her friends, and Rob disappears upstairs again. Jo slumps on the sofa. Why does she always want Christmas to be perfect?

At least this year, Jessie's illness has given them the perfect excuse not to see Rob's parents. They usually visited his parents' house for lunch the day after Jo's mum had gone home. Jo has always dreaded it.

Their house is huge and the decor wouldn't look out of

place in a designer magazine, but it's not a house she would ever want to live in. When the girls were young, she was always worried they might make a mess or break a vase that had cost hundreds of pounds. Even in the equally immaculate garden, the girls were restricted. It's just as well they weren't keen footballers, because Rob's father would never have let them kick a football on his lawn. Not that David did the gardening … he paid people to do that for him. One year it had snowed and the girls had been desperate to make a snowman, but David forbade them to go on the lawn to roll balls to make a body and head because they would damage the grass. In the end, the girls had made their snowman in the front driveway while Rob fumed and Jo tried keep the peace, telling the girls it would be much better in the front of the house because everyone walking past would see it.

Jo had understood from very early on in their relationship that Rob had rebelled against his father, who'd expected him to follow him into the finance industry, like Justin. The measure of success for both David and Justin was how much money they earned. 'Are you a professor yet?' his father would ask sometimes, as if he couldn't consider Rob had a successful career until he achieved this senior academic position. That barb always hit home and put Rob in a foul mood. He would scowl as Justin and his wife talked about all their homes: a six-bedroomed house in Hertfordshire, a holiday villa in Tuscany, an apartment in Val-d'Isère. And every year his brother would tease Jo: 'You haven't lost that accent yet', as if he could think of nothing original to say. She always smiled while thinking, *I'd rather have my accent than your ridiculous posh one.*

In the quiet of the living room, Jo allows herself to think

of her mum, of all her childhood Christmases – how special they'd been even though they didn't have much money.

When she and Rob were first married, they'd always spent Christmas at her mum and dad's house. Rob hated going to his parents' house as much as Jo did. Her parents didn't quiz him. They showed an interest in his research not his status, and her mother always made a fuss of him: Had he had enough to eat? Was he warm enough? Was there something he would prefer to watch on the TV? Her dad was such a mild man in comparison to Rob's father. He didn't need to dominate the conversation or make his presence known. So Rob could relax in a way he never could in his own parents' house.

The only time her parents and Rob's parents ever met was at their wedding. Once had been enough for Jo's parents. After the Registry Office ceremony, Jo and Rob had booked lunch in their favourite restaurant for immediate family and a few friends. They had told everyone there were to be no speeches; they wanted it to be very low key. It was such a relief for her dad, who'd been dreading having to give a speech. As Jo had feared, her mum and dad shrivelled in front of Caroline and David, not knowing what to say. At the end of the meal, ignoring Rob's request, David stood up, gave a short speech, then toasted the bride and groom. Rob had turned red with anger and Jo's dad looked confused and embarrassed. Justin was completely plastered by the time they left the restaurant and Jo heard him say to her dad, 'Ee ba gum, I enjoyed that', in an appalling imitation of a Barnsley accent. If it hadn't been their wedding, Rob would probably have floored him.

After her dad died, Jo decided Christmas was too much work for her mum and persuaded her to spend it with them.

She remembers last year and the tears she has been fighting back all day pour down her face. But then she reminds herself that a few weeks ago, they had nearly lost Jessie and here she is at home on Christmas Day. She has a lot to be thankful for. She wipes her face and blows her nose.

Jessie slinks into room and drops into one of the armchairs. She fiddles with the Bakelite bracelet, running her fingers over the beads. 'I love this,' she says. 'It's such a cheerful colour. Is it from Zoe's shop?'

'It is. I'm pleased you like it.'

'Can you read more of Alice's diary?'

Jo is glad Kate isn't in the room as she would have been sure to accuse Jo of being too soft, of letting Jessie get away with her earlier bad behaviour. But Kate doesn't understand how this diary has created a bond between them. And she thinks of the final lines in Seamus Heaney's sonnet:

> *I remembered her head bent towards my head,*
> *Her breath in mine, our fluent dipping knives—*
> *Never closer the whole rest of our lives.*

She picks up the diary from the coffee table.

### Sunday, 18 May 1941

Today I went to Boars Hill with Margaret. The photograph Pat had taken of me last year had reminded me how lovely it was, and I wanted to show Margaret. We took the bus part of the way, then walked through fields of buttercups to the top of the hill. We could see the spires of Oxford below us as we ate our picnic. I felt as if I had taken a step out of my current life filled with war and destruction into another more peaceful life.

Margaret talked constantly about her new job working for the Department of Education. Initially she had been in the typing pool, but within two weeks, she was plucked from there to be a secretary to one of the managers. I wasn't surprised. Margaret is clever and diligent and the most organised person I know. But I'm clever too and I couldn't help feeling Margaret was streaking ahead of me. I have to admit I was rather jealous. I wasn't going to tell her about my decision to become a nurse in case she told her parents, and it got back to Mum. But I had to tell her to prove I had a future too. Margaret looked surprised.

'But isn't nursing a very caring profession?' she said.

I frowned. 'Do you think I don't care about making people well?'

'It takes a lot of patience to care for sick people.'

'I know I don't suffer fools gladly, but I have a lot of patience when I'm working in the lab, and I have other qualities: I have stamina and one thing I've learned is that nursing is sheer hard work. I learn fast. And I *do* care. I imagine it's very rewarding helping someone to recover. Just as it's satisfying when the penicillin we've made cures someone.'

She had spoilt our walk and we barely spoke on the way home. When we said goodbye, she laid her hand on my arm and said, 'I'm sorry. I didn't mean to offend you. If this is what you really want, then you should do it. One thing I do know about you is that if you're determined to do something, you generally succeed.'

I thought about her words when I got home and regretted getting angry. She knows me well. I am dogged. That's why Mum and I don't get on.

**Wednesday, 21 May 1941**

When I came home from work there was another letter from Dad. Peter had already pored over it and discussed it with Mum. He'd probably even read it to her. So I took it up to my room to read. I haven't replied to his last letter yet. This one arrived much more quickly.

Underneath these words is a pocket made from plain paper and inside a flimsy airmail letter.

'Look, another one,' Jo says, holding up the diary for Jessie to see. This is the third letter from Alice's dad that she has found in the diary. Each time just touching the letter makes her feel she has stretched her hand back through history. She holds her breath as she eases it out and unfolds it carefully. It's a privilege to hold such a precious document and she worries it might fall apart in her hands. Jessie moves from the chair and curls up beside her, leaning her head on Jo's shoulder so she can see the letter. She is quiet and Jo can sense her intense interest. The writing is small and spidery, but although the ink has faded over the years, it is easy to read.

*My Dear Family*

*After five days leave, I'm back in the thick of it. But those five days were so wonderful that my memories of them will keep my spirits up. After months in the desert, where all the colours except the sky are fawns and duns and dusty green, visiting*

*Cairo was overwhelming. Not just the colours – the blue of the Nile edged with lush green borders – but the sounds of the place. Cars and the rattle of horse-drawn carriages mixed with donkey carts and trams overloaded with barefoot peasants. All life, rich and poor, rubs shoulders in the streets. It hums with so many different languages, overlaid five times each day by the Islamic call to prayer. The mosques are beautiful, like nothing I have ever seen before.*

*I spent one day and one night in Cairo at a cheap hotel. I visited the pyramids at Giza. Their size is unbelievable, 450 feet high and constructed from millions of stones. They are, in effect, giant burial mounds thought to be shaped to resemble the rays of the sun falling to earth.*

*I caught the train to Luxor where I stayed for three days. I went first to the Valley of the Kings, where tombs were cut into the rock for the pharaohs, over 3,000 years ago, then to the Karnak Temple, a vast open-air complex, overwhelming in size. The most impressive was a large hall with over 130 colossal stone pillars, each carefully carved with hieroglyphs, and on the walls, images of pharaohs making offerings to gods, as well as pictures of teams of oxen, ducks and geese, resembling scenes I had seen by the Nile. How little has changed. These Ancient Egyptians believed in the survival of the spirit – if you can believe that, then there is no need to fear death. It's a creed I could quite willingly adopt at the moment.*

*This war is appalling, but when I was in Luxor, I thought that if I had a choice between the opportunity to see this place, even with the possibility of death, and my old life in Oxford, I would choose this. That doesn't mean I don't love any of you any less, but I never felt so alive in all my life.*

*Love Dad*

'Wow,' Jessie says.

Jo slides the letter back into place, 'Shall I continue with the diary?' Jessie rubs her head on Jo's shoulder, which Jo assumes means yes.

I wrote back straight away and told him the images he described have been flitting round my head all evening. I love that he has had some pleasure, some respite from the fighting and the terrible things he has witnessed. I would hate to be fighting like Dad, but how I ache to be able to travel to see such places: to see those tombs, those temples, those cities. My life seems so small, so humdrum, and I want so much more. Perhaps one day, when this war is over, I can escape this dull life and travel further afield.

**Sunday, 25 May 1941**

HMS *Hood* was sunk yesterday with the loss of all but three men – 1,415 lives all gone. I was glad it was a Sunday today and I could pray for them and their families. Mrs Page, the woman who lives opposite, has lost her only son. I remember seeing him when he was last home on leave looking very handsome in his navy uniform. He was only two years older than me. I was truly shocked. He should have had his whole life ahead of him. It's made me think. I need to grab hold of life while I've got it. I've finished two chapters in the book Dr Heatley lent me and I've started reading some of the other chapters now. It's so interesting and has reminded me how much I like learning. It has convinced me I've made the right decision about nursing.

All the curtains are drawn in Mrs's Page's house. Mum went to see her before church and said she was in a terrible state. She lost her husband a few years ago. He'd been badly gassed in the last war and was never a well man afterwards. So she's completely alone now. How do you keep going when you've lost so much?

I've been feeling very guilty all week about my argument with Margaret. I was so glad she was at church today. I'm still cross with her, but I don't want to fall out. She's the only true friend I have. I had some material left from making my dress, so I spent yesterday afternoon making her a toiletry bag, with a red ribbon for a drawstring. I was rather pleased with it. I wrapped it up in a piece of the brown paper that the draper had used to package the dress fabric. Very little is thrown away in this house: envelopes, bits of string, paper bags … they all have a use eventually. I waited for her outside church. She seemed to take ages and I wondered if she was deliberately trying to avoid me. Finally, she appeared with her parents, who stopped to talk to the vicar. I rushed up to her, rattled out my apology and gave her my present. She smiled and said she was sorry too. We leaned against the churchyard wall while she opened it. She seemed genuinely pleased and when her parents joined us, her mum admired my gift so much, I decided I would make one for her too.

**Friday, 30 May 1941**

Johnny Cox died. How can I believe in a god that can do such a thing; to give his parents such hope and then snatch it away? He had continued to improve after I last saw him, but then a few days ago, he had convulsions, meningitis was confirmed and he slipped into unconsciousness. The doctors gave him more penicillin, but it didn't help. I'm feeling very wretched tonight.

Jessie squeezes Jo's arm. 'If they hadn't discovered penicillin, I would have died, wouldn't I?'

Jo hesitates before she answers. It's so hard to be truthful. 'Yes.'

Jessie stares out of the window her lips pressed together.

Outside a mist hangs low over the garden. Two blackbirds are quarrelling. Jo has avoided telling Jessie how they nearly lost her. One of the doctors had said to her when she came round from the sedation, 'You had us worried for a while, Jessie'. Jo had been sure the meaning of his words hadn't registered. But it's clear now that Jessie is well aware of her close brush with death and unsurprisingly, has been frightened by it.

Jessie emits a quiet sob. Her shoulders are hunched, and tears are slowly running down her face. Jo wraps her arms around her, just as she did when she was a small child, and this time Jessie doesn't push her away.

# 11

# Jo

Jo pulls back Jessie's curtains and light floods the room. Jessie groans. 'Why is it so bright? It's January.'

'It snowed overnight.'

Jessie is suddenly awake and interested. She pushes back her duvet and lowers her stick-thin legs gingerly to the floor. She shuffles across the room to the window. Snow blankets the front garden, drapes the shrubs and edges the top of the fence. There are no human footprints, but an animal print, a cat possibly, trails across the lawn.

If Jessie was fit and healthy, she would be out there building a snowman. She has always loved the snow and at eighteen that passion has not diminished. Jo sees in Jessie's eyes her longing to be out, but then suddenly it dies. 'What's the point? I can't go out there.' She flops on her bed and pulls the duvet up to her ears.

'No, but it's pretty to look at. Come down to the living room and you can admire it through the French windows.'

'I'm never going to improve.'

'Nonsense! You're a little better every day.' But although Jo can see she is clearly recovering, it has become difficult to convince Jessie, and she doesn't know how to overcome Jessie's resistance. She needs professional help, but every time Jo suggests this, Jessie refuses.

'I'm just going to pick up my dress from the dry cleaners. Then I'll drop into Zoe's shop to say hello. Dad's working from home today. I won't be long.' Jo had been immensely relieved to discover that Kate had taken Alice's red and grey dress to the dry cleaners when they'd returned from the hospital. It has languished there ever since. She phoned the dry cleaners to let them know it might be sometime before she could pick it up. They told her not to worry, they would keep it safe. She immediately told Jessie who said, 'That's so cool, Mum. You actually have the dress that Alice described making in her diary.'

For Jo it's a rare opportunity to leave the house. She pulls on her walking boots, a warm coat and gloves and steps outside. It's like entering a different country. The world is utterly changed and there is that strange quietness that comes with heavy snow. There are a few footprints on the pavement, but the road is pristine and white. Some children must have been up early because there are already snowmen in some front gardens. One has a maroon scarf around its neck, another a lime-green bobble hat.

She catches up with a woman pulling a toddler on a blue plastic sledge behind her. 'That looks fun,' she says and the child beams back at her. It seems like it was only a few years ago that she was pulling first Kate, then Jessie on a sledge whenever there was snow.

Jo decides to head for Zoe's shop first. As she wanders down Swan Lane the shop name shouts out. VINTAGE. In gold capitals on a black background; a stylish imitation of the gold and black on the ancient Guildhall clock. She's been a regular visitor since the day she'd discovered it with Jessie in a buggy and Kate toddling beside her. She'd stood before the window and admired a grey 1940s' gaberdine coat, pleated at the back with a narrow waist, and wished she had enough money to buy it. For the first time she'd felt at home in the prosperous market town, oozing wealth from its centuries-old buildings with red-brick facades and overhanging gables, so different from the northern mining town she still thought of as home. It was like finding water in a desert. She'd become a regular visitor and one day, when both her girls were at school and she was admiring the window-dressing, she'd noticed a small sign pinned to the glass *Part-time assistant required. Enquire within*. The job had kept her sane and she and Zoe had become firm friends.

Jo pushes open the door. A yellow-silk evening gown hanging on the wall ripples as a draught of cold air snakes in. The shop always smells of Zoe's musky perfume, but she is nowhere in sight. There are no customers and stepping from the busy street into a place of quiet is balm to Jo. She stands and inhales the smell and the tension in her body trickles away. It's so good to be here, away from the sickroom, doing something for herself for once.

From the back room, separated from the shop by a Lucienne Day curtain, comes the sound of rustling and a metallic clink. Jo examines some of the dresses, picks up a grey quilted beret and tries it on, peering at herself in the mirror. It's gorgeous, but when would she ever wear it? As she places the hat back on the mannequin head, the curtain swings back and Zoe appears in dungarees with a pink land-girl scarf around her head.

'Jo,' she says. 'What a lovely surprise. How's Jessie?' She wraps her arms around Jo. A really tight embrace, not those air kisses some people insist on. Zoe is a big woman, tall and broad – or 'big-boned', as she likes to say. Her hugs are like being wrapped in a warm blanket and remind Jo of her mum.

'She's on the mend. A bit deaf, but considering what she's been through, she's escaped relatively unscathed.'

'Come in the back.' Zoe leads Jo gently into the room behind the shop and sweeps the curtain closed. Jo sinks on to the old sofa.

Zoe sits beside her. 'Is Rob looking after her?'

'If you can call it that. He's working from home and will keep well away. But Jessie will let him know if she needs anything. She's very challenging. It will do him good to have to cope with her constant demands.'

Zoe looks bemused. 'I've never heard you talk about Rob like this before.'

'I thought we were going to lose her, Zoe. And when I needed him most at the hospital, Rob would vanish. He was never there when decisions had to be made and as soon as he could, he went back to work and left me to it. I always thought we were a team, that I couldn't cope without him. But you know what? I coped *better* without him. When he was there, he just seemed needy, and I had enough to deal with without looking after him too.'

Zoe is smiling.

'What?' Jo says.

'You've always been the stronger one of the two of you. You've just never realised it before.'

Jo stares at the faded knees of her jeans. 'He's nagging me again about putting Mum's house on the market. When am I supposed to find time to do that?' She is silent for a moment. She knows she isn't being entirely honest. 'The truth is. I don't want to sell her house.'

Zoe rests her hand on Jo's arm. 'Why the rush?'

'There are costs associated with keeping it. But there are so many emotions tied up with that house. I just can't deal with them right now.'

'Your focus is bound to be Jessie.'

'I have to admit, I'm getting rather bored of being a full-time mum again.'

'Why don't you use the time to work on your idea of retraining? Weren't you thinking of picking up that career in science you always wanted?'

Jo sighs. 'I don't know any more. I don't know why I can't decide. I helped my children make decisions about their university courses, but when it comes to me, I'm totally incapable of moving forward.'

'Perhaps you can't make up your mind because you're considering the wrong area. You're trying to turn the clock back to your aspirations twenty-one years ago. Why don't you focus on what you enjoy doing now?'

Jo lets this thought settle in her mind. Maybe she is looking at it the wrong way.

'How's the dress?' Zoe says.

'I'm just going to collect it from the dry cleaners. I've discovered from reading Alice's diary that she made the dress herself.'

'That explains why there was no label in the dress. She was a good dressmaker.'

'I've been reading the diary to Jessie. It's the only thing she's interested in, other than children's cartoons. And she's desperate to see the dress.'

The doorbell jangles. Zoe sweeps back the curtain. A young woman has entered the shop with a small child and hangers squeak along rails as she examines the dresses and blouses.

Jo glances at her watch. 'I'd better go. Seeing you has recharged my batteries.'

Zoe steps into the shop then turns back to Jo. 'When Jessie is a little better, perhaps we can have a day out in London, just the two of us? Maybe the V&A Museum?'

'That would be a real treat.'


Jo is greeted in the dry cleaners by the owner's dog, a fat Labrador, who nuzzles her hand like a long-lost friend. Behind the counter the hangers of polythene-clad garments flutter as she closes the door. The owner squints at her ticket, then goes through all the clothes searching for a matching number. When he's been through the whole row, he disappears into a room at the back. He seems to be taking a long time. What if he hasn't kept it despite his assurances? But just as she's starting to worry he reappears with her dress on a hanger. He folds it in half and tapes the bottom of the polythene sheath to the top. 'You take care now,' he says. 'It's slippery out there.'

When Jo returns Jessie is dressed and sitting on the sofa eating toast smothered in mashed banana. Comfort food. At least she's eating now. When she first came home Jo was happy if Jessie ate anything, even if it was just a bowl of ice cream.

'Did you make that yourself?' She tries not to express surprise in her voice.

'No, Dad did.'

'Really?' Now she can't help but show her astonishment.

'I had to give him strict instructions on how to make it.

He's useless. If you ever left him, he'd starve to death.'

Jessie puts down her plate and waves a letter. Her expression has changed to a scowl. Jo guesses what it is and what is coming next.

'The post came … from my college.'

Jo swallows. She'd been hoping to be with Jessie when she opened the letter.

'They're deferring my course until next year. But presumably you knew that.' Jessie is shouting now. 'Did you contact them? Don't you think you should have discussed it with me first?'

'That's not what happened. It was the doctor at the hospital – she told you she would be writing a letter to your college explaining your illness, and that you would need to postpone your studies.' But Jo knows that Jessie wasn't absorbing much information then. 'I'm sorry, I should have explained it again to you. I was waiting for the right moment. But you've been so fragile. I didn't want to set you back.'

'What about all the friends I've made?' Jessie wails. 'They'll all be a year ahead of me.'

'You'll make new friends, and you'll still have your original ones.'

'It won't be the same,' Jessie moans. 'And what am I going to do with myself until October?'

'I'm sure when you're up to it we could get a reading list from the college and then you would have a good start next year.'

'But what if my brain stays like mush? I might never be able to go back to college.'

Jessie is crying now and Jo knows this is going to be the setback she'd been worried about. 'You're so much better.

When you first came home, you couldn't read and you barely said a word. Now look at you – bossing your dad about, and you didn't have any problem reading the letter.' Jessie manages a smile and wipes the tears away with the back of her hand.

'Are those my socks?' Jo says staring at Jessie's feet. One sock is blue-striped, the other is patterned with large navy spots.

'Sorry, I was getting bored with mine.'

Jessie always wears odd socks, a habit which began in her childhood. When Jessie and Kate were children, socks disappeared at an alarming rate, but it was always just one of a pair, not both. She's no idea where they went. It used to annoy Kate when one of her favourites disappeared, but when this happened to Jessie, she just paired it with another one and she rather liked that they didn't match. After Jo read the *The Borrowers* to them, they both exclaimed when another sock went missing, 'It's the Borrowers'.

At junior school Jessie painted a picture of a scene under the floorboards where socks were used for covering furniture, making snug beds and even clothes. She won a prize for it and Jo bought a clip frame. It still hangs on her bedroom wall.

'I picked up the dress. I'll show you when you've finished,' Jo says glancing at Jessie's greasy fingers.

I won't touch it,' Jessie says. 'Please.'

Jo hesitates, then feeling guilty about the letter, she relents. She fetches the dress and carefully pulls the polythene over the hanger so it can be replaced later. It has cleaned well.

'It's lovely. Can you put it on?'

Jo slips out of the room to the downstairs bathroom. When it slides over her body she has the same sensation that she'd had in Zoe's shop when she first tried it on. The feeling that she is a different person. She dampens a flannel and picks up a towel for Jessie's hands. Sometimes she feels as if the clock has turned back to Jessie's childhood. Is Jessie really so tired that she can't get off the sofa to wash her dirty fingers?

Jessie cleans and dries her hands without comment. Then Jo walks up and down and twirls round in front of Jessie as if she is a model on a catwalk.

'What's it made of? The material hangs really well.'

'It's rayon crêpe. It's beautifully made. I can't imagine many of the clothes made today lasting for over seventy years.'

'I fancy a dress in that style. Do you think Zoe might have something that would fit me?'

'I'm sure she would. Why don't we pay her shop a visit?'

'When I'm a bit stronger.'

'I could drop you off nearby so you don't have far to walk.'

Jessie shakes her head.

There's that pushback again. Jo carefully straightens the back of the skirt before sitting in the chair nearest Jessie. 'Well, it's something to look forward to when you're better.'

Jessie is quiet for a moment, then says, 'It's very fashionable to buy second-hand clothes – to save the environment.'

'I'm a bit fussy. I only buy 1940s' clothes.'

'But why only that period?'

'I fell in love with 1940s' clothes when I was a child. My nan used to love telling me stories about the war.'

'What sort of stories?'

'She was a clippie on the Barnsley buses. It was a hard job; her shift started at 5 a.m.'

Jessie raises her eyebrows. 'That's tough. I couldn't do that.'

'I think in the war you didn't have much choice. Everybody was expected to work as part of the war effort. But she played hard too, going to the dances, the cinema, walking on the moors with her friends.'

'Like Alice?'

'Yes. And when she told me her tales about going to a dance in Sheffield, where the Joe Loss band was playing, walking out with a GI, the VE party, she would illustrate them with the clothes she wore: a dress, or a hat or a particular pair of shoes.'

'How old was she during the war?'

'She would have been twenty in 1940, so not much older than you. Nan was a hoarder, and when she showed me the clothes that she still had from that period, I asked her to give me some of them for a dressing-up box. She was soft-hearted; she would do anything for her only grandchild, and I loved those clothes with a passion.'

'I remember you made a dressing-up box for us. Kate and I always argued about who got to wear the bridesmaid's dress. I think Kate usually won.'

'I was a bridesmaid to one of my cousins on Grandad's side of the family. It was rather horrid, cheap satiny material.'

She remembers wearing the dress and how much she hated it. She must have been about ten and had already formed a strong opinion of clothes she liked and definitely didn't like. Her mother had to cajole her into it. 'One day,' she'd said, 'you'll get married, and you can choose your own bridesmaids' dresses.' But that never happened: there were no bridesmaids at their Registry Office wedding, and she was already four-months pregnant with Kate.

'But when did you start wearing 1940s' clothes as an adult?'

'I thought I'd grown out of dressing-up until there was a 1940s' fancy-dress party at university.'

'That was in Brighton, wasn't it?'

'I hunted through the vintage shops in the Lanes and found a navy-blue day dress with a waterfall wrap skirt. I researched the make-up and hairstyles of the era, bought some seamed stockings and platform shoes. Even your dad entered into the spirit of it. I found him some wide turn-up flannel trousers which he wore with braces, a white shirt and a fedora.'

'Really? I'm seeing a whole other side to Dad. I'm going to tease him about this.'

Jo smiles. 'I became a bit addicted and bought more until I had a whole wardrobe of them. Then Kate was born and I rarely wore them again.'

She remembers wearing one of her favourite dresses to a birthday celebration at Rob's parents' house when Kate was a baby. She'd been so pleased she'd got her figure back and fitted into it. His mother had looked Jo up and down when she'd taken her coat off. 'That's an unusual dress,' she said. When Jo told her it was second-hand, she was appalled and said, 'But how can you wear something someone else has worn?'

'It has been cleaned,' she replied.

When she told Rob about this conversation in the car on the way home, he said, 'I don't like you wearing old clothes. It makes us look like we can't afford new ones.'

'Well, we can't,' she'd replied.

'I don't want you wearing them anymore when we visit friends and family.'

She hadn't said another word on the journey. But the next day she'd taken all her vintage clothes to the Oxfam shop and immediately regretted it. She had mourned their loss until she'd found Zoe's shop and her love had been rekindled.

Margot Shepherd

'It's so beautiful outside,' Jo says. She stands at the window and watches the meltwater drip from the cherry tree and pit the snow beneath. Being outside has driven away some of the despondency that has been troubling her. She knows it would help Jessie too, if only she could persuade her.

'Will you read me some more of the diary?' Jessie says, making it clear she's not going to engage in this conversation.

'Let me put the dress away.'

'Can't you keep it on, just while you read the diary?'

'Like we've travelled back in time?'

'Something like that.'

Jo removes the diary, sandwiched between two books in the waist-high bookshelf, and settles in the chair beside Jessie.

**Thursday, 26 June 1941**

How things have changed in the space of a few days. I arrived at work this morning to discover that Dr Heatley and Professor Florey have left for the USA, to find a drug company to scale up the manufacture of penicillin. Seeing Dr Heatley is the highlight of my day. It was like a black cloud had descended on me when I heard.

Professor Florey is prepared to give up all the information about how to produce our antibiotic in return for a kilo of it. He's desperate to continue clinical trials, to demonstrate the drug's effectiveness. You would have thought that now he has shown it works, companies in this country would be eager to get involved. But they're not interested. George said their trip had been kept very secret, even about how they are getting there. No-one knew until they arrived this morning and opened the letters that had been left for them by Professor Florey. Even Dr Chain didn't know. He was hopping mad to have been left behind. He thinks he should have gone instead of Dr Heatley, but as George said, 'It's Dr Heatley who knows how to make penicillin, not Dr Chain, so what use would he be?'

I shall worry until we have news that they have arrived safely. It is so dangerous trying to cross the Atlantic with the Germans waiting to pick off any planes and ships.

I was in low spirits all day – we all were. And to make things worse the professor left instructions for Dr Chain to take over the making of penicillin. He followed us around all day wanting to know exactly what we were doing, and kept muttering about efficiency and how he thought we could change a few things so we could produce more – no doubt to prove he was better than Dr Heatley. Everything works like clockwork, so why fix what isn't broken? We know our jobs. The hardest bit is the extraction which George is going to take over. There's a great sense of working as a team with Dr Heatley. He's always telling us how important we all are and what a good job we are doing. There wasn't a single word of praise from Dr Chain today.

**Monday, 7 July 1941**

News has filtered down to the lab from Dr Jennings that Professor Florey and Dr Heatley arrived safely in New York. There was a combined cheer when this was announced by George, and I think we will all sleep better now.

George and the other girls don't like Dr Jennings. She's quite reserved and they take that to mean she thinks she's above them all. But I think she doesn't understand the banter that goes on between the girls and our chief technician. I rather admire her. Not many women have a degree in science, least of all a higher degree. She's been testing whether penicillin has any harmful side effects in mice. It's clear that the professor has enormous respect for her. She's often referred to as 'Mrs Jennings', because she's married, but she is a doctor just like Dr Heatley and we don't call him 'Mr' Heatley. I think it's rude and demeans her. If it was me, I would be furious.

Everyone knows she's having an affair with Professor Florey and there's general disapproval in the lab because she's married. But then so is the professor, yet all the disapproval is directed at her, as if it's acceptable for a married man to have an affair, but not a married woman. It's such hypocrisy.

**Tuesday, 15 July 1941**

More news from Dr Heatley in a letter to George from Peoria, which apparently is near Chicago. It seems Professor Florey has been successful in persuading the US Government to help with the production of penicillin. The Department of Agriculture Research Lab agreed to help, as long as Dr Heatley stayed on to get the mould culture started. Dr Heatley said, '*Everyone is very hospitable here. People love to hear English, and one shopkeeper told me it's beautiful to listen to. I couldn't get the mould to grow to begin with, but now it is growing as well as it was in Oxford. Everyone in the department is kind and do what they can to help but I miss you and "the girls" and all the help you gave me. You and "the girls" have become quite a legend.'* We all giggled at that. It was strange to think we were famous in America. It helped the day go by, and we didn't get upset when Dr Chain shouted at us.

### Sunday, 20 July 1941

Yesterday I went to another dance at the Carfax with Margaret. It was a late night, and I was too tired to write in my diary before bed. Margaret has become friendly with a man called Arthur, who works in the same department, and she asked if I minded if he came too and brought a friend, John, to be my partner. I was glad of it as I didn't want to be a wallflower. I wore the same dress and make-up as last time. Mum was out when I left. I wonder if that was deliberate, so we didn't have another row, but Peter was home. He looked so miserable, I asked him if he wanted to come with us. 'You love dancing,' I said, but he shook his head. He interrogated me about who John was, when I told him he was to be my partner, but I wasn't very forthcoming because I didn't know much about him. All I knew was he worked at the town hall like Margaret and Arthur.

'Will you dance with me before you go?' he said. 'Like we used to?' I smiled and said that of course I would. We pushed the sofa back in the parlour and turned on the wireless. There's always some music on at seven o'clock.

'Can you remember the steps?' I said and he

nodded. When we were children, he danced with Mum and I danced with Dad, then we would swap partners and dance with each other. There wasn't much space, so only one pair could dance at a time. Peter turned up the volume and waltz music blared through the speaker. He rested one hand on my waist and we circled the room. It is a long time since we have been so physically near to each other – not since he used to curl up in bed with me when he had a bad dream, before we had separate rooms. Our relationship changed yesterday and the closeness that we used to have returned. I hope it lasts. It was the best part of my evening.

John was a good dancer. He was a pleasant and polite man, but I felt no romantic connection with him, as I had with Frank. I missed Frank even more and just wanted it to be him, not John, dancing with me. I was glad at the end of the evening that he didn't ask to see me again as I wouldn't have known what to say. Arthur caught the bus with us and made sure we got home safely. He is a gentleman, and I can see why Margaret is keen on him. It is clear that he adores her.

'Didn't you used to have an old record player?' Jessie says. 'I vaguely remember you showing me when I was studying the Second World War at school.'

'It's in the cupboard under the stairs. And there's a box of old shellac records. They were my nan's and when she died, Mum kept them for me until I had a place of my own to keep them. I haven't played it for a long time, but it would be rather nice to listen to the records, to complete our time travel.'

Jo carries the record player into the living room and

places it on the floor beside the sofa. She wipes the dusty carrying case with a damp cloth and opens the lid to reveal the turntable and silver playing arm.

Jo passes Jessie a small painted tin that is chipped and rusting.

Jessie stares at the lid. 'His Master's Voice. I used to love the picture of the dog.'

'Do you want to put the stylus in?' Jo says. Without any encouragement Jessie leaves the sofa, her daytime comfort zone, and crouches on the floor. She flips the lid of the tin open, removes a needle and pushes it into the playing arm.

Jo turns the crank in the side of the case to wind up the player and Jessie watches. 'Wasn't something like this rather expensive back then? How could a clippie afford it?'

'It was a gift from an American soldier she went out with for a while.'

'So why didn't she become a GI bride?'

'She said it was fun while it lasted, but she never took it seriously.'

'I wish I'd known her. She sounds a character.'

'She was,' Jo says. 'I'll just get the records.' She hauls a cardboard box into the living room and slits the packing tape sealing it. 'What would you like to hear?'

'Something that Alice might have danced to.'

Jo pulls out a record in a brown paper sleeve. The red centre label reads His Master's Voice: Joe Loss and his band playing 'Oh Johnny'.

After slotting the centre hole over the prong in the middle of the turntable she releases a switch and the record starts turning. Carefully she lowers the stylus onto the edge of the record. Within seconds the tinny noise of a big band fills the room.

'What would you dance to this?'

'The foxtrot. Shall I show you?'

Jessie nods.

She holds out her arms as if she has an imaginary part-ner. She hasn't danced for such a long time, but she quickly finds it's like learning to ride a bike, as her feet remember the steps. Back with her right foot, back with her left, side with the right, close with the left. Slow, slow, quick, quick. The dress sways against her legs and she has a sudden yearning to return to dancing classes.

'When did you learn?' Jessie says.

'I joined the Dance Club at university, but I could never interest your dad, so I stopped going. I used to dance with you and Kate when you were babies. It seemed to soothe you when you were colicky. Why don't you dance with me now? I'll show you the steps.'

Jessie shakes her head. 'When I'm feeling better.'

The door flies open. Rob stomps in and the needle on the record jumps. 'I'm trying to work.'

'Dad,' Jessie says, 'that's really mean. It's only been playing a minute.'

'I can tell you're feeling better,' he snaps. 'I was working at home because I thought I would get some peace and quiet.'

Jo waits for him to make a rude comment about her dress. Thankfully he doesn't, but that's probably because he hasn't noticed. 'You should be pleased that Jessie is showing an interest.'

'Is it for her, or for you – your bizarre interest in a period of history that was filled with death and destruction, when half a million people in this country lost their lives?' He jabs his finger at her, his expression one of disgust. 'I don't understand why it's glorified. I don't think you would have liked living then. It was a hard life.'

Jo flinches as if his words are body blows. Jessie is right. He is mean. That's a good word to describe him. He begrudges her little bit of fun with Jessie. 'That's the point,' she says. 'Despite all the hardship, people got on with their lives and coped.' He glares at her, anger radiating from him, but he doesn't respond, perhaps because of Jessie's presence. He turns and marches out of the room. As she watches his departing back, she can't help but be surprised that for once she stood up to him.

# 12

# Alice

When Alice wakes at six in the morning she can't understand why she's awake so early on a Sunday, the one morning when she doesn't have to get up for work. Then she remembers – Peter has asked her to go fishing with him today. After a quick breakfast she makes some Spam sandwiches for both of them. Her previous experience of complete boredom the last time she went fishing means she is well prepared. She takes two library books, Frank's last letter and some paper and a pen so she can reply. She packs the sandwiches and some drinks into a knapsack, and they leave before their mum is up.

The day is hot and sultry and by the time they've cycled to the stretch of the river by the Perch Inn, her blouse is glued to her body with sweat. They find some shade under a large tree where their only neighbours are some ducks dozing and preening themselves. Alice pulls her shoes and socks off, dips her feet in the cool water, then lies back. The grass, still a little damp from the overnight dew, is refreshing.

Peter has been working on a farm during his summer holidays. picking fruit and vegetables. He's volunteering – his contribution to the war effort – but he also gets free meals and is given produce to bring home. He's always gone before she gets up and she's missed having to chivvy him out of bed. The house is too quiet. Her mum wanted him to work at the munitions factory where he would be paid; with more and more men being called up they are desperately short of workers. But Peter was adamant he wanted to work outdoors and hated the thought of working in a factory. He's not shy of hard physical work, but he isn't used to doing it every day. He was exhausted at the end of his first two weeks and spent most of his Sundays in bed. He loves working on the farm; there are two land girls who clearly spoil him, and the farmer's wife makes a fuss of him too, always making sure he's had enough to eat. He's such a good-looking and easy-going boy that everyone can't help but love him. Now he's decided he doesn't need to sleep on Sundays anymore. Sundays are for fishing.

Their peace is disturbed by the gravelly staccato drone of a Tiger Moth crossing the sky. Even Alice is interested, knowing these were the planes their dad helped to build before he joined up. It always seems such a flimsy aircraft. She remembers her dad saying they were used mainly for training pilots. But Peter says some are fitted with light bombing racks now and are being used to protect our shores if any enemy aircraft try to land.

She moves into the sun, feeling the grass under her heels, and stares up through the branches at fragments of cloudless blue sky. She can hear the ducks quarrelling and some shouts of children in the distance and feels such peace. She wants to wrap up that moment, put it in a box and take it out whenever she's feeling low. But then the sense of well-being slips away. How can she feel contented when in Europe and Africa fierce battles are being fought and ships are being torpedoed in the seas around this country? Frank and Dad could be in the throes of combat right now.

It's hard to believe how only two weeks ago, she was barely speaking to Peter. The discord between them had arisen after an incident on Peter's sixteenth birthday. It was a Saturday and she had been at work as usual in the morning, He'd had the day off from the farm and had agreed to work Sunday instead. As the weather was dry, they had a picnic in Port Meadow. They'd arranged to meet at one of the areas that was like a beach, where they could sit by the river. George let her go a little early when she explained it was a special day and she thought she might beat them to their favourite spot. But Mum, Gran, Vivien, Pat and Peter were already sitting on a picnic blanket already eating sandwiches when she arrived. She was a bit miffed they hadn't waited for her. They were all laughing and for a while she'd watched and felt like an outsider. But then she approached them, and a space was made for her on the blanket, food was offered and the conversation began again, only now she was included. She couldn't help thinking about what it would be like not to have this family, to walk away from this life into another. She's not sure if it was her decision to apply for nursing school or her dad's letter that made her have such strange thoughts.

Pat was dressed in high-waisted trousers, quite wide in the leg, made of lightweight cotton drill. As she's very tall and slim, they suited her figure. Alice found herself watching how Pat and her aunt behaved with each other. But there was nothing unusual; they were just friendly in the same way that she would be friendly with Margaret. She dismissed the thoughts she'd been having since finding the strange photograph of them, deciding she was being unnecessarily suspicious.

Shortly after they'd eaten Alice and Peter went swimming. All morning, in the heat of the incubation room, she'd been thinking about slipping into the water. She'd put her costume on under her dress in the toilets before she left work, so there would be none of the bother of trying to get changed when wrapped in a towel.

She set off across the river wanting to swim alone, to lose herself and let the current take her. But Peter decided he wanted to lark about and kept grabbing her and pushing her under. He was considerably bigger than Alice now and working on the farm had made him very strong. It was impossible to stop him. And the more he did it, the more annoyed she became. But because it was his birthday, she had to stop herself from yelling at him – not something she found easy. In the end she left him in the river alone. He'd spoilt the swim she had been so looking forward to.

She lay on her back for a while to dry off before she put her dress back on, anger coiled within her like a compressed spring waiting to be released. Then two spitfires sliced through the sky with a thunderous rasping noise. She watched Peter stare up at them and knew he wished he was up there. She understood. It must be thrilling to fly at such speed. Although she was still cross with him it was tempered by a concern that one day he could be one of those pilots hurtling through the sky, giving his life to save their poor island.

She had spent the evening of the following day at Margaret's house and when she came home Peter was already asleep. She discovered he had left a small punnet of raspberries on her bed. It was as if he knew he'd crossed a line. And since then, every morning before leaving for work, he has washed up his dirty breakfast bowl and plate, instead of leaving it for her to do, and laid a place at the table for her. It's a small gesture, but she knows it's his way of apologising.

Now by the riverbank, Alice takes Frank's letter out of her bag and rereads it.

*Dear Alice*

*I'm so glad of the photograph, because I was starting to forget what you look like. I brought a sketchbook with me and have been drawing whenever I can. You keep appearing on the paper as if my hand has a mind of its own. I will be drawing the feathery leaves of a palm tree and suddenly there you are, peering out from behind it.*

And next to these words is a sketch of palm tree with Alice beside it. It still makes her smile, even though she has read the letter at least three times.

*I have been ill with what I thought was flu but was, in fact, sandfly fever.*

There is a picture of a sandfly sticking its proboscis into his arm with 'Ouch' beside it. She giggles again and Peter glances over at her.

*I was sent to a nearby RAF hospital for a week, but I'm now back in camp. I managed to get into a nearby town on leave and have bought you a silver necklace. I wish I could send it with the letter, but it would be sure to go astray. We are about to move from the plain into the mountains and I'm looking forward to a change of scenery. We seem to spend a lot of time taking guns apart and mending them. Write soon. Your letters always cheer me up.*

*Love Frank.*

He sounds bored. But that's better than fighting in a battle like her dad. He seems such a gentle soul; she can't imagine him killing anyone.

She pens him a letter, telling him about Professor Florey and Dr Heatley going to the USA, and her thoughts about a career in nursing. She starts telling him how she is sitting by the river while Peter fishes, and then feels guilty that she is having such an enjoyable day. She folds the letter and puts it in her bag. She'll finish it at home, and write to her dad as well. They've heard nothing from him since May and she hangs on to her mum's words – that no news is good news. She remembers how in one of his letters her dad said he liked to imagine he was by the river, so she will describe the fishing trip with all the details: the ducks and the weather, even the Tiger Moth. If he can picture it, it might give him some pleasure.

Eventually, Alice loses herself in *Jamaica Inn* and is only vaguely aware of Peter sitting beside her with his rod and line, the float bobbing on the water. Barely any words are spoken, but it is a comfortable silence. She puts aside her book while they eat and talk for a while about what it will be like after the war. Peter says he is still determined to join the RAF when he's eighteen. Alice wants to tell him of her decision to apply for nursing school. She debates with herself: Should I? Shouldn't I? Can she trust him? She decides that if he asks what her plans are for the future, she will tell him. But he doesn't ask. Still, the bond that was broken all those years ago is gradually beginning to heal.

As they cycle home, Peter races ahead and she can't keep up. But she doesn't mind. She's too happy to care. Coming over Osney Bridge she's surprised to see her aunt hurrying down a side street. She calls out, but Vivien doesn't hear. Alice follows, wondering where she's going. Terrace houses with large bay windows line both sides of the road and before she catches up, Vivien turns into the tiny garden of one of the houses. The front door opens revealing Pat, her face gilded with a broad smile. Vivien disappears inside and the door closes. Alice knew Pat lived somewhere near the river and it seems strange, now that Pat has spent so much time with her family – at her gran's house, on excursions and at family celebrations – and yet the family has never been invited to Pat's home.

She wonders about knocking on the door and saying hello, but hesitates, feeling she wouldn't be welcome. A movement in the room upstairs draws her attention. Through the window she sees Pat pulling Vivien towards her and kissing her passionately, her aunt pulling back and quickly drawing the curtains. She looks away, feeling like a peeping tom and hurries towards Botley Road. Her mind is in turmoil. Of course, it all makes sense now: the photograph, Vivien's reaction when Alice found it, the secrecy around Pat's home, the numerous occasions when her aunt spends the night there. She wonders if her mum knows. If she does, Alice can imagine her reaction – her narrow-mindedness will make her cruel. Alice is shocked, but her aunt's love life is her own affair and now she knows, she will tread more carefully. It is a secret that could ruin Vivien's life.

# 13

# Jo

*12 February 2018*

Moonlight creeps around the edges of the blind. Jo glances at her bedside clock. The red numbers blink in the gloom: 3.10. She's wide awake, flashbacks of Jessie's first few days in hospital filling her head. Going back to sleep is not going to happen until she's calmed her mind. She should be sleeping better now that Jessie's nightmares are less frequent. But this early morning waking seems to be happening every day now. She eases her feet out of bed onto the rug. The house is submerged in sleep, the only sound the distant hum of the refrigerator in the kitchen. Jessie's door is partly open and in the dim glow of a nightlight, Jo can see her humped shape under the duvet, her hair strewn across the pillow.

On her first night back home, Jessie insisted on leaving her bedside light on. She said she'd got used to the dim lights in the hospital at night and couldn't possibly sleep in complete darkness. Jo had hunted in the kitchen drawer where she kept all the bits that had no obvious home: Allen keys, a roll of picture wire, rubber bands, curtain hooks, and there at the back she found the old plug-in night light she'd used when Kate and Jessie were babies. She presented it to Jessie like a trophy, thrilled that she hadn't thrown it out, as if she'd known it would be useful one day.

The door to Kate's old room is wide open, the bed empty.

Rob is at a conference in Paris for five days and Jo loves having the place to herself. It's as if she can breathe freely. She doesn't have to worry about saying the wrong thing or listen to him nagging her about jobs she hasn't done: 'Have you phoned the plumber yet?' 'When are you going to clean the cooker? It's disgusting.' 'I'm not moving back into our bedroom until you've tidied up your clothes. Why can't you put things away when you take them off?'

In the kitchen she pours out a glass of milk and opens the slats of the venetian blind. Silvery light creates stripes of white across the sink and worktop. She stares out at the other-worldly place the garden has become. She had been planning to return to bed to read for a while, but the urge to step outside and be bathed in this magical light is irresistible. She pulls a fleece from the hook on the back door and slips her feet into her garden clogs. Rob would think she was mad if he was here. But he's not and she knows she wouldn't even consider going out if he was. When did what Rob think become so important to her? When did she lose her autonomy to be herself?

Outside the world is monochrome. The full moon, startlingly bright, hangs vast, like a stage backdrop. She steps across the lawn, grey with dew, her feet leaving imprints, a trail of her meandering. A moth blunders into her face and she stops and watches it flit away. She feels at one in this ghostly place. Lately she feels like she's in one of those old photographs where the colour has leeched out as they age. She has become colourless, like the garden. Her mind has been so focused on Jessie that there seems no time or energy left for her. All her hopes for her own future seem to have been rubbed out.

Beneath the cherry tree the white flowers of the snowdrops hang like tiny lamps. A conifer casts an elongated shadow across the grass and the moon shimmers on the leaves of the laurel. Her mind settles, all her dark thoughts rinsed away by the soft-hued light. A female tawny owl calls out, *ke-wick*, *ke-wick*, and a male hoots in reply.

Her feet are cold. She thinks she will sleep now. But after closing the back door and locking it, she is perplexed by a cold draught circling her ankles. Frowning she checks she really did shut the door, then hurries into the hall. The front door is ajar, the key fob is swinging. Her stomach plummets and she sprints upstairs. Halfway up she trips, banging her knee. 'Damn!' she shouts out loud. Jessie's door is wide open, and she's not in her bed. Sleepwalking? Jessie must be sleepwalking again. Back down the stairs she is cursing herself for not going out of the front door straight away. Her mind is racing. Which way would she go? Turning left would take her deeper into the housing estate and was a route they rarely took. So she turns right, towards the main road, running and half-limping, her knee throbbing. She wishes she'd put some proper shoes on. The clogs are not designed for running. But too late now.

She'd found Jessie sleepwalking last week. A noise had disturbed her downstairs, and she was about to wake Rob, terrified they had burglars, when she realised Jessie's bed was empty. She was standing in the living room, eyes open, but not seeing. She'd read somewhere that you were not supposed to wake sleepwalkers so she had guided her back to bed. The next day Jessie had no recollection of the incident. Jo had worried about Jessie's safety on the stairs, but had never imagined she would leave the house.

She turns the corner onto the main road and there in the distance is a ghostly figure in pyjamas. 'Jessie,' she yells. She has to stop her; she could easily step into the road. A car is speeding towards her, headlights illuminating the road. 'Stay there! Jessie!' she yells. But Jessie is oblivious to everything: to her, to the car, to where she is.

Jo has almost caught up with her when Jessie stops, as if unsure of where she is, and steps into the road. A car horn hoots, jarring the quiet of the night. It swerves. Jessie steps back, her eyes staring in terror and Jo grabs her and holds her tight. She half-expects Jessie to struggle and wonders where she is in her mind in this sleeping state.

'It's okay,' she keeps saying. 'I've got you. You're safe now.' Jessie's hands are cold and clammy; her feet are bare and there is a thick smear of blood across the toes of one foot. Jo removes her fleece and drapes it over Jessie's shoulders. She hesitates, wondering what to do about her feet. Her clogs are too small for Jessie, but they are better than nothing and she's relieved that Jessie doesn't struggle when she slides her feet into them. Her heels hang over the back and she shuffles as Jo guides her back to the house. Grit grinds into the soles of Jo's feet and she thinks she can bear the pain, but then has an idea. 'Wait, Jessie,' she says and surprisingly, Jessie stops walking, like an automaton. From her fleece pockets Jo yanks out a pair of mittens that her mum had knitted. She pulls them onto her feet. They will give her some protection, but she will ruin them. 'Sorry, Mum,' she says. 'Needs must, as you would say.'

'We must look a comical pair,' Jo says. But Jessie is still who knows where, in her sleeping world.

Jo guides her to bed, then examines Jessie's feet. Tiny

pieces of grit are embedded in her heels, the balls of both feet crisscrossed with thin red stripes, and there is a deep gash on one big toe. She tweezers out the grit, cleans them and applies antiseptic cream, then cleans her own feet. The mittens are filthy and there are holes where the wool has frayed.

So much for going back to sleep. She lies awake in bed haunted by the thought that if she hadn't been awake, she wouldn't have known Jessie had left the house. She gets up, takes the keys out of the front and back door and pushes them under her pillow. She closes her eyes and imagines she is walking round the garden in the moonlight again until sleep finally sucks her in.

It's mid-morning before Jessie gets up. Jo is in the kitchen making a coffee. 'Mum, my feet are really painful.' She lifts one foot and shows Jo.

'Do you remember anything about what happened last night?' Jo says.

Jessie shakes her head and Jo explains the sleepwalking and her stepping into the road in front of the car.

'Jesus, Mum.' Her eyes are wide with alarm. 'What's happening to me?'

'I don't know, but I've made an appointment with the GP for this afternoon.'

Jessie frowns. 'That means I have to go out.'

Every time Jo has suggested that Jessie goes for a walk, Jessie pushes back. 'I'm not ready yet. I get too tired.' A meander round the garden is all she's achieved, and the garden is only 200 square metres. Whenever Jo suggests they go for a short walk, Jessie complains that her legs are like jelly and she would collapse if she attempted to walk to even the end of the road and back.

'You were out last night. You managed to walk quite a long way.'

'Yeah, but I didn't know what I was doing.' Jessie grabs a box of granola from the cupboard and pours some into a bowl.

'I'll drive you. All you have to do is walk from the carpark to the surgery. It will take less than two minutes.' Jo takes the milk out of the fridge and passes it to her.

'I'll think about it,' Jessie says, emptying the contents of the plastic bottle onto her cereal. She picks up the bowl and limps out of the room.

'I'll clear this up then,' Jo says to her receding back. She washes out the plastic container and drops it into the recycling bin, then wipes up the drips of milk that dot the worktop. 'See, I do tidy up sometimes,' she says to an imaginary Rob standing in the kitchen.


It's late afternoon. The receptionist looks up and smiles at Jo.

'We have an appointment to see Dr Burton,' Jo says. 'Jessica Collins.' She glances behind at Jessie, who is hanging back just inside the main door as if she is not with her.

The receptionist checks her screen and taps her keyboard. 'Please, take a seat in the waiting room. The doctor is running a few minutes late.'

Jo starts walking towards the waiting room, then stops. Jessie is not following. She is still standing in the same place as if her feet are stuck to the ground. 'I'm not going in there,' Jessie says. 'It's full of sick people.'

The waiting room is quite full. Someone is coughing, a woman holds a small child on her knee who looks hot and lethargic, and an elderly woman, leaning against a man, is ashen-faced. Jo turns back to Jessie.

'I'll wait outside,' Jessie says. 'Can you text me when the doctor calls me in?' Jo watches Jessie open the glass-panelled door, walk a few metres and lean against a wall.

Jo sighs. At least Jessie is here, and by gentle leading she is hoping Jessie's mental health will be raised with the doctor.

She picks up a well-thumbed magazine, flicks through the pages then glances at the wall-mounted screen where patients are called for their appointments. Their names appear with a room number accompanied by a fanfare. The sound seems faintly ridiculous. She's glad Jessie didn't come in; she would be saying what Jo is thinking out loud and everyone would be staring.

She thinks about the progress Jessie has made. Her physical health has gradually improved, she is eating properly and has gained some weight, but her state of mind is still concerning. Jo believes the sleepwalking episode is a manifestation of an underlying mental-health issue. But whenever Jo suggests counselling, Jessie says she's not ready yet.

Jessie's name flashes up on the screen and Jo texts her. She watches Jessie enter the surgery, and how she carefully keeps her distance from other people. Outside the doctor's room Jessie grabs the sleeve of her coat.

'Would you prefer if I don't come with you?' Jo says.

Jessie shakes her head.

Jo opens the door and Jessie edges in beside her, still holding her sleeve. Once inside the room Jessie lets go and drops into the chair beside the doctor's desk. Dr Burton smiles.

She has cared for Jessie ever since she was a toddler, so is a familiar face, which Jo hopes Jessie will find reassuring.

'Hello, Jessica, I've just been reading the notes from the hospital. You had a tough time. How can I help you today?'

Jessie shrugs. 'I'm fine. It's Mum who thought I should have a check-up because apparently I went sleepwalking last night.'

Dr Burton glances at Jo.

'She's had a lot of nightmares,' Jo says, 'but the sleep-walking is new and quite terrifying because she walked into the path of oncoming car. It was lucky that I'd followed her.'

'Were you aware of this?' the doctor says to Jessie.

'No. I just noticed my feet were sore this morning.'

'Shall we have a look?'

Jessie removes her trainers and socks, and the doctor inspects her feet. 'The damage is just superficial, but I'll give you an antibiotic cream.'

Jessie frowns. 'Is that necessary? I thought you didn't dish out antibiotics now unless you really needed to.'

The doctor frowns. 'And you don't think you need it?'

'Isn't that how you develop antibiotic resistance? By over-using them? I only want them when I really need them.'

'I wouldn't be prescribing the cream if you didn't need it.'

The doctor performs a routine physical exam: listens to her chest, takes her blood pressure, asks questions about her sleeping, about the nightmares. Does she have any concerns?

'Just that I nearly died,' Jessie says.

'And that's very frightening. Do you have flashbacks?'

'No, just these terrible dreams and now it seems sleep-walking as well.'

When Doctor Burton asks if she's managing to do some

short walks outside, Jessie says what she always says to Jo: she's just too tired. 'We'll book you in for a blood sample, just to check all is well. Meanwhile, I really do recommend you try going out. Just walk a little bit each day.'

Jo can see Jessie has closed down. She has put up a mental screen. In a moment she's going to say she's fine, can she go now?

The doctor suggests antidepressants and counselling, but despite her patient explanation – that depression is a common side effect of meningitis – Jessie is adamant. 'No,' she says.

'I'll give you a list of counsellors in case you change your mind,' Dr Burton says.

Jo takes the list knowing Jessie will refuse it. The appointment is over.

Jessie doesn't say a word in the car on the way home. She stares out of the passenger window so Jo can't see her expression. Once they're back at the house she goes straight to her bedroom and shuts the door. Jo makes herself a cup of tea and sits at the breakfast bar. The feelings of helplessness she had at the hospital wash over her again. She wants to help Jessie, but doesn't know how. She'd been hoping the GP would persuade her, but while Jessie might be withdrawn and quiet, her stubbornness has returned.

At least the trip to the GP has confirmed what she has always suspected – Jessie doesn't want to go out because she is frightened of getting ill again.

Jessie sidles into the kitchen and puts on the kettle. Her nose is red and her face is blotchy.

'I'm going to sit on the sofa and read some more of Alice's diary,' Jo says. 'Perhaps we could read it together?' Jessie is certainly capable of reading it herself now, and although Jo rather likes reading it to her, she needs to stop treating Jessie like a child.

'Okay.'

Jessie settles on the sofa beside her with a mug of hot chocolate. 'It was cold outside. I don't envy Alice living in a house with so little heating. Although I'm interested in her life, I wouldn't want to have lived like that. I like being warm.'

Jessie is still underweight, something the doctor had commented on, so is bound to feel the cold more acutely. 'Just because I like the clothes and textiles from that period doesn't mean I would have liked to live then. But there was a spirit I admire. I can see it in Alice,' Jo says.

'When I go back to Oxford, I'm going to see the city completely differently,' Jessie says.

'You mean you'll see it through Alice's eyes?'

'Yes, I suppose so,' Jessie says. She looks thoughtful for a moment. 'Is the Radcliffe Infirmary the hospital I was in?'

'No, I looked it up. The Radcliffe Infirmary was in Woodstock Road in North Oxford. The John Radcliffe Hospital is in Headington in East Oxford, and wasn't built until 1979. In 1941, there was a sanatorium for tuberculosis and a convalescent hospital where it stands. But here is an interesting coincidence: Alice lived in Headington. She mentions the road where she lived, Winter Street, in her diary. And there's something else. Just before the doctors took you off the ventilator, I went for a walk to clear my head and I found a church. I went inside. I was so on edge, you can't imagine, and it was so peaceful.'

'Poor Mum. Where was Dad? Why were you on your own?'

'What I've realised is that the church must have been where Alice went with her family.'

'Really? Haven't I got an appointment to see my consultant soon?'

'In five weeks.'

'Could you take me to the church afterwards?'

'Of course. What a lovely idea.'

Jo had been wondering if the visit to the doctor was a mistake, or at best a waste of time. But now she senses a shift in Jessie. Is she thinking about the doctor's advice?

**Monday, 15 September 1941**

It's chaos in the labs. There's an infection in the incubation room and Dr Chain just gets annoyed with everyone. It's everyone's fault but his. We have made very little penicillin for the last two months. Everyone is desperate for Dr Heatley and Professor Florey to come home. Now I've decided to apply for nursing school, I need Professor Florey to come home more than ever. I need a reference from him if I'm to stand a chance of being accepted. Only two months until I'm eighteen and I can apply.

I've been really tired lately, so George sent me to the Radcliffe Infirmary last week for a blood test. Apparently, I'm very anaemic. It's a known effect of the amyl acetate that we use in the extraction procedure. So I'm not allowed to do any more of the extractions until my iron levels are back up. The tablets I have to take are like horse pills. Mum says I have to eat lots of liver. At least that's not rationed, although it's not often the butcher has any.

There are some days when it's hard to get out of bed and just keep going to work. The only positive feature in my life is Peter. I can't believe how much our relationship has changed.

**Sunday, 21 September 1941**

It's four months since we heard from Dad and I'm frantic with worry. The news from the campaign in North Africa is not good. Mum has forbidden all talk of the war when she's in the house. She doesn't want to know. Peter hides his newspaper in his room, and I go to Gran's to listen to the news on the wireless. I wonder if Mum is ever frightened about working in Cowley. It's such an obvious target for the German bombers.

I keep writing to Dad, in the hope he's receiving my letters. Today I wrote to him describing all the problems at work, how much I dislike working for Dr Chain and how I long for Dr Heatley to return. I told him how I keep thinking about the time we all used to dance in the parlour. I said that I worried about him every day and how much we all missed him. I told him about Frank's letters and how much they made me laugh. I was worried then that he might think I preferred Frank's letters to his, so I said that I loved his letters because they were so beautifully written. 'I think you could have been a writer, Dad, and may be you will be one day. I hope you will let me read your journal when you come home.'

I told him how horrible the weather is here at the moment: cold and wet. And that he's going to get a shock when he comes home. He must be so used to it being hot all the time.

**Thursday, 9 October 1941**

Finally, Professor Florey is back but Dr Heatley has stayed in the US to continue work on penicillin production with a drug company. When I asked when he was coming back, George said he'd heard it would be several more months. I moaned out loud. The professor was horrified when he discovered how little penicillin we'd made in the last three months. He said he would take charge of manufacturing from now on. Dr Chain seemed very grumpy for the rest of the day. We've still got an infection in the incubation room, so the professor told us to throw all the culture medium away, sterilise all the incubation pots and start again, with everything completely clean. So that's what we did today. It's going take a week to be up and running again.

My anaemia is improving but not enough to be able to help with the penicillin extractions. At least I'm not really tired anymore. Professor Florey has enlisted the help of Dr Gordon Sanders to do the extractions who, like Dr Heatley, is a bit of a whizz with inventions. The whole mood of the place has changed with the professor's return. He calls us the 'Brewing Department'. Now Professor Florey is in the lab he's much more approachable than when he was in his office most of the time. He's not as easy to talk to as Dr Heatley, but I'm not afraid to ask the professor questions when I don't understand something.

**Monday, 20 October 1941**

Professor Florey says we need to find a way of increasing our yield of penicillin and if none of the drug companies are interested, then we just have to mass produce it ourselves. That's a tall order. But Dr Sanders has discovered that doubling the length of the glass columns in the extraction machine increases the amount we can extract and he has made our very own production plant in what used to be the autopsy room behind the lab. A bathtub is used as a tank for the crude filtrate, there are hundreds of feet of glass tubing and the extracted penicillin is collected into eight ten-gallon milk churns.

**Tuesday, 4 November 1941**

My birthday at last! It was work as usual but during the afternoon tea break Megan produced a cake made with carrots which sounds weird but was delicious. Someone had bought a card and George and all the girls had signed it. I felt a pang of guilt about my plan to leave when they were being so kind. It was strange knowing I was about to step into another life. Professor Florey wasn't in today but as soon as he's back I will ask him for a reference and apply to nursing school.

There was a celebration tea at gran's house, and I opened my presents afterwards. Peter gave me a very expensive-looking fountain pen which must have taken him ages to save up for. He said it was for writing my diary. I have been complaining that my current pen is very scratchy. That he'd been listening gave me a warm feeling inside. He even let me give him a hug. I shall treasure it always. Gran gave me a bottle of dark blue ink, Mum, some chocolates and Vivien of course bought me a book: *Testament of Youth* by Vera Brittain.

She said I would understand why she had chosen it when I read it. I am intrigued.

**Friday, 7 November 1941**

I was so relieved today when I saw there was a letter from Dad. But my excitement faded as I started to read. He's been injured and was writing from a hospital in Jerusalem. He said, 'I really needed some of the penicillin you're making, Alice. I had a very nasty infection. I'm over the worst of it now and starting to get stronger every day. The nurses here are like angels. They're rushed off their feet, but still find the time to sit and talk to their patients. They hold the hands of dying men and whisper words of comfort.' I knew he was letting me know he approved of my career choice without giving the game away.

He didn't say much about the injury, just that he's lucky to be alive. He was the only one in his patrol to survive and he said that, for a while, he thought he was a goner too. He said he wasn't sure how long he would take to recover. I'm worried about the tone of the letter. It's so different from the last one. He says he's coming home, but I'm not sure I want him to be shipped home. Ships are not safe places. I know this is an irrational thought when he almost died in battle. And I do want him home. He said his head isn't healing. I presume the trauma of what he has been through has affected him mentally, like shell shock. Poor Dad. I wanted to reach out and hug him. Mum was quiet when I read the last part out. She had that closed-in look on her face and I knew there would be no discussing the meaning of his words when she was around. I wondered if she thought he was weak for succumbing to this. Physical wounds are acceptable but mental wounds are not.

Underneath this entry is another paper pocket and tucked inside is the letter from Alice's dad. Jo opens it, skips the first part, which Alice had described in her diary, but reads out the section that had clearly alarmed her.

*Please write to me, Alice. I need your letters to keep me sane. Although my body is healing, my head is not. I feel as if I am walking a razor edge, and on one side is insanity. Keep writing; your letters keep me on the right side. I've been told I'm going to be shipped home, but it's not clear when. And when I'm home, I will need more hospital treatment, so I don't know when I'll see you all.*

Jo looks at Jessie. 'I'm not mad.' Jessie says.

'No, neither was Alice's dad. I think he was suffering from post-traumatic stress disorder. It was called shell shock then.'

'Do you think I've got PTSD?'

'I think you've suffered a huge trauma, both to your body and your mind. But I think there's something else going on. You're afraid to go out. That was clear today.'

'I'm just tired. I'm exhausted walking round the garden.'

'But whenever I suggest we go out somewhere and walk a similar distance you push back.'

'I'm just not ready yet.' She slides sideways on the sofa and puts her head on a cushion.

'Jessie, the doctors and your body have done a wonderful job to heal you, but your mind is a different matter.' Jo takes

Jessie's hand. 'Are you afraid that stepping out of the house might put you in contact with another deadly disease?'

Jessie frowns and worries her sweatshirt between her finger and thumb. 'It's scary out there.'

'Not as scary as it would have been for Alice. We have antibiotics now. The death rate from infectious diseases in this country is the lowest it's ever been.'

Jessie says, 'I know, but still—'

'You need to try to take some steps forward and that means going for a walk every day. We are surrounded by beautiful parkland and countryside. Being outside will help you.'

But Jessie is plugging her earbuds into her ears and fiddling with her phone, making it clear she's not discussing it anymore.

# 14

# Jo

Jo manoeuvres her car into a space in the carpark of Claremont Landscape Gardens. It's a perfect day for walking in a park. There's a cloudless sky and the light touch of frost on the grass sparkles in the sunlight. Every twig on the bare branches of the trees is laced in white.

Jo was surprised when Jessie announced this morning that she would like to go to Claremont. It was a favourite place to visit when she and Kate were children: picnics in the summer, kicking through leaves in autumn, tramping through snow in the winter. Their discussion yesterday had clearly sown a seed in Jessie's mind. Jo hadn't commented. She'd just said, 'That's a lovely idea. Just make sure you wear lots of layers, as it's even colder than yesterday.'

The path skirts the lake's edge. Jo is wary, not wanting Jessie to walk too far. This is a huge step, and she doesn't want it to have a negative impact. After twenty minutes she directs Jessie to a seat with a view across the lake to the amphitheatre of grass terraces cut into the hillside. Although many of the trees are bare, a majestic cedar dominates their view. The lime trees bordering the amphitheatre sprout globes of mistletoe, like strange Christmas decorations.

'I'd forgotten how beautiful it was here,' Jessie says. 'Did Dad used to come with us?'

'When you were small, he came. When you were teenagers, he'd always find an excuse not to come.'

When did Rob check out of their lives? It must have happened by gradual degrees, so slowly that she wasn't aware it was happening. His role in their marriage has gradually diminished. She'd always thought that their shared past bonded them together, but in truth the bond between them has been dissolving slowly as each year passed. She often wonders if they would have married if she hadn't become pregnant. Had he felt trapped? He's back from his conference and Jo mourns her loss of freedom. When he's in the house he seems to fill all the space, so she's pushed to the edges.

The lake is so still it acts like a mirror, reflecting the trees so perfectly that it's hard to tell which is the real image. Has she been looking at the reflection of their marriage instead of the real image? What she thought it was, rather than what it truly is? She wanted to believe that the reflection was real, she wanted that stability, but like a stone thrown into a pond, the reflection has faltered.

Jessie appears to be mesmerised by the view. Hands thrust into her pockets she leans forward. All the colours seem enhanced: the sky, a cerulean blue; the grass, hung with drops of thawed frost that catch the light, is a startling emerald-green. She is quiet as if she is content to just observe the world.

In another month the first leaves will begin to appear, more bulb shoots will sprout from the soil, winter will pass and another cycle will begin. Jo thinks that both she and Jessie have been wintering for too long. It's time they moved forward like the plants and trees.

'I've been reading about antibiotic resistance,' Jessie says.

'Did you know that farm animals are given antibiotics even when they're healthy?'

'Yes, I did know,' Jo says. Is Jessie reading about this because she's frightened? It's happened before; it could happen again. And saving her life depended on the availability of effective antibiotics.

Jessie pulls her hat down over her ears. 'I'd never realised before how lucky my generation and your generation are. I guess reading Alice's diary brought that home.'

There's not a lot wrong with Jessie's brain. 'So you can concentrate long enough to read this stuff?'

'For short bursts. It's very tiring though.'

Jo leans forward. 'Prior to the development of penicillin, millions died from bacterial infections.'

'But we're heading back there, turning back the clock,' Jessie says.

Jo doesn't want to say that there is a potential catastrophe hurtling towards modern man, that most people seem oblivious to. It will just frighten her even more.

'I've been thinking,' Jessie says. 'I want to change my degree to Microbiology. I want to do something about this.'

'That's very commendable. But don't make a hasty decision. You have plenty of time to think about it. Do some reading. You chose Physics because it was a subject you really enjoyed. Is Microbiology a subject you will enjoy, or are you doing it because you think you should?'

Jessie shrugs. 'It makes me feel I have a purpose.'

Jo ponders this. It could be helpful in pulling Jessie out of her depressive state, if she feels she has something to work towards. But it seems like a very sudden decision.

'Do you think they will let me change course?'

'I don't see why not.'

A breeze corrugates the surface of the lake and blows a strand of hair across Jessie's face.

'And if you're wondering what to do with the rest of the year, if they let you switch courses, you'll have plenty to read to get up to speed.'

Jessie looks cold.

'Let's get a hot drink,' Jo says. 'We can keep coming back here and walk a bit further each day, until you can walk all the way around the lake.'

Jessie stands. 'That sounds like a good plan.'

As they walk towards the coffee shop Jessie says, 'What about you, Mum? You said you were planning to restart your career. Didn't you do a degree in biosciences?'

'Biochemistry,' Jo says. 'I was going to be a clinical bio-chemist.'

They sit in the café warming their hands on their mugs of coffee. And Jo tells Jessie the story she told Rob when they first met, about all the tests she had and her fascination with how they had been able to work out what was wrong with her from her blood.

'What was wrong with you?' Jessie says.

'I had terrible stomach pains, but they couldn't find any-thing wrong with me. The blood tests didn't help in the end. But they ruled out lots of sinister possibilities. It was my GP who got to the bottom of it. It was caused by stress. I was being bullied at school by a gang of girls. They used to follow me home from school and threaten to beat me up. I don't remember why I couldn't tell my mum. Perhaps I thought she'd make a fuss and contact the school, or the parents of the girls, and I thought that would make it worse.'

'So what happened?'

'The GP told my parents and the headteacher. I suppose the school must have spoken to the girls, because the bullying stopped. The pains receded. But I had decided what I wanted to pursue as a career. Your dad thought I was a bit odd being so sure at such a young age. And then all my plans went off the rails when I had Kate.'

'Couldn't you still have trained?'

'It's different now. It's much easier for people to do part-time courses and combine careers with having a family.' Jo pauses. 'That's a bit of a cop-out. I think I lost my confidence. I never had much to start with. That's always been my problem. You, on the other hand, always had plenty until you were ill.'

She'd told herself her career was just on hold until Kate was of an age when she could start her training to be a biochemist. Then Jessie was born and she decided that she would pick up her career when both children were at school. But milestones came and went: Jessie started primary school, secondary school, sixth-form college … And each time she raised the subject, Rob persuaded her it wasn't the right time, they couldn't afford the cost of training courses – she should wait.

'But you could go back into science now,' Jessie says. 'Didn't Gran leave you some money?'

'She did. She knew she was dying and told me that she had some savings that I would inherit. Gran and Grandad were always careful with their money, saving for the *just in case* times, but I had no idea just how much they'd put aside. She said that it was for me to retrain for a career that I would love.'

Jo swallows. 'I'd told her many times that what was what I wanted to do.'

'Well, now you can.'

Jo shakes her head. 'I think I'm too disorganised to be a scientist.' It was Rob who had convinced her of this. At the same time, he'd made it clear that if she wanted to work it would have to fit in around school hours.

'But that's nonsense,' Jessie says. 'Just look at Alexander Fleming and the discovery of penicillin. And I'm not exactly an organised person, but you don't think I shouldn't have a career in science.'

Jo considers this. Of course Jessie is right. But when Rob persuaded her, he was so convincing. But why was he so against her trying to get into a career in science? Financially it would have been more comfortable having two substantial incomes. When he told her about female colleagues who'd combined a career with having children, she could hear the admiration in his voice. She should have stood her ground; if she had, he would have had some respect for her and maybe their marriage wouldn't be in such a sorry state.

Was he against her having a career to make his life easier, by having a wife who didn't work? Or was it to keep her dependent on him? How many times has he thrown at her that he was the major money earner, so it was up to him what his income was spent on? It is as if she has been wearing blinkers and they have suddenly been removed.

'Mum?' Jessie says. 'Are you okay? You look as if you were a very long way away.'

'Just thinking. And you're right. I need to make some decisions about my future career.'

# 15

# Alice

**1 December 1941**

*What luck,* Alice thinks as she steps from the platform into a compartment with an empty window seat. It's even facing the direction of travel.

An elderly lady with a fox fur round her neck steps in shortly after Alice and sits facing her. 'Travelling backwards makes me a little sick,' she says. She clearly expects Alice to volunteer her seat. Alice hesitates for a moment wanting to be magnanimous, but also desperately not wanting to give up her prize. The seat beside her is taken, but there is another forward-facing seat adjacent to the corridor. Why doesn't she sit there? The woman glowers at her and Alice decides if she's going to be unpleasant about it, she's definitely not moving. Mrs Fox-Fur should have gone first class instead of third.

The bench seats soon fill up; at least half the occupants are servicemen and all of them smoke, so the air soon becomes a smoky fug. She wonders about opening the window, but decides the sooty smoke from the train will be worse. There's a hiss of steam, a whistle and the guard waves a green flag. The guard, Alice is astonished to see, is female. She smiles at this encroachment of a woman into a man's world. The train chugs forward and slowly gathers speed; its rhythmical exhaling, the *clackety-clack* on the rails and the swaying motion irons out her anxiety about her forthcoming interview at the nursing school. At last this is her chance to step into a new life.

She wants this so much that she can't believe she will be lucky enough be offered a place. She stares out of the train window mesmerised by the unfolding scene: the houses that back onto the railway line, then, as the train edges out of Oxford, a field of cows, endless hedges, a river. She can't understand why all the other passengers are engrossed in their newspapers when there is so much to see outside. After a while the train stops at a station in another town. She has no idea where; the station sign has been removed. All that remains are rusting enamelled signs pinned to the picket fencing advertising Camp Coffee and Wild Woodbines. At least Birmingham is the terminus, so she doesn't have to count the stops and hope she alights at the correct station.

Alice smooths out her dark-blue skirt, lifts her jacket over the revere collar of her cream blouse and fastens the jacket buttons. The last thing she wants is her blouse to be spoilt with sooty smuts. When the train dives into a tunnel she can see her head and shoulders reflected in the window. Very stylish, she thinks, especially her aunt's felt hat with a bow on the back. She glances down at her shoes: sensible lace-ups that Vivien had advised and polished to a shine.

In the last three weeks, her life has undergone a momentous change. She finally plucked up the courage to talk to Professor Florey about nursing school. He didn't seem surprised. He said she would make a very capable nurse.

'Of course, I'll miss you,' he said, 'but I will fully support your application. I recommend Queen Elizabeth Hospital in Birmingham. It's a voluntary hospital which opened three years ago and is one of the most modern hospitals in the country. Draft a letter with your qualifications, listing any prizes you won at school and detailing your experience at the Dunn. Show it to me before you send it.'

Alice spent that evening drafting what she wanted to say. Then, after her mum had gone to bed, she took a single sheet of her dad's white writing paper from the bureau in the parlour and wrote the letter in her best handwriting without a single mistake.

The next morning, she hurried to Professor Florey's office as soon as she arrived. He said he wouldn't change a single word. 'Leave it with me and I will send it with a letter of support.' She wanted to dance down the corridor when she left his office. Her first step on the road to freedom. She kept humming as she worked, and George said, 'You're in a good mood today, Alice.' Even the mundane jobs weren't a chore. It rained all day and on her way home there was a torrential downpour. By the time she walked through the back door she was sodden. But she didn't care.

It was fourteen days later when the letter arrived inviting her for an interview in a week's time. She had got to the post before Peter, but her mum had spotted that it was an official-looking letter with a typed name and address. Of course, she wanted to know who it was from. Alice had told her it would be from the Infirmary with the result of the repeat blood test she'd had, to check whether her haemoglobin levels were back to normal. She hated lying, but what else could she do? She was not going to be thwarted again in her ambition. She opened it in her bedroom, her hand shaking with anticipation and when she read it, wanted to whoop for joy. The only person in the family who she has told is her aunt, who promised to keep her secret.

Professor Florey gave her the day off for the interview, but asked if she could work an extra hour each day for a week to make up for lost time. That meant on the interview day she could tell her mum and Peter she'd been given the day off because of working an extended day, which was true.

When Alice alights from the train the platform is packed with people disembarking. Porters rush between them with luggage trolleys, steam hisses from the engine, a whistle blows. She is jostled and pushed. It's like a tide moving forward and propelling her out into the street.

The devastation around the station makes her stop in her tracks. The shock of the scene is so unexpected. She knew there had been some bombing in Birmingham, but had thought it was the factories that had been targeted. Hoardings have been erected around the bomb sites, but the partial remains of blackened buildings rise above her. She stares at the desolation in horror. If anyone had been inside when the bomb was dropped, they couldn't possibly have survived.

The road is potholed and the pavement ruptured in places. She treads carefully, watching where she places her feet. Between the cracks there are shards of glass, a small broken button, a few shreds of dirty blue fabric.

People rush by her, seemingly oblivious to the wreckage, or just numb to it, getting on with their lives. She doesn't have to wait long for the bus to the hospital and goes straight to the top deck where she can get a bird's-eye view of the town. When she tells the clippie she wants a ticket to Queen Elizabeth Hospital, the woman sitting across from her says, 'That's where I'm going'. She's wearing a maroon-felt trilby tipped onto the side of her head and a coat in a matching colour.

Alice says, 'I'm going for an interview to be a nurse.'

She soon realises that revealing this was a big mistake. The woman begins to tell Alice her whole medical history. Alice half-listens, telling herself she will have to get used to this in future. It will be good practice for her to be patient. The woman pulls a pack of Craven A cigarettes from her bag and offers Alice one. Alice shakes her head but watches as she lights it with a silver lighter, opens the window and blows a plume of smoke towards it.

As the bus trundles through a leafy suburb, Alice admires the pebble-dashed semi-detached houses with their neat and tidy front gardens, while the woman's description of her ailments drones on in the background. She imagines living in such a place rather than in a back-to-back terrace with an outside lav. The bus pulls into a stop and her eye is drawn to a gaping hole in a row of houses. One house has been reduced to a huge heap of rubble: bricks pulverised to dust, wood splintered to matchsticks. But the party wall is still standing with a stub of the upper floor. She feels rather disrespectful staring at the inside of a stranger's house: the wallpaper with large pink flowers on a turquoise background; a chair, completely undamaged; a brown and red dress hanging from a picture rail. As the bus moves off and draws nearer to the bombsite, she can see the dress isn't brown at all, it's just smothered in dust. She must have looked horrified because her neighbour stops relating her medical problems and says, 'It's very sad. The family had taken shelter in the cellar. They all died, including a ten-month-old baby.'

Alice is appalled. The woman takes a long drag on her cigarette and exhales another cloud of smoke. 'I heard from my brother who is an ARP warden that they all looked as if they'd just gone to sleep. The bomb blast had sucked all the air out and they'd been asphyxiated.' The woman stares out of the window, silent for a moment, as if contemplating the awfulness of her story.

Then the clippie calls up the steps: 'Queen Elizabeth Hospital.' There's a rush of people, emptying most of the top deck. She walks with her companion to the hospital, and is glad of her presence because the woman knows exactly where to go. Alice can't help noticing her shoes: high-heeled, black with a peep toe. 'I like your shoes,' she says. 'Are they crocodile leather?'

'They are,' her companion says. 'I always believe in creating in a good impression when I see a doctor. They take you more seriously.'

Alice wonders if one day she will be able to afford stylish shoes and hats like this lady and her aunt. But then this thought is gone because she can see the hospital ahead and all she can think is how big it is, how impressive. Built of brown brick, five storeys high and rising above it a fat-stepped tower, faced with a square clock.

As they approach the wide stone steps to the main entrance, Alice notices two nurses tripping down the steps of a building opposite.

'That's Nuffield House,' her companion says. 'The nurses' hostel.'

The building looks so new and modern that it makes Alice pause and try to imagine living there. She's sure they don't have squares of newspaper for toilet paper. The thought of escaping her home, of beginning a new life, makes her stand straighter and lift her chin. She feels like a bird in a cage with the door open – all she has to do is flap her wings and she can take flight into another world.

At the main entrance Alice parts company with her companion. 'Thank you for your help,' she says.

'My pleasure. Good luck with your interview. Maybe I'll see you again. And the next time, you'll be in uniform.' She smiles and Alice watches her walk down a corridor, her heels clopping on the linoleum floor.

Just inside the entrance is a reception desk where a man gives her directions to the matron's office. Somewhere she must have taken a wrong turning for she is soon lost and ends up outside a ward. Through the glass window in the door, she can see six beds lined up on each side of a long room and, at the far end, a gas fire, beside which sit two male patients in their dressing gowns. A nurse bustles through the door.

'It's not visiting day today,' she says. Alice explains she is here for an interview with Matron, but must have taken a wrong turning. 'Follow me,' she says and sets off at such speed that Alice has to run to keep up.

'Here we are,' the nurse says, stopping outside a door with a sign that reads 'MATRON' in black capital letters. 'I hope it goes well.' She smiles and glances at Alice's feet. 'Matron will be impressed with the shoes.' And she disappears at the same lightning speed.

Alice is grateful for her help because she would have been late otherwise, which would not have created a good impression. She knocks on the door and hears a faint, 'Come in.'

Matron is behind a large desk surrounded by paperwork. 'And you are?' she says pointing at a chair in front of her desk.

Alice gives her name and sits.

Matron puts down her pen. 'Ah, you're one of Professor Florey's Penicillin Girls.'

'Yes,' Alice says.

'So why do you want to be a nurse?'

Alice is well prepared for the question. With Vivien, she had practised her answers to all the questions they could think of. 'As part of my job, I often have to deliver penicillin to Oxford Infirmary, so I've come into contact with the nursing staff and seen their dedication to the care of their patients. And I've seen how rewarding it can be.'

Matron tips her head to one side. 'Any other reasons?'

'I want to have a career where there's a structure which will enable me to progress to higher levels through hard work. My ultimate goal is to be a sister.'

'You're ambitious,' Matron says and Alice wonders if she has made a mistake admitting to this. But Matron continues, 'I don't see that as a problem. It's good to have some drive and determination, as long as the patients always come before the aspiration.'

Then she asks about her work on penicillin. Alice explains in detail what she does, how much she has learned about infections and about the book that Dr Heatley had given her. Matron nods from time to time, but doesn't interrupt.

'And what do you think is the nurse's most important duty?'

Alice remembers overhearing a lecture from one of the sisters to a junior nurse at the Infirmary. She can recall it practically verbatim. 'A nurse's duty is to maintain a high standard of cleanliness, in themselves, in their patients and in the wards.'

Matron inclines her head. 'Your background gives you valuable insight into infection control.'

'Cleanliness is paramount in the incubation room,' Alice says. 'An infection can set back the production of penicillin for weeks.'

'There are a lot of lectures to attend, exams to pass. A lot of our girls don't stay the course because they find this too onerous.'

'I'm eager to learn,' Alice says.

'Yes, Professor Florey indicated that in his letter.'

Then Matron says, 'Thank you for coming,' picks up her pen and starts writing notes in a large book. Alice assumes this means the interview is over and stands to leave. As she walks to the door, she hears, 'It's nice to see some polished shoes.'

In the corridor Alice glances at a clock and is amazed at how long she's been in there. It felt like the interview was over in a few minutes, but it had taken over half an hour. She takes this as a good sign, and as she walks back to the main entrance, she relives the interview. It seemed to have gone well. She hadn't had any trouble answering the questions and Matron seemed interested in her answers. But now she has to wait for days, maybe even weeks, to find out if she has been accepted. How cruel that is.

She is extremely hungry by the time she arrives back at the train station as she hasn't eaten since breakfast. She wanders up and down streets nearby, trying to find a teashop that is affordable. Eventually, she finds one with a boarded-up window and a sign saying, 'WE ARE STILL OPEN'. It's a tiny place with only five tables, but is busy with customers. A table is vacated by a young couple just as she enters. A waitress rushes over.

'Just a moment, madam. Let me clear the table for you.'

Alice doesn't think she has ever been addressed as 'madam' before. She sits up straight, shoulders back like a lady, and orders baked beans on toast and a pot of tea. Sitting in the café at a table on her own, she feels as if at some point during the day she has crossed an invisible boundary and become an adult.

Her mind is full of the day's events, her body still tense with the excitement. She really wants this job. She loves the modernity of the hospital. She loves the kindness of the nurse, who took time out of her busy job to show her to Matron's office, and she even likes the matron, who she was expecting to be severe and highly critical, like the sister in the Oxford Infirmary.

Two hours later she opens the back door of her home and as she steps into the kitchen she is swamped by the smell of last night's cabbage. Glancing around she sees the room as a stranger might: the threadbare rug by the fire, the peeling paint on the window frames, the ceiling yellowed with her mum's constant smoking. She wants to turn round and walk out again. But she can't because Peter is sitting at the table eating toast and margarine.

'You're looking a bit posh,' he says with his mouth full. 'Where you've been?'

'Just out for the day,' she says and hurries upstairs to get changed. She'd been hoping she would be home before him and now she's consumed with guilt. Hiding the truth from Peter is profoundly uncomfortable. She wishes she could trust him, but just doesn't know if he will keep her secret. He won't be happy that she's planning to escape Oxford, so might tell her mum as a way of stopping her. She has a story ready to tell them, a lie, if she is grilled about spending the day with a friend – a visit to the cinema and afternoon tea.

# 16

# Jo

*20 February 2018*

Jo is in the kitchen when the doorbell buzzes. A spoon she has just washed clatters to the floor. 'Damn!' she says picking it up and putting it back in the bowl of soapy water. As she walks to the front door, she calls out to Jessie in the living room. 'That'll be Caroline.'

Jessie groans. 'Do I have to see her?' She's sitting in her usual place on the sofa minus the duvet and pillow, which Jo persuaded Jessie to leave in her bedroom.

'I won't let her stay long. I promise.'

As Jo opens the front door, she prepares to be engulfed in the heady smell of perfume. Caroline is standing on the doorstep with a bunch of pink roses and two small Harvey Nichols bags. She's wearing a beautiful cream coat, her hair is, as always, immaculate, as if she's just walked out of the hairdresser. But she looks tired.

Caroline puts her gifts on the hall table and mutters,' My coat?' as if she's just walked into a restaurant.

'Shall I take it?' Jo says, bristling with irritation. As Caroline slips her arms out of the coat sleeves, Jo sees how thin she is. Caroline has always been slender, always been careful about her figure, but she's as thin as Jessie. Jo ushers her into the living room, where Jessie is staring at the open laptop on her knees.

Jessie puts the laptop aside and smiles at Caroline, who hands her the roses and one of the bags. 'Thank you, Caroline. The flowers are lovely.'

'I'll put them in some water,' Jo says, taking the bunch from Jessie.

Rob told Jo, not long after they met, that Caroline was a cold mother, more interested in being a social butterfly than in her children. And yet she seems to adore Kate and Jessie. She once told Jo that she wished she'd had girls instead of boys. She always remembers their birthdays and buys them lavish gifts. Once when Jessie was opening one of Caroline's presents, Rob said that his mother had forgotten his tenth birthday. He waited all day, thinking she was going to surprise him at teatime, but when it was evident that no presents were forthcoming, he had reminded her. Caroline denies it, of course. But Jo can quite believe it.

When Jo returns with the flowers in a vase, Caroline is sitting in a chair beside Jessie, looking very settled.

'Look what Caroline has given me,' Jessie says showing Jo a Charlotte Tilbury make-up set.

'That's very generous.' Jo says, knowing there wouldn't have been much change from £200.

'And I've got something for you,' Caroline says to Jo and hands her the other Harvey Nichols bag.

'Oh. Thank you.' She reaches into the bag and pulls out a pot of La Mer body cream. It's a very generous gift, but just the sight of it makes her skin prickle. Has Caroline never noticed she has eczema and that all the soap in the house is perfume-free? She smiles the pretence of being very grateful for something she can't use and tells herself that Caroline was trying to be kind.

After twenty minutes of Caroline's chatter, Jo interrupts. 'Jessie gets very tired. Come and have a coffee in the kitchen.'

'Of course, I don't want to wear you out, Jessie.'

'You're our first visitor. Jessie just hasn't been up to seeing anyone before.' She hopes Caroline takes that as a compliment.

As Jo steers Caroline out of the room she glances back at Jessie, who mouths, 'Thank you.'

In the kitchen, Jo turns the kettle on. 'Tea or coffee?'

'Do you have any decaffeinated?'

'I have lemon tea.'

Caroline's face brightens. 'Lovely.' She perches on a stool at the breakfast bar and places her Louis Vuitton Handbag on the counter.

Jo opens the glass-fronted cupboard where she keeps the Poole pottery tea set that had belonged to her nan. It's a sleek, twin-tone design in sepia and mushroom; the height of modernity in the 1950s. It must have been an expensive purchase for Nan and was only used for special occasions. Caroline never uses mugs and whenever she visits, asks if she can have a cup and saucer. But today Jo shuts the cupboard and selects a white mug from the draining board.

She hands Caroline the mug of tea and sits beside her. Caroline wraps her hands around it as if they are cold and Jo notices that the varnish on her nails is chipped. 'I'm sorry that you couldn't talk to Jessie for very long,' Jo says.

'I understand. I was very worried about her when she was in hospital. It was so hard to find out from Rob what was happening. I knew she was ill, but he wouldn't tell me how serious it was.'

'She nearly died.'

Caroline's eyebrows lift. 'I had no idea. Rob never told me.' She puts her hand on top of Jo's. It is the most affectionate gesture she has ever made. Jo studies Caroline's face. Her mascara is smudged, as if she's been crying, and her lipstick has been applied in such a hurry it bleeds over the edge of her mouth.

She puts her hand over Caroline's and is surprised at herself. Despite her intense dislike of Caroline, she is a human being who is clearly distressed.

'Has something happened?'

It is as if she has touched a hairspring, for tears well up in Caroline's eyes. She apologises and reaches for a handkerchief in her sleeve. 'This is so embarrassing. Can you promise not to tell Rob what I'm about to tell you?'

Jo frowns. 'Of course.'

'A week ago, I was in London shopping for a present for Jessie. I'd just been to Harvey Nics and thought how lovely it would be to meet David for lunch. He's been working late nearly every night and often works weekends as well, so I feel I hardly ever see him.'

*Sounds familiar*, Jo thinks.

Caroline takes a sip of her tea and places the mug down. 'I rang his office and his personal assistant said he'd just left for lunch at the Oxo Tower. I asked if he was alone, because I know he often has business lunches. She said there was nothing in his diary, so she assumed he was. I hailed a taxi and was at the restaurant in ten minutes. It was very busy. I didn't spot him straight away. Probably because I was looking for a man on his own. But he wasn't alone. He was with a young woman I'd never seen before. Younger than you Jo. Long blonde hair.' Caroline stops and exhales loudly as if she's trying to control herself. 'I started to walk towards them. Then I saw she had her hand on the table and he was holding it. I turned and walked away as quickly as I could.' Her eyelashes are spiky with tears and she reaches for her handkerchief again.

Jo can hear her mobile phone ringing somewhere in the house. She can't remember where she left it. Then Jessie calls, 'Mum.'

'I'll just see what she needs,' Jo says and slips out of the room. In the living room Jessie is holding Jo's phone. 'It rang, but I didn't want to bring it to you in case I got sucked into conversation with Caroline.'

'Who was it?'

'Zoe.'

'Did she leave a message.'

'Shall I play it?'

'No, I'll listen to it later.' She slips the phone into her trouser pocket.

As Jo walks back into the kitchen, Caroline is hurriedly pushing a hip flask into her handbag. And when Jo slides onto her stool, she detects the unmistakeable smell of gin.

'I'd better go,' Caroline says. 'I'm sorry about my outburst.'

'You don't have to go. Have you confronted David?'

Caroline stares miserably at the countertop. 'It's happened before and he always promises he won't do it again. But he always does.' She sighs. 'Yes, I confronted him. He confessed he'd been having an affair for the last year. I'm afraid I was rather drunk. I'd been waiting a long time for him to come home. Do you remember his Lalique tiger that sat on the coffee table?'

Jo remembers the tiger well, especially David waxing lyrical about how much it must have cost. It had been a gift from a client; crystal, with a few black stripes and facial features that made it quite lifelike. The girls always wanted to stroke it, even when they were teenagers. What child wouldn't be fascinated by such an object? Jo had been terrified one of them would knock it to the floor and smash it.

'I threw it at him,' Caroline says. 'Luckily I missed him and hit the wall behind. It could have killed him. It's rather heavy.'

'Did it break?'

'Oh yes. Into many pieces.' Caroline presses her lips together and stares into her tea. 'I expected him to say he was sorry, but instead he said, "I want a divorce. I'll leave in the morning. My lawyer will be in touch."'

'I'm so sorry, Caroline,' Jo says, trying hard to mean it.

'He slept in the guest room and when I woke the next morning with the most excruciating headache, he'd gone.' Caroline runs her hands through her hair. 'How can I live on my own? We've been married for forty-five years.'

Jo is not sure how to respond. Does Caroline really expect her to answer this question? She waits. Caroline's silence lengthens and Jo decides she needs to answer honestly.

'One thing I've learned from Jessie's illness is that we have reserves we never knew we had, until we needed them. I never thought I could cope with the dread that she might die. I thought at least I would have Rob to support me. But your son left it to me to talk to the doctors and to be with Jessie when she needed physical and emotional support. He didn't tell you how serious it was because he never faced up to the magnitude of Jessie's illness – he couldn't deal with it.'

Jo takes a deep breath. She thinks she might have just gone too far. But if Caroline can pour her heart out, then why can't she? Caroline frowns, shifts in her seat but still says nothing.

'Why don't you want Rob to know?' Jo says. 'He'll find out soon.'

'I just prefer him to hear it from me. I'd better go. Thank you for listening. That was kind when you clearly have a lot on your plate right now.'

'You need to get some help. Find a counsellor who will help you get through this – and a good lawyer.' Jo pulls out a drawer and removes the sheet of paper with a list of counsellors the doctor had given Jessie. She's even thinking she might use one herself. 'This might help you. I'm trying to persuade Jessie she needs more psychological help than I can give her.'

'But don't you need it?' Caroline says.

'This is a copy. I gave Jessie the original list.'

'Thank you,' Caroline says putting the paper in her hand-bag. 'Can I say goodbye to her?'

'You might want to wash you face first.' Jo says noting the streaks of mascara under her eyes.

After Jo has closed the front door, her first reaction is guilt for not being more sympathetic. But Caroline has friends. Why did she need to pour her heart out to a daughter-in-law she doesn't like? She wanders back to the kitchen and washes Caroline's mug. As she stares out at the garden, a thought occurs to her. Have I just been played? When she said 'Don't tell Rob', it wasn't what she meant at all. She assumed I would tell him. She doesn't want to tell Rob herself, but she wants him to intervene, to persuade David to go back to her. Well, she's read me completely wrongly, because I'm not telling him.

She pulls her phone out of her pocket and listens to Zoe's

answerphone message. *It's Zoe. Give me a call when you've got a spare minute. It's not urgent.*

*Zoe you are just the tonic I need*, she thinks, as she phones Zoe back.

'Hi, Jo. How's Jessie?'

'Getting better, slowly.' Just hearing Zoe's voice lifts Jo's spirits.

'You'll never guess. I've managed to get two tickets for a tour of the Clothworkers' Centre, in Kensington, in two weeks' time.'

'That's amazing. Aren't they like gold dust?'

'It's a stroke of luck and, of course, one of the tickets is for you.'

Jo is thinking fast. Surely Jessie will be okay to leave on her own now, and it would do them both good. Jessie needs to realise she can fend for herself, and Jo needs to get out of the house and have some time for herself. After months of a humdrum existence, it's like a light has been turned on.

# 17

# Alice

**14 January 1942**

Alice sits at the kitchen table, her stomach taut with anxiety. Her mother is finishing a cup of tea. Peter is chattering about his day at school. Their plates are empty and in a moment, Alice knows her mother will ask her to clear all the crockery and wash up. Alice has barely said a word. She has to tell them now. She can't delay it any longer.

When she came home from work yesterday, there was a letter from Queen Elizabeth Hospital, offering her a place starting at the beginning of March. She was glad her mum wasn't home when she opened it. But ever since, she's been putting off telling her. Her mum will be angry, especially when she finds out Alice discussed her decision to apply with Vivien. Today she told Professor Florey and handed in her notice. He was delighted for her. He even shook her hand and said she'd made an important contribution to the production of penicillin and that he and the rest of the team would miss her. All day she's been churning with a mixture of excitement about her future, and dread at the prospect of revealing her news to her mum and Peter.

She takes a deep breath. 'I've been offered a place at a nursing school and I've accepted.'

They are both silent, their faces expressionless, as if they don't understand what she is saying. She waits. The fire crackles and spits and finally her mother says, 'What are you talking about?'

'I'm afraid I haven't been entirely honest with you both and I'm sorry for that. But I decided some time ago that this was what I wanted to do. I discussed it with Professor Florey and he helped me apply and wrote a reference.' She thought showing she had the professor's support might help her mum accept it.

'He had no business doing that,' her mum says, her voice rising in volume. 'You can just write to that nursing school and tell them you've changed you mind.'

'No. You can't stop me doing this. I've handed my notice in and I start in six weeks.'

'That's where you were when you had the day off work and you were all dressed up,' Peter says.

'I'm sorry. I wanted to tell you.' she says looking at Peter so he knows she means him and not her mum.'

'Where?' her mother says.

'Birmingham.'

'You're definitely not going there. Have you any idea how many bombs the Germans have dropped on Birmingham?'

'I'm fully aware, but nowhere is safe. Where you work is definitely not safe, but you still work there.'

'And what's wrong with your job? I thought you liked it. You're always saying how important your work is.'

'It is important. But there is no future. No career. I want a job that is more satisfying and where I can progress into more senior positions over time.'

'How will I cope without your salary?'

Alice knew she wouldn't say, 'Congratulations, Alice'. That was too much to expect, but at least she isn't shouting.

'I'll send you what I can. I will be earning considerably less than I am at the Dunn, but I'll get free food and lodgings.'

'Why didn't you discuss it with me before you applied?'

'Because I knew you would try to stop me.'

'You always do what you want, Alice Lawrence. You're a selfish girl.'

*I suppose I am*, Alice thinks, *but Mum made her choices a long time ago and I'm sure she regretted them*. Now it's time for Alice to choose her own path in life. She will never forgive her mother for making her give up school.

'I suppose you asked Vivien's opinion?'

'I made my own mind up. But I did tell her.' Alice waits for the explosion. But it doesn't come. Her mum pushes her chair back, and without another word, goes upstairs.

Alice clears the table and starts washing up. Peter picks up a tea towel and dries a plate. She knows then, it has hit him hard; he rarely helps. They are both strangely silent. Alice washing, Peter drying, like an old married couple.

Eventually, he says, 'Can I come and visit you?'

'Of course,' she says. 'I'm going to miss you.' She rinses a plate under the tap. 'You do understand why I'm doing this? I don't want a life like Mum's. If she'd let me stay on at school and become a teacher like Vivien, maybe I would have stayed in Oxford. But she took that away from me.'

'But why not train here, in Oxford?' he says.

'Professor Florey recommended this hospital and I like the idea of going somewhere new.' She stops washing and looks at him. 'If you were in my shoes, what would you do?'

'That's different,' he says, 'You're a girl.'

She despairs at this point and when she's put all the dry crockery and cutlery away, she says, 'I'm going to Margaret's house.' At least she will congratulate her and share her excitement.

As she walks down Winter Street, she worries Margaret might not be in; she seems to spend more and more time with Arthur. And she needs to see her, not just to share her news but because she is beginning to have doubts about the enormity of her decision. She needs Margaret to reassure her that she isn't making a huge mistake.

But Margaret is at home. And her parents, as always, are very welcoming, treating her like family. Margaret's mum has made a tea loaf and insists Alice has a piece, even though she explains she's just eaten. As expected, they are all delighted with her news and Margaret sweeps away the niggling doubt. She stays until nine o'clock.

Peter is still up doing his homework at the kitchen table. She says, 'Goodnight', and gets a grunt in response. He's cross because she's leaving him again, just like at junior school. Her mum's bedroom door is closed and there's no light showing underneath. She's glad. She doesn't want another confrontation tonight, although she's sure there will be an argument tomorrow. Alice isn't sure which manifestation of her mother's anger is worse: her silence when she completely ignores her as if she doesn't exist; or her flinging abuse at her. At least it's only for six weeks. Then she doesn't have to endure it ever again.


Three days later her mum has barely spoken to her. Not another word has been said about the nursing school. She's not even asked which day she's leaving home. There's a very frosty atmosphere between her mum and Vivien. Peter has forgiven her and seems more concerned that they will still see each other. She has tried to reassure him. How could she walk out of his life? It would be like severing part of herself.

On Saturday she'd bought herself a case and hidden it under her bed after filling it with a few things she wants to take: a couple of her favourite books –*Rebecca* and *The Mill on the Floss* – her dad's letters and a photo of Peter and her dad. She doesn't want one of her mum. Alice hates her. It's horrible living here. How can a mother treat her own daughter like this? She wants to leave home now and never see her again.

At least there is some respite this evening; her mum has gone to the cinema with Vivien to see *Moon over Miami*. A peace-making offer from her aunt no doubt. They won't fall out for long.

Thank goodness for Peter. He makes it bearable. But he isn't feeling too good this evening. He didn't eat his tea. That's not like him. And he was complaining of a headache. While Alice is clearing the table, he says he's going to bed. When she has washed up, she goes upstairs to make sure he is alright. He's fast asleep. She hopes he's not getting the flu. But he's never ill. She tiptoes back downstairs again and sits beside the fire. The back door opens and her mum walks in, past Alice as if she's not there. As her mother hangs up her coat in the passage, Alice wonders if she should mention that Peter is unwell. But when she turns to speak to her, she's gone and she hears her mother's bedroom door close quietly.

# 18

# Jo

'And this is a mid-nineteenth-century muslin dress decorated with beetle-wing cases,' the curator says, as she slides out a deep drawer from the storage unit and removes the protective paper.

There's an audible gasp from several women on the tour. Jo glances at Zoe and grins, then turns her attention to the dress. She is fizzing with excitement.

The wing cases, an iridescent blue-green, are stitched onto the white muslin with gilded thread and arranged in floral patterns along the hem, around the neck and sleeve cuffs.

'You can see how the dress would have shimmered in candlelight,' the curator says. 'The cases are from the jewel beetle and are shed naturally, so are a perfect renewable resource. In this period, they were a major export from India.'

'They look very fragile,' Zoe says.

'They are. That's why they were only used on the edges of the garment.'

'May I take a photograph?' Jo says.

The curator inclines her head and Jo takes out her phone. It's such a pity Jessie can't be here. But at least she can share the photographs with her.

At the start of the tour, the curator had introduced herself as Angela. She said the centre had 7,000 storage drawers and

500 metres of hanging rails. They had textiles from all over the world from more than 3,000 years ago to the present day. Jo was stunned by the vastness of the place, the immensity of the archives.

When Angela then said, 'It provides a resource for students to study', Jo had a peculiar feeling as if a sudden connection had been made in her brain.

Zoe's words in the shop last November come flooding back: 'Perhaps you can't make up your mind because you're looking in the wrong area. You're trying to turn the clock back to your aspirations twenty-one years ago.'

The next drawer reveals an eighteenth-century gown made from Spitalfields silk. It has a cream background and is elaborately patterned with pear-shaped fruits and exotic flowers in crimson, gold and dark green. 'One of the design-ers of the floral patterns for Spitalfields silk was Anna Maria Garthwaite, who signed her name A.M.G., on her designs, to disguise she was a woman,' Angela says. 'Many of her original watercolour designs, dated and annotated with the name of the weaver to whom they were sold, are in the V&A Museum.'

Jo makes a mental note of the name. She will look for these the next time she's in the museum. She takes more photographs then lays her hand on Zoe's arm. 'Thank you for persuading me to come. It's amazing being so close to these costumes.'

Angela begins to walk towards another area. 'If you follow me, ladies, I'm now going to show you some garments from the last century. I notice that two of our party are wearing 1940s' dresses. They look genuine vintage.' She turns to Jo and Zoe and smiles.

The curator turns a wheel on the side of the vast storage unit, which opens to reveal row upon row of drawers. She tugs on the middle drawer to reveal a very different dress from the last two exhibits. Tomato-red with three-quarter-length sleeves, it is tightly gathered at the waist, with two external pockets just below the waist band. 'This is an Edward Molyneux day dress in rayon crêpe from the Utility collection. Raw products were in short supply in this period, so Utility products had to use economy of material.'

'But despite that, it's still elegant and beautifully made,' Jo says.

'I'm sure you could imagine wearing it today,' Angela says.

*I wish I could*, Jo thinks, and wonders if she could make such a dress. It's a long time since she's made her own clothes, but she's bored at home with Jessie. She needs something to focus on. When she was a teenager, she used to bargain in the market for inexpensive material and make her own dresses with her mum's sewing machine. It's still there, sitting in her mum's house. She knows exactly where it is and aches to be back there.

Jessie doesn't need her anymore. In fact, she needs the opposite. Her confidence is steadily building, and she has had her first appointment with a counsellor. It seemed to go well and she's talking to friends again on the phone.

Perhaps it's time Jo went back to Barnsley to make sure the house is alright and get some agent valuations. She could bring the sewing machine back with her.

The curator is opening another drawer. Nestled among the protective paper is a ladies' maroon-wool suit, nipped in at the waist with a pleated skirt and collarless jacket. 'The jacket would have been worn with a fur stole,' Angela says.

'Does anyone want to guess which decade this is from?'

'1930s,' Zoe says immediately. Jo laughs. Her friend probably knows precisely which year it was made.

'I shall now bring us right up to date,' Angela says and starts walking to another part of the centre. Jo and Zoe follow. There's an excited chatter in the group which echoes in the cavernous building. Angela stops. 'The next exhibit was unveiled at the V&A in 2012.' She pulls out yet another enormous drawer to reveal a glossy cape the colour of butter, covered in embroidery of flowers and spiders. 'This wonderful fabric is made of undyed raw spider's silk. It took 1.2 million spiders and 3 years to make.'

'It must be a special spider,' Zoe says.

'The spider is found in Madagascar; it's the size of a human palm and weaves webs that gleam golden in the sun. What is amazing about this silk is that, weight for weight, it is five times stronger than steel. It's a similar product to silk made by silkworms, but is softer and lighter.'

'Who would have thought that something so delicate could be so strong,' Jo says. 'It's like something from a fairy tale.'

'Spider silk has some other interesting properties, which have been known about for centuries,' Angela says. 'Apparently, the Greek and Roman soldiers used pads of spider silk to staunch wounds. It is believed to have antiseptic properties and increases blood clotting.'

'I must tell Jessie. She'll be fascinated,' Jo whispers to Zoe.

The cape is the last item on the tour and one by one the tour members thank Angela and gradually drift away.

Zoe suggests a nearby Italian restaurant for lunch. After they've ordered, and while Zoe visits the ladies, Jo sends a message to Jessie. *Just finished the tour. It was brilliant Are you okay?*

Jessie responds within seconds. *Glad you're having a good time. I'm fine. You don't need to rush back for me.*

A contentment Jo she hasn't felt for months rinses through her. She responds. *We were shown a cape made of spider silk! Apparently, pads of spider's webs used to be applied to wounds. It was thought to be antiseptic and aided healing.*

Zoe slips into the seat opposite Jo. 'Is she okay?'

'Yes. She's so much better. There was a time when I couldn't ever imagine this semblance of normality.'

'It's been a long haul. You deserved a day off.'

The waiter appears with a lasagne for Jo and cannelloni for Zoe. Jo picks up her fork. 'This is such a treat. Lunch out.' She leans towards Zoe. 'The tour was a completely different experience from visiting the museum. I can actually imagine wearing those dresses. In fact, I'd like to be locked in there overnight and have a free run of the place. Could you imagine trying them on? I'd be like a kid in a sweet shop.'

Zoe smiles.

Jo continues. 'And when she said students could come and use the archive for researching textiles and clothes, I could a feel a tingling running up and down my spine. How amazing to be able to do that, or to help to preserve the garments. That would be my dream job.'

'You say it as if it would be impossible, but I'm sure there are courses that can train you for such a career.'

Jo rubs her forehead and exhales. 'Conservation is a type of science. Do you think my degree might help me get on to a course?' Zoe nods enthusiastically. Jo feels as if her mind is on a roller-coaster, going too fast. She needs to slow down, to think this through. That tiny shoot the curator had planted in her brain is growing fast like those speeded-up films.

Zoe puts down her fork and scrolls through the internet on her phone. 'Look,' she says showing Jo her screen. 'You could study Textile Conservation at the University of Glasgow, or the V&A has its own diplomas. I'm sure there are more.'

Jo rubs her fingers over the white tablecloth, feeling the warp and the weft.

Zoe reaches across and puts her hand on Jo's. 'I've said it before, but now Jessie is recovering, it really is time to think about what *you* want to do for the rest of your working life.'

Jo contemplates Zoe's words. Of course, she is right. Ever since Kate was born, she has put herself second. Her children and her husband came first. But now it's time to be who she wants to be. And whereas once this leap into the unknown would have been scary, now it's exciting, as if she's been asleep for a long time and has just woken up.

They eat in companionable silence until Zoe says, 'What's happened about Caroline and David? Does Rob know about the impending divorce yet?'

Jo had told Zoe about Caroline's visit when she phoned after Caroline left. She wanted to know if Zoe thought Caroline had been disingenuous.

'Justin phoned to tell him. Once Rob knew, I told him Caroline had told me when she came to see Jessie, but had made me promise not to tell him.'

'What was his reaction?'

'He's furious with his father. He thinks it's all very sordid – a man of his age having an affair with a woman of thirty. But he's not getting involved. He says it's none of his business and anyway, his father has never taken any notice of what he thinks. And then he said something which stunned me.'

Zoe tilts her head.

'He said a few years ago, he'd been at a conference in a hotel in London and he'd seen David coming out of the hotel with a young woman on his arm. I don't know if it's the same woman, but I can't believe he never told me.'

'I'm just amazed his mother has put up with it for so long and that she doesn't want a divorce.'

'Perhaps she's frightened of the unknown. I can understand that. David is going to let her keep the house. They have an apartment in London where he's living now. It's probably a fair division. Rob doesn't have any sympathy for her. He's been urging her to get help for her alcoholism for some time, but she's in complete denial.'

'Maybe this will make her face up to it,' Zoe says.

Jo had once wondered if Rob was having an affair with one of his colleagues. It would have explained all the weekend working, his gradual pulling away from the family. But there was no evidence, no strange smell on his clothes, no unusual phone calls or secretive behaviour. She'd decided that his research was his mistress. He has a determination to succeed, to make that important discovery that would make his name. He has become like his father; the only difference is he isn't fixated on earning a lot of money like his father. But he is mean. They say that before men marry, they should look at their girlfriend's mother to see what they will be like as they age. But surely it was the same for women. Jo should have looked at Rob's father and seen that, no matter how much Rob tried to go against the grain, in the end, he would be his father's son. He has the same need to be at the top of the ladder. But his struggle to win grants to fund his research means the university loads him with more and more teaching which he hates. His research is squeezed into weekends and evenings, his dream career slowly slipping away. And his failure to achieve this is making him a bitter man.

'She bought me this,' Jo says pulling the pot of Crème de la Mer from her handbag.

'Caroline?'

'I can't use it, but wondered if you would you like it.'

'Don't you want to take it back and buy something else?'

'Not if it's something you would get pleasure from.'

'I would love it. Thank you.'

As they leave the restaurant, Zoe says, 'The V&A Museum next?'

'Why not,' Jo says and links her arm through Zoe's as they walk to the bus stop. 'We can look for those designs by Anna Maria Garthwaite. She sounds like an impressive woman.'

Jo's phone pings. It's message from Jessie. *Check this out. Apparently scientists have made spider-silk bandages with an antibiotic embedded in it. Isn't that amazing?*

# 19

# Alice

**21 January 1942**

Alice is in the processing room helping Dr Sanders with the extraction apparatus. One of the pumps has failed and they are replacing it with a new one. Her stomach grumbles. It seems a long time since breakfast.

'Alice.' A woman's voice. Alice, head bent over the new pump and holding a length of rubber tubing, looks up. Dr Jennings is standing in the doorway. 'There's someone to see you in reception,' she says.

'Who?' Alice says frowning, but Dr Jennings doesn't wait to reply. Her back is already receding.

Alice is puzzled. Who could it possibly be? She glances at Dr Sanders. 'I can manage on my own now,' he says.

As she walks out of the room, she has a dawning realisation. It must be bad news about her dad. Why else would anyone come here? And with this certainty she rushes down the stairs blood pulsing in her ears.

Her mum is sitting on the hard wooden bench where Alice has seen visitors waiting before. As soon as she sees her mum's reddened eyes, her stomach twists.

'Is it Dad?' she blurts out. 'Have you had a telegram?'

But her mum shakes her head. 'It's Peter. He's got diphtheria.'

Alice stares at her, struggling to take in what she's saying.

'He's in the isolation hospital. Gran realised and got him an ambulance.'

It all suddenly makes sense. Just before she'd left this morning, Peter had said he had a sore throat and felt a bit sick. She'd told him to go back to bed and as her mum was on an early shift she said she'd call at her gran's house on her way to work, and ask her to pop over and check on him. He didn't argue, just went straight back upstairs. His voice sounded hoarse, which she thought was caused by the sore throat. She was sure he had flu and went to work a bit worried, but she knew her gran would look after him.

'But why have you come to the tell me? Why isn't Gran here?' Alice says wracked with guilt for leaving Peter. 'Surely, you want to be with Peter.'

'You've been telling me how marvellous penicillin is,' her mum says. 'Well, as you've been working on it, they should let you have enough to treat him. I don't care how you get it, just get some.'

Alice looks at her mother in horror. She hadn't come to break the news of what had happened; she'd come to pressurise Alice into getting some penicillin for him.

'Don't get all precious about this,' her mum says. 'He's going to die if you don't help him.'

Alice has never seen her look so vulnerable, as if the hard protective layer she wraps herself in has been ripped away.

'I'll wait here while you acquire some,' she says.

'I can't just go to the lab and help myself to a vial of it. I'll speak to Professor Florey. You should go back to the hospital, to be with Peter. He needs to know you're there.'

Her mother hesitates, then stands. 'I'll see you at the hospital then. But don't come without it.'

Alice waits for her mum to leave then goes straight to Professor Florey's office. The red light outside his door is on, meaning he doesn't want to be disturbed. But Peter's life is in danger, and she doesn't care if he's busy. She knocks out of courtesy but has every intention of going in if he doesn't answer. When there's no response, she puts her mouth near the door and says loudly, 'I'm sorry to disturb you, but my brother is very sick.'

'Come in,' he says.

She bursts into the room. 'Please can you help me? My brother has diphtheria.' And as soon as she says that dreadful word, tears gather in her eyes.

'Sit down,' he says, offering her the white handkerchief he always keeps in the breast pocket of his jacket.

'He needs some penicillin or he's going to die,' she says.

'I'll talk to my wife,' he says. 'She's in charge of the clinical side of things now. What's your brother's name?'

'Peter,' Alice says. 'He's in the isolation hospital.'

Professor Florey takes the top off his fountain pen and jots this down. He puts the pen down. 'Leave it with me. I promise I'll do what I can. But right now you should be with your brother and family.'

Alice is about to ask if she should tell Dr Sanders that she won't be working anymore today. But before she can say anything, he says, 'I'll tell Dr Sanders.'

As she runs to get her coat, she sees Megan in the corridor. 'Are you alright?' Megan says. Alice shakes her head and keeps running. There's no time to stop and explain. Outside the world seems too bright, the sky too blue. Her mother's words keep repeating in her head. 'He's going to die unless you help him.'

She cycles so fast the journey to the hospital on her bicycle is a blur. She wants to scream at everyone who gets in her way. She wants to shout at God. 'No, not Peter. Please, God, not him.'

When she arrives, the hospital receptionist says 'It isn't visiting time yet.' There are a few chairs in the reception area all filled with anxious looking people. She feels like she's suffocating, and all the people seem to be staring at her. She steps back outside and leans against the wall gulping in air. There's a lady hovering near her.

'Are you alright?' the lady says.

'I just want to see my brother.' How can they be so cruel?

'Didn't you know the visiting times?' the lady says. 'You're lucky it's a Wednesday. We can only visit on Wednesday and Sunday afternoons and then only for one hour.'

'Is that all?' Alice says. 'How heartless.' She supposes she should be thankful that it's a Wednesday. It must be a good omen, she tells herself. She needs something to hang on to, something to stop her from falling apart.

It soon becomes clear that the lady visitor has been waiting for someone like Alice to talk to while she waits. Alice wants to tell her to go away. She just wants to be on her own.

But the lady is prattling on, oblivious to Alice's distress. 'I have to get two buses and the timing of them means I'm always early,' she says. 'My little girl has scarlet fever. She's only three and it breaks my heart every time I have to leave her. She cries and cries.' The lady fiddles with the scarf around her neck as if her nervous fingers have to be busy. 'I can only talk to her through the big window in the corridor that overlooks her room. It's like she's in a glass prison. She's too young to understand.'

Alice lets her mind wander, unable to focus on the barrage of words. Where is her mum? Why didn't she tell Alice about the visiting times? Then the lady takes a handkerchief out of her sleeve and dabs her eyes. This woman is suffering too. She should try to listen.

'The nurses seem kind,' the lady continues. 'And she is getting better, but the hardest thing is not being able to care for her myself. It's instinctive for a mother to care for her children. I do think they should let us visit more often. I mean, what harm can it do? It's just easier for the staff not having us here. Mind you, I've been told you know when they are not going to survive, because they let you visit every day.'

Alice thinks her head is going to explode. She wants to scream at her to be quiet. It is a relief when at that moment a nurse pokes her head out of the door. 'We're open to visitors now,' she says. The lady rushes to the door and edges past the nurse. But as Alice approaches the nurse says, 'We usually limit the visitors to parents.'

'My dad is fighting overseas, so there's only Mum and me.'

The nurse hesitates and Alice thinks she's going to refuse her entry and she can feel the tears welling up again. 'Please,' she says.

The nurse hesitates. 'As there's only you visiting, I suppose I can let you in.'

When Alice reaches Peter's room, she gasps in shock. Her mind is so unbalanced, she'd forgotten he would be isolated. There is a huge window on one side so all she can do is stare at him through the glass. She feels so helpless. He's under a white sheet and blanket in a black metal bed, his face flushed and sweaty. She wants to hold his hand, to hug him. To put a cold cloth on his head to cool him. She understands now what the lady visitor had meant. It is instinctive to care for those we love.

Alice has no idea if Peter can hear her, but she puts her mouth to the glass and explains how she has tried to get him some penicillin and that she's hopeful. He must have heard her because he turns his head towards her. Through the glass she can hear the high-pitched whistling noise of his breathing. And she remembers how Dr Heatley had told her what a terrible disease diphtheria was and how the toxin produced by the bacteria narrowed the throat so it was like being slowly strangled.

As she stands staring at him trying to convey how much she loves him, the nurse appears by her side. She says, 'We're treating him with antitoxin. He's a strong lad. I'm sure he can beat it.'

But Alice knows diphtheria is a killer; they are vaccinating babies against it now, but that's too late for Peter. She has seen the posters. *Diphtheria is deadly, Immunisation is the safeguard.*

Then her mum comes running towards her with her aunt. 'Have you got it?' she says.

'I've been to see Professor Florey. He's going to try to help.'

'That's not good enough,' she hisses. Vivien tries to calm her, but she becomes even more agitated, grabbing Alice's arm, holding it so tight it hurts. 'You go back there and don't return until you've got it. Steal it if you have to.'

'It's not that simple. It has to be injected. It has to be given by a doctor who will want to know where it has come from. And it isn't just one injection. It will be several over four or five days. It will be a lot of penicillin.' And as Alice explains, she realises that the chance of there being enough to treat Peter is miniscule. One thing she knows is that you have to keep giving penicillin until the infection has cleared up, and patients aren't being treated unless there's a good chance of success, which means there has to be enough for a full course of treatment.

But Alice's mum keeps yelling at her, and the nurse says if she doesn't calm down, she will have to leave the hospital. In the end, Alice goes. It's the only way her mum is going to stop shouting. She cycles to the Radcliffe Infirmary and heads straight to the ward where Dr Ethel Florey has an office. She's about to knock on the door when a nurse stops her.

'You can't go in there,' she says with a severe expression on her face.

'I work on penicillin at the Dunn,' Alice says, 'and I need to talk to Dr Florey urgently.'

The nurses face softens. 'What's your name?'

'Alice.' The nurse knocks on the door and enters.

After a few moments she reappears. 'You can go in now'

Dr Florey is sitting behind her desk, holding her ear trumpet. She smiles. 'Hello, Alice. Professor Florey has spoken to me about your brother. Most of the penicillin we have has been allocated, but we're going to try to make some available for Peter. Leave it in our hands. I can't promise, but we will do our best.' She removes her ear trumpet, and Alice knows the conversation is over.

She thinks about going back to work, but how can she possibly concentrate? She trusts the Floreys to help if they can; she believes what they have said. There is nothing more she can do, so she cycles home. All the way back she tortures herself with guilt. How could she have left him alone this morning when he was so ill? Should she have known it was diphtheria? Gran knew – that hoarse voice was the clue.

Should she have alerted her mum last night when she came home, told her that he wasn't well? But since they weren't speaking, she didn't. Would her mum have known last night and taken him to hospital? Would he have had a better chance? When she enters the house it is full of silence like a thick fog. She keeps seeing her mum's face and can't help feeling that her mother wishes it was Alice and not Peter that is lying so still in the hospital bed.

# 20

# Jo

***13 March 2018***

The front door clicks shut. Perplexed, Jo glances out of the window and sees Jessie walking quickly down the front path to the road. Strange. She didn't mention she was going out, especially as it's the first time she has gone out on her own since she's been ill. Jo picks up her phone, planning to text her, then stops. The last thing Jessie needs is her mum continually keeping tabs on her. Upstairs, she pauses by Jessie's open bedroom door. It's back to its usual messy state: discarded clothes litter the floor and her desk is overflowing with paper and books. There is a dirty plate and glass balancing precariously on the edge of her bedside table, so she enters the room to retrieve it.

Alice's diary is lying on the floor beside the bed as if Jessie has just dropped it there. Jo is surprised. Jessie lost interest in it after Jo suggested she might have PTSD. Jo was disappointed that this connection between them had been severed, but there's no reason why Jessie shouldn't read it on her own. And if she is reading it, they can renew their chats about Alice and her family. But Jo is irritated that Jessie has left the diary on the floor, knowing how important it is to her. It's already in a fragile state, the cover edges are ragged and some of the pages are coming loose. Staring at it, abandoned, she realises how much she's missed losing herself in Alice's life. She picks it up eager to read it again. The plate and glass can stay there for now. In her bedroom she makes a nest of pillows against the bed headboard and settles down. When she turns to the page she'd last read with Jessie she realises there are only a few written pages left; the last pages are blank.

She loses herself in the diary, completely absorbed, then suddenly stops reading. She feels as if she's been holding her breath and needs to breathe for a moment before she continues. Her connection with Alice is so strong she feels like she is in Alice's head and it's hard to break the spell and bring herself back from the past into the present. She glances around the room, sucking in its familiarity, trying to anchor herself. She dreads what she suspects is coming next in the diary, but she has to read it, there are only two pages left.

**Thursday, 22 January 1942**

I didn't know what to do today. I barely slept last night. When I did sleep, I dreamt I was in the culture room in a sleeveless nightdress and as I pipetted the culture medium, the mould started to expand over the edge of the container, sliding down the sides and onto the bench. It slithered onto my hand, and I stared in horror as it climbed my arm. I tried to brush it off, but it had embedded itself in my skin. Slowly it wrapped itself around my neck and as I opened my mouth to scream, it slipped into my mouth and began to fill my throat until I couldn't breathe. I woke with a start and sat up in bed. My heart was pounding and I was gasping for breath. I got up then. I had thought sleep would take the fear away, but it was even worse than being awake. I went downstairs, lit a fire and sat beside it in Dad's chair, wrapped in a blanket. I wished Dad was home instead of being thousands of miles away. He would have comforted me; he would have understood that I'd done everything I could. Mum didn't come home. I assumed she'd gone to Gran's house.

Once it was light, I dressed, had a cup of tea, but couldn't face eating. I had to do something, so I went to Gran's. She was up and said there was no news. Mum and Vivien were in bed. 'There's nothing for them to get up for. They can't see him until this afternoon. It seems so cruel.' I was surprised they were allowed to visit again. Then I remembered the words of the woman I had met outside the hospital: 'They only let you visit more often if there is little hope of survival.'

I cried and Gran held me, but then said, 'I don't understand why you couldn't get him the penicillin.' I explained how I'd spoken to the Floreys and they had promised to try to help. But she still didn't understand – just like Mum. Then Mum came down. Her face was grey with tiredness. She stared at me with a look of disgust and started bellowing at me again. Her words were like physical blows.

I love Peter. I will do anything for him. Why can't she understand that?

I think my hate for her is ballooning into something monstrous. Distraught I went back to the Dunn to plead once more with Professor Florey. It was a wasted trip. He wasn't there. He'd gone to London for a meeting at the Medical Research Council. I cycled to the Infirmary, but couldn't find his wife either. Nobody knew where she was. I tried to visit Peter at the Isolation Hospital, but was told Mum and Vivien were already there and only two people were allowed to visit. I feel as if I have spent all day chasing shadows. I'm home again in an empty house. Thank God Mum isn't here yelling at me. I need some peace. I am so tired.

**Friday, 23 January 1942**

I have so much to write I don't know where to start. I wasn't sure if I could write what has happened, but I'm in such a state, it might help calm me down. It is late evening. I am at Margaret's house and I cannot sleep.

Peter is gone. I can't bring myself to write that word. How can it be possible? Where has he gone to? Mum came home this morning. I had spent another night alone at our house and woke early after a restless night. I was pacing up and down my room, not knowing what to do, when I heard the back door open. I went downstairs, eager to hear if there was any news. But Mum was doubled up on the hearth rug sobbing. I knew then that it was over. I didn't cry, not then. That came later. I knelt beside her and tried to put my arm around her. But she flung me off. 'Don't touch me. You failed him. Your own brother.'

'I did all I could.' I protested. 'I begged them to help him. I would have done anything to save him.'

'If you weren't leaving, they would have given that drug to him. But you were disloyal to them. Why should they be loyal to you?' she screamed at me.

I shook my head. 'No, they aren't like that. They're good people, just trying to do the best they can with a limited supply of antibiotic.'

She glared at me with such hatred then, her face red and puffy. 'I despise you,' she spat at me. 'I don't want you in this house anymore.'

I ran up the stairs to my room. I pulled out the suitcase, shoved in all my clothes, my diary and the pen that Peter had given me for my birthday. It gave me something to do. It distracted me, as I tried to focus on a course of action. I wanted to get out of the house away from her and that empty bed in Peter's room. I didn't want to go to Gran's. There would be more blame there, I was sure. I felt as if I was drowning, and I had nothing to cling on to keep me afloat.

I turned up on Margaret's doorstep this morning. I didn't know where else to go. Margaret had already left for work, but her mother put her arms around me while I cried until I was so exhausted, I fell asleep in an armchair. When I woke, I was covered in a blanket and Margaret was home, kneeling beside me with a look of genuine concern. 'I am so sorry, Alice. You must stay here until you go to Birmingham.' Every time Margaret and her family said something kind, my eyes filled with tears again. They are mystified as to why my mother should behave in such a heartless way.

'She's deranged by grief,' Margaret's mother said. 'She will regret what she said, I'm sure.'

I think she's wrong. Something has hardened in me against her, against my family. Not one of them has taken my side, not even Vivien, who should know better. She's an educated woman. She should understand that what Mum was asking of me was impossible. She should have explained to her.

I've been thinking about Dad a lot this evening. I need to write to tell him, but I'm not sure about his mental state. Would it be a good idea to tell him or wait until he comes home? I know my letters are important to him and I can't write and pretend that all is well. That would be a lie. I can imagine Mum saying that's what I should do. But I will wait until I'm at the nurses' home, so I can give him my new address.

This will be my last diary entry.

Poor Alice. Jo wishes she could step back in time and give her comfort. She understands her loneliness. Having to cope with such profound grief without the support of her family must have been devastating.

Had Jessie read to the end of the diary? Is that why she went out? She has submerged herself in Alice's life in the same way that Jo has when she couldn't face reality. But going for a walk to think it through, to deal with her emotional reaction to it … that's a healthy response, another sign of recovery. Jessie will have seen the parallel with her illness. She survived, but Peter didn't. A few years later and he would almost certainly have survived, but in 1942, they just couldn't make enough penicillin.

'Have you read it?'

Jo looks up. Jessie is standing in the doorway. She was so lost in her thoughts she hadn't heard the front door. 'Yes,' she says. 'It's heartbreaking.'

'It was a shock. And rather too close to home.'

'I know.'

Jessie slumps onto the bed next to Jo. 'Did you notice the writing in the last entry? How erratic it was?'

Jo opens the diary at the last page. There are spots where the writing is blurred, and the paper is crinkled. Alice's grief is laid out on the page. 'I felt like an intruder, like one of those people who have a morbid curiosity in tragedy.'

'In some ways I wish I hadn't read it,' Jessie says. 'But it's made me even more determined to work on penicillin resistance. I've decided to do my Physics degree first. I think my degree could bring different skills to the problem.'

To Jo it is refreshing to hear Jessie talk with such resolve.

Jessie plumps up a pillow behind her and sits beside Jo. 'Her mother was so cruel. Do you think Alice ever forgave her?'

'We'll never know. But I think Alice was tough. She was much stronger than I was at that age. And I didn't have all the obstacles in my way that she had. I think she would have been even more resolute to train as a nurse. The thing I like about her is that once she decided she was going to do something, she did it. She reminds me of you.'

Jessie grimaces. 'Not anymore.'

'Yes, it's still there – you just said it yourself.'

Jessie rubs her forehead. 'I think it's time I started to see my friends again. I know this sounds very ungrateful, but I'm getting rather bored with being at home.'

Despite her sadness about Peter, Jo feels a lightness in her body that has been weighed down with worry. 'That sounds very normal.'

# 21

# Jo

**19 March 2018**

In the car, Jessie is subdued. Jo has become used to this new version of her daughter. She's meeting up with friends and outwardly, she seems to have fully recovered. But the fun-loving, chatty Jessie has been replaced by a more serious, contemplative Jessie, who only talks if she has something important to say. It's not surprising that coming to terms with her own mortality has had this effect on her. Jo listens to the radio, happy to let Jessie quietly stare out of the window.

They are on their way to Oxford for Jessie's check-up with her consultant. While Jessie is at the hospital Jo wants to spend some time walking the streets where Alice lived, looking for the places she mentioned in her diary. She feels as if she got to know Alice during the period documented in the diary. She often finds herself thinking about her, wondering if she had a happy life. There is no doubt in her mind that Alice would have grabbed life with both hands and let nothing stand in her way.

Jo has allowed plenty of time for the journey; she doesn't want to rush. The route cross-country to Winchester then north on the A34, is longer than travelling via the M40. But memories of her last journey on that motorway are still raw and she couldn't face that route. In time she will, but not yet.

The sun was shining when they set off meandering through the country lanes. The trees are now tinged with green and patches of wild daffodils light up the roadside. There's a smell of spring in the air, the organic smell of warming earth and freshly mown grass.

As Jessie's mental and physical health has improved, so has Jo's sleep. Her anxiety levels have dropped as well. But there is something else she is keenly aware of: a steely resolve to make some changes in her life.

She drops Jessie at the entrance to the John Radcliffe Hospital then drives to the carpark in the Old High Street in Headington.

They have agreed that Jessie will message her after her appointment, and they will go to the church that Jo had visited when Jessie was in hospital. It's the churchyard Jessie wants to visit – she's convinced that is where Peter will be buried. She may be right, but it's the church that Jo wants to see again. It gave her such comfort when she was at a low ebb. She wants to show Jessie the stained-glass window of the angel and tell her the story behind it that she has now researched.

As she steps out of the car Jo smooths down the front of her flannel trousers. High-waisted with a wide leg, they were one of her first purchases in Zoe's shop. Until now, Rob's distaste of her second-hand garments had made her self-conscious, so she only wore them when meeting Zoe or other friends who understood her love of 1940s' clothes. She remembers when she tried the trousers on in Zoe's shop. How Zoe had said how lucky she was to have the figure to wear them. Her conversations with Jessie about Alice's diary have made Jo determined to wear these clothes more often. They are part of who she is. And why should she let Rob deny her this pleasure because of his ridiculous concern that it makes them look poverty stricken?

She removes her coat from the back seat, a hip-length swing coat, and fastens the single large button at the neck. She pushes her hands into the voluminous side pockets, locks the car and heads towards the street where Alice used to live. How she wishes there was a rent in the fabric of time that would let step her back to 1941. Or some mind-altering drug that would take her there like in Daphne du Maurier's *House on the Strand.* And of course, if she went back in time, she would want to take Peter the penicillin that would save him. It seems so unjust that he died and yet Jessie lived. But that still happens all over the world. Life is unfair. There has been a change in Jessie since she learned that Peter died, as if she's decided that she has been chosen to survive so she must make the most of her life.

Jo has studied the map, done her research on the internet, so she knows exactly where she is going. When she arrives in Winter Street, she is surprised by how similar the row of terrace houses is to her old home in Barnsley. Brick rather than stone, but the same sash windows, typical two-up, two-down houses, with a tiny front garden a few feet deep, behind a low brick wall. It must have changed since Alice lived there: solar panels on the roof, satellite dishes on chimneys, cars parked nose to tail along one side. There are no children playing hopscotch, but she can hear the *thwack* of a football and the shouts of some boys in a garden nearby. A door bangs shut somewhere behind her. A dog barks. A young couple exit a house to her right and walk towards her holding hands; the woman is chatting, the man has his head inclined towards her, a half-smile on his face.

Alice had written on the inside leaf of her diary, *This belongs to Alice Lawrence. If found, please return to 12 Winter Street, Oxford.*

Jo stands in front of number 12. It has two planters in the front garden filled with hyacinths. She can smell their heady scent from across the road. The front door is painted blue and it has PVC sash windows, yellowed with age. Of course, Alice would rarely have gone in and out of the front door. When she did this on the evening of the first dance, it would have been unusual. She would normally have exited through the back door, just as Jo had done in her old home. She takes some photographs to show Jessie, then walks to Windmill Road – the route Alice described when she cycled to work. The next stop is the Co-op, where Windmill Road meets London Road. This is where Alice had read the sign with her new glasses and discovered the world was no longer a blur but full of minute detail. The sign and Co-op have gone, but the building remains, now an estate agent and nail bar. On London Road she finds Ager's the Drapers, where Alice had bought her dress pattern and fabric. Of course, it is no longer a drapers; now it is a Chinese takeaway. What would Alice think if she walked down these streets now, changed beyond all recognition from when she left in 1942? Did she ever come back? Jo's childhood home has such a pull on her, like a magnet, that she can't imagine Alice not wanting to return. But perhaps her violent rupture from the place had tainted it forever in her memory. She will never know.

A WhatsApp message from Jessie interrupts her thoughts. *Just leaving the hospital and heading for the church.*

Jo retraces her steps along London Road and turns right into Osler Road. She joins the route she'd taken from the hospital on that day four months ago, when she'd felt as if she was suffocating, and half-expects to see Jessie ahead of her. But she doesn't see her until she approaches the church. Jessie is waiting on the pavement, leaning against the stone wall surrounding the churchyard. She holds a bouquet of flowers in one hand: white daffodils and purple hellebores with stems of pussy willow. Jo raises her eyebrows.

'For Peter's grave,' Jessie says

'What if it's not here?'

Jessie shrugs. 'Then I'll donate them to someone else.'

Jo takes a deep breath. There are so many different emotions flashing through her head: her fear when she last visited, juxtaposed against the hope she now has of Jessie's future and her own. Jessie is smiling, 'Did you find her house?'

'I did. I took some photos to show you.' Jessie opens the wrought-iron gate onto the flagstone path that leads to the church door. They step off the path onto the mown grass of the cemetery. Jo steps slowly among the gravestones. Mottled with lichen, some names barely readable: mothers, fathers, daughters, sons, a child aged only two years old. All that loss, all that grief. And her own grief, still unresolved, drives an urgent desire to visit her mum and dad's graves. She hasn't been there since Jessie became ill. Perhaps she'll go there in the next few weeks. Jessie doesn't need her support anymore. She has decided which path she'll tread, has put all her fears behind her, whereas Jo is still standing at the crossroads certain she knows which way to go, but with a barrier in her way – Rob. She knows he won't be supportive, and a big battle lies ahead.

Jessie has gone ahead. There is only one gravestone she wants to find.

'Mum,' she calls. 'Over here.'

Jo joins Jessie by a grave with wilting flowers clearly laid recently. The gravestone reads, *Peter Lawrence 1926–1942. Forever in our hearts.*

Jessie removes the decaying flowers and replaces them with her own, so tenderly as if she knew Peter personally. 'I wonder who left the flowers.'

'The granddaughter perhaps on her grandmother's behalf. Have you noticed the adjacent grave?'

Jessie turns and reads the stone engraving out loud. *'Harriet Lawrence, mother of Peter, sister of Vivien, 1900–1948. Peace at last.'* There are wilting flowers on this grave too.

'Don't you think you should put some flowers on this one as well?'

Jessie frowns. 'But she was so horrible to Alice.'

'She was in pain. Whoever put flowers on Peter's grave placed some on hers too. They look identical to the ones you removed.'

Jessie stares at the drooping flowers in her hand. 'Okay, I'll donate a few.' She bends and removes three daffodils from Peter's grave and places them on Harriet's grave.

'Do you want to see the church?' Jo says. She remembers that the door is stiff and pushes hard when she turns the door handle. Inside it is just as she remembered. The sun has even come out and is shining through the south windows. She shows Jessie the stained-glass window depicting Raphael and they stand before it. 'When I was here before, it was very early morning and the sun was on this window. I was admiring it when Kate messaged me to say you were going to be taken off the ventilator. I ran all the way back to hospital.'

'Poor Mum,' Jessie says and rests her arm around Jo's shoulder.

'I've been thinking about the window a lot lately,' Jo says. 'I decided to find out the meaning of what he's holding. Do you see he has a staff in one hand and a fish in the other? There is a story in the bible that Tobias healed his blind father with the bile from a fish, under the guidance of Raphael. In ancient times, and even now, blinding conjunctivitis is common in the Middle East. It causes an abnormal growth over the cornea, which was treated with bile for over 2,000 years. I don't know how effective it was. There's little information. But what will interest you is that it's caused by a bacterial infection. I read that two million people in the developing world are blind because of this bacteria. And it's completely curable with antibiotics.'

'That's terrible.' Jessie stares at the window. 'I told the consultant about my ambition to work in antibiotic development. He said that the world needed more people like me.'

'Does that make you feel confident you've made the right decision?'

'I knew it was the right choice before I told him.'

Jo thinks about her original goal when she was at university and how she'd lost her way. Jessie is different. She has tenacity, a determination to succeed. 'Stick to your goal. Don't be like me.'

'Do you think Alice is still alive?'

'I don't know. Zoe might still have the contact details of her granddaughter. She might phone her if I ask.'

'Do you mind if I ask her?' Jessie says.

'No, not at all. But are you sure? Wouldn't you rather remember her as she was in the diary?'

'She's touched our lives in a profound way. And if she *is* alive, I want to tell her that.'

# 22

# Jo

**23 April 2018**

Jo dumps her handbag in the hall and hangs up her coat. The house seems strangely empty without Jessie, who is now on a train to Bath to stay with friends. It had been gratifying to see how excited she was in the car on the way to the station. How things have changed. For Jo, life is no longer focused on Jessie's well-being; she can focus on herself once more. After the visit to the Clothworkers' Centre, she knew what she wanted her future to be. And of course, the money she's inherited from her mum can be used to fund a diploma or a postgraduate degree. She's had many imaginary conversations with her mum over the last few weeks. Not that she's ever told Rob about these. He would think she was crazy.

She's researched possible courses, read about the type of jobs she could pursue once qualified, talked at length to Zoe, who dispels any doubts and urges her to pursue this new ambition. For the first time in twenty years, she's thinking about herself, her future. It's like the flame that had been lit at the exhibition is now a raging fire. But there is one hurdle she hasn't cleared. She still hasn't told Rob. She's been putting it off, assuming he's not going to be supportive. He's working at home today trying to write a research paper, so with Jessie out of the house, this is the perfect opportunity to discuss her decision with him.

He's in the kitchen. She can hear the kettle being filled, the rattle of a cup and saucer. She takes a deep breath. Just do it now. He has his back to her and is spooning instant coffee into a cup. Beside him on the worktop is a plate on which he's placed two digestive biscuits.

'Did she catch the train?' he says, half-turning towards her.

'It was just pulling into the station as we arrived.' Jessie is back to her old ways of leaving at the last minute.

Rob turns back to the kettle which has just started to boil, emitting a whistling noise which at this moment Jo finds intensely irritating.

When the noise stops, she says, 'I've been thinking. I want to use some of Mum's money to go back to university.'

He tips a spoonful of sugar in his cup and begins to stir. She can see the tension in his body, the way he holds himself rigid. Maybe she should have picked a better moment. He stops stirring, places his spoon carefully in the saucer and turns towards her again. He frowns. 'And what would you study?'

'Textile conservation.'

Rob looks at her as if she's gone mad. 'You'll spend all that money on a degree? Then what? Do you really think at your age you'll be able to step into a new career? You'll be competing with all those young people who have not had a twenty-one-year break. Why don't you get another data-clerk job?'

'It hardly taxes my brain.'

'It's empty nest syndrome. You just need to get through it.'

'I don't know why you're being so difficult. I finally have a chance to have a career,' Jo says.

'You could have had one before. You chose a different path.'

'I chose?'

Rob's eyes are a hard grey, like the colour of those marbles the girls used to play with. She normally considers him to be still quite good-looking, but when he's in this *nasty* mood, his face becomes quite ugly. 'You chose not to have an abortion.'

Jo stares at him in dismay. She's beginning to wonder who this man is that she married. 'We discussed it, we agreed,' she says.

He shrugs. 'I thought at the time that it was deliberate, you forgetting your packet of pills on the holiday in Greece.'

It was only her second holiday abroad. They were in their final year and decided to have a short break at Easter before they got down to the hard slog of revising for their finals. Her parents took holidays in the Yorkshire Moors or the Dales. Rob, of course, had been all over the world. He couldn't believe it when she said she'd only ever left the country to visit France on a school trip.

'But we still took precautions', she says. 'Don't you remember you bought those condoms at the pharmacy in Tolon? We couldn't find the Greek word for condoms in the phrase book and the pharmacist couldn't speak much English. You had to use sign language. It was hilarious.' She smiles as she remembers how they'd both fallen about laughing afterwards. But then one evening they'd had too much to drink and the condom had been forgotten.

It's clear from Rob's face that he doesn't find the memory amusing. 'It was extremely embarrassing,' he says.

'But the pregnancy was an accident.'

'Was it?' he says. 'You seem to forget that I wanted you to have an abortion. If you remember, I'd been offered a place to study for a Ph.D. We couldn't live on the income from one studentship and bring up a child. Let's face it, Jo, it gave you a get-out. You didn't have to face the uphill struggle of a career. You could just slip into motherhood and pretend you were a martyr, giving it all up for Kate.'

Jo can't believe what he's saying, the cruelty of his words. But as usual with Rob she starts to believe what he's saying. She is sure forgetting to take her pills on the holiday hadn't been deliberate, but she can remember the relief when the decision had been taken that she would keep the baby. And was part of the relief that she didn't have to forge a career? She doesn't think so, but as always, he has planted a seed of doubt in her brain.

'We had no money and were dependent on my parents,' Rob says. 'You have no idea how much I hated having to accept their offer of a flat.'

'But we managed. We were happy, weren't we?'

She had enjoyed those early years. They didn't have much money, but then she'd never had much growing up. She had slipped into her mother's shoes. She knew how to cook cheap meals, how to shop for bargains. Rob didn't have a clue. He'd always had money and he'd rather admired her thrift then. She'd earned a bit of extra cash coaching children for their GCSEs at the weekends when Rob could babysit Kate.

'I don't understand why you suddenly feel a need for a career,' he says.

'When did you stop being kind?' Jo says.

Rob looks at her as if she is a nobody, a piece of dirt on his shoes. 'I don't understand what's going on,' he says. 'For once we have some extra funds from your mum's estate and now you rock the boat with this announcement.'

Jo closes her eyes and sighs. This is even more difficult

than she was expecting. 'This is what I want to do. It is my money. Mum left it to me.'

'Actually, a court of law would say it's *our* money.'

'Then at least half of it is mine.'

'That's not how we decide things in this family. Mine. Yours. We share things.'

'No, we don't. We only share things when it suits you.'

She can't believe what she just said. Normally she would have just thought this, internalised it and avoided a confrontation. She can see him swell with anger and knows there will be a violent reaction. He picks up the nearest object to hand, his plate, and smashes it to the ground. As tiny pieces of pottery and fragments of biscuit skitter across the floor, Jo walks out of the kitchen, grabs her handbag and coat and leaves. She feels battered by his anger and the way he belittles her. She's sick of avoiding confrontations. After twenty-one years, this is what her marriage has become. When did the love that had borne them aloft in the early years, slowly diminish, until now there is a barely a thread holding them together?

She starts the car engine, and hands shaking, heart pounding, she drives, not thinking where she's heading, just needing to get away. She wonders about going to see Zoe. But there's a much stronger draw on her emotions, like a magnet pulling her in. She had been planning to go to Barnsley to check the house and put some flowers on her mum and dad's grave. So why not go now? Spending a few days in her mum's house will help her think things through. And once she's on the M1, she decides there is no going back. The nervous tension in her stomach eases and her shoulders drop.

At Toddington she pulls into the service station and heads for the café. As she eats a sandwich, she watches the cars speeding by and mulls over Rob's anger. Did I provoke a reaction? That's what he will say in his defence. But what she said is true: he has never shared in bringing up the children or running the house. And he always makes the decisions about what they spend their money on.

She pulls her phone out of her handbag. She feels an urgent need to connect with her daughters. Just to hear their voices. Glancing at the screen she sees there are three missed calls from Rob and a text message: *Where are you?* It's clearly bothered him that she's walked out.

She'd talked to both Jessie and Kate about her plans to train in textile conservation, but made them promise not to say anything to Rob until she'd had a chance to discuss it with him. Kate said she felt very uncomfortable with this, and that Jo shouldn't put off telling him. Easy for her to say. Jessie just said, 'Fine.' She dials Kate's number.

'Do you think my idea about retraining is bonkers?' Jo says.

'No.' Kate says, 'Are you getting cold feet?'

'Your dad is worried it will be money wasted, doing a degree at my age.' Jo says.

'He'll come round. You should do this. I've heard the way you talk about it. Where are you? It sounds noisy.'

'I'm in a service station on the M1. I'm on my way to Barnsley.'

There's a pause before Kate answers. 'I thought you weren't going for a couple of weeks.'

'I changed my mind.'

'I've a lecture in ten minutes. I'd better go. Can you ring me tonight? I'm not doing anything.'

She suspects Kate has detected something is wrong. Jo doesn't usually make sudden decisions. She doesn't phone

Jessie. Much as she would like to speak to her, Jessie definitely knows there was no plan to travel to Barnsley today and she doesn't need to be unsettled at the moment.

Now she's calmer, she's able to think a bit more clearly. For once she's going to take control of her life, instead of it being controlled by circumstances – and by Rob. He will try to persuade her by all means possible that's she's making the wrong decision. But she's not going to give into him and she needs to find the strength to make a stand – the argument with Rob is about much more than her mum's money and her future. It's a demonstration of all that is wrong with their relationship. She has tiptoed round the edge of the chasm that has opened up in their marriage for too long, gingerly feeling her way, careful of her step. If she steps too near, the edges will crumble and either the chasm will become larger or their marriage will collapse and there will be no return. Does she care? She used to think she needed Rob, that without him she would fall apart. But not anymore.

She phones Rob and he answers almost instantly.

'I've decided to go to Mum's house for a few days.'

'Does that mean you're going to put it on the market?'

'No,' she says. 'I've told you before, I'm not ready to do that.' She can hear him sigh.

'Okay here's the deal,' he says. 'If you sell your mum's house, I'll agree to you retraining for a year … two years max.'

'I'm not selling Mum's house. Not yet.'

'You can't have everything.'

She can hear the tension in his voice, his anger building again. And she doesn't want another argument. 'I'll phone you tomorrow,' she says and ends the call.

Back in the car, she slips in a CD and the freedom to play

whatever music she likes, without Rob's objection to her 'crappy taste', makes her catch her breath.

'I'm going home,' she says out loud. She drives from the slip road onto the motorway as Queen's 'Don't stop me now' blasts out of the speakers, filling her car with the sound of Freddy Mercury. Jo feels as if the years are peeling away as she sings along just like she used to as a teenager.

# 23

# Jo

**24 April 2018**

The burial ground is quiet; all Jo can hear is the wind rustling the leaves in the trees. She closes her eyes and lets the calmness of the place seep into her. A robin in a beech tree above her begins its plaintive song. It's like a hymn, an ode to her parents. She arranges her flowers carefully on the graves: dark-blue iris for her mother, so perfect it's hard to believe they're real, and for her dad, deep-red tulips, like the ones he had grown on his allotment. When her dad died her mum had bought the two plots in a green burial site.

'It's a comfort,' her mum had said, 'to know that one day I will be beside him.'

To Jo, who couldn't imagine a life without her father, the thought of losing her mum as well had been more than she could bear. She had wept copious tears at her mother's words. *How selfish I was*, she thinks. *I should have been trying to understand my mother's pain instead wallowing in my own*. Her mother had outlived her father by only five years and the day the phone call came from the hospice, that her mother only had days to live, Jo had wanted to scream at the world. She had spent those last few days with her.

'Don't be sad,' her mother had said. 'I'll be with your dad again.' But how could she not be desolate? Her parents had rooted her to the ground. Having no brothers or sisters, there was no-one now she could share all her childhood memories with. Like the day she fell from her bedroom window, her life saved by the kitchen lean-to. Or the day in Debenhams when she'd wandered away from her mum to feel the fabric on the racks and racks of clothes and lost her. The terror of her aloneness, that fear, percolated her childhood. And her mother gave her such wise counsel. How could she survive without her?

Rob didn't seem to comprehend her grief. Maybe because he didn't have a close relationship with his parents, he couldn't understand the pain she was in. Or maybe it was because he had never lost someone to whom he was inextricably bound.

Jo drops to her knees. Last year's leaves blanket the ground and dog's mercury encroaches from the woodland floor. She pulls it away from the edge of the graves and clears the leaves with a broken piece of branch, uncovering the primroses her mum had planted on her dad's plot. Keeping it tidy makes her feel useful; this small action is all that she can do for them now. The primroses have multiplied, and she wishes she had a hand fork so she could divide and transplant some on to her mum's grave. Perhaps tomorrow she'll come back. Her dad's gardening equipment is still in the shed, all hanging neatly, a place for each tool. Her mum had tried to keep the garden under control after her dad had gone. It had always been his domain, whereas the house was hers. Her neighbour mowed the lawn for her, and she manged to keep it weeded. She'd said she felt in touch with him when she was out there on her knees pulling up dandelions and thistles.

'Hello, Mum. Hello, Dad,' she says making sure there is no-one else around who might think she's deranged. She doesn't know why she's worrying about it. She's heard others talking to their dead relatives, who clearly don't care what anyone else thinks. She has spent her whole life caring about what others think of her, especially Rob. It's time that stopped. 'My life has been a bit of a roller-coaster since I last visited,' she says. 'I've decided to train in textile conservation. I can't remember the last time I felt so energised.' She hesitates. 'But I've got an even bigger decision to make. I don't think I want to be with Rob anymore, but it's difficult making that leap.'

She remembers the other leap she had made from Barnsley to university. She had managed that and survived, although in those first few weeks, there were several occasions when she'd almost gone home. It was only her parents' pride in her achievement, the first in the family to go to university, that had stopped her. She had to succeed, for them.

The ground is damp, and the knees of her jeans are now dark patches. She stands and leans against the tree over-hanging the graves. When her dad died, she always came with her mum on his birthday. But she'd missed it this year because of Jessie's illness. As she leaves, rain begins to fall and the tree drips onto the graves. She turns away quickly, not wanting to see the flowers spoil.

Half an hour later Jo unlocks the door to her mum's house. When she arrived yesterday evening, she felt like she was coming home. And it's not just the house, it's the place that shaped her. If she can spend time here, she knows she can make sense of who she is and what she wants – decide whether she wants to build a life apart from Rob. Since Jessie has been home the gulf between them has widened. Their marriage has been fractured for some time, so why is she only now considering the possibility of leaving him? Familiarity? Too fearful of stepping outside? But Rob isn't the man she thought she'd married.

She stands in the bay window of her mum's lounge. The street is deserted under a slate-grey sky and pouring rain. It's hours before sunset, and yet many windows are rectangles of yellow light. She turns round and takes in the familiarity of the room, barely changed since she was a teenager: the floral-patterned sofa and matching curtains, the green carpet, the fringed standard lamp. And sitting in the corner the Singer sewing machine in its bentwood case. She opens the case and takes out the machine. It is still threaded with the reel of navy-blue cotton used when her mum made herself a dress a few months before she died. Jo runs her fingers over the cold black metal, pictures the needle nodding up and down, her mother easing the cloth through as the line of stitches grew. Then she remembers Alice making her dress for the dance. How little some things have changed. Tomorrow she will go to the market, buy some material and make a dress. She wants to feel that connection with her mum … with Alice.

Her mother's spirit still inhabits this house. She couldn't imagine her spirit anywhere else. She doesn't normally believe in such things, has never believed in an afterlife, but her mind is not rational at the moment.

Her mother was never still, not until the end, when the pain sucked all the energy from her. Even when she was sitting her hands would be busy, sewing or knitting. When she remembers her mother, she's always in the kitchen, standing by the cooker, making jam with the blackberries and raspberries her dad grew on his allotment, or with her arms smothered in flour, hands plunged into the Mason Cash mixing bowl, making pastry.

The house hasn't changed much on the outside: the stone is still grimy with coal dust, the same windows and door, unlike the neighbour's house where they are now plastic. The door is painted dark red now, her mum had painted it herself after her dad died. She'd hated the green colour Jo's dad insisted on painting it. It was one of the areas of conflict that wasn't worth fighting over, she'd once said. 'Pick your battles,' she'd told Jo when she asked for advice a few years after she married Rob.

Yesterday evening on the phone Kate had asked outright, 'Are you and Dad splitting up?' Jo explained she just needed some time, dodging the questions that she doesn't know the answer to. Kate had been subdued, probably shocked.

She hasn't phoned Jessie yet and she can't put it off any longer. She judges that Jessie is strong enough to cope with her news now. Three months ago, she wouldn't have dreamt of walking out. The phone rings and goes to answerphone, but almost immediately Jessie rings back. 'Hi, Mum. Everything okay?' Jo can hear the sound of voices and laughter in the background. She explains she's in Barnsley. It was a sudden decision, but she needed some space away from Jessie's dad to work out whether their marriage had a future. Jessie seems less shocked than Kate. 'I'm not surprised, Mum. It's been a long time coming.'

'You will need to ask Dad to pick you up from the station when you get home.'

'No, I don't, I can get a bus. I don't need mollycoddling anymore. How long are you staying?'

'I don't know. At some point I need to go back to the

house to pick up my things. I left without anything, not even a toothbrush.' She smiles at her boldness.

'Blimey, Mum. It must have been a mega row.'

'Yes, I guess it was.'

'If you're going to be there more than a week, can I come and stay? Dad's never around much and his cooking is useless.'

'Of course. Whenever. I'm sorry to land this on you when you're only just recovering.'

'Don't worry. Really. I'll phone you in a few days.'

Jo has a twinge of guilt and squashes it immediately, remembering Zoe's words: 'It's time to think about yourself.'

She sees the young girl who lives next door run into the ginnel between the two houses and remembers the innumerable times her footsteps had echoed as she took that path, before she unlatched the back gate and pushed open the back door. She can feel the warmth of the kitchen, the smell of drying clothes on an overhead airer, the tick of the clock on the dresser and sees her mum waiting for her. She can feel that relief she always felt at coming home after school.

The rain stops, clouds thin, the light brightens. The road gleams and in the tiny front garden drops of water sparkle on the shrubs and garden ornaments. If she's going to stay for a few days, she needs some more food. She'd bought enough provisions to get her through twenty-four hours at the last service station before she left the M1, but now she needs to get something for her dinner. She can't face anymore driving but there is a convenience store on the main road she can walk to. She was a regular visitor when she lived here, running errands for her mum. As she walks down the front path, Carol, who lives in the neighbouring house, is just coming out of her front door.

'Jo, I was just coming to see you. I saw your car. How are you?'

Carol had been a good friend to her mum, helping her out with shopping when she became too ill to go out. She'd helped prepare the food for the funeral and Jo regrets that she hasn't contacted her since sending a card thanking her for all her help.

'I'm sorry I've haven't been in touch. Jessie has been very ill with meningitis. This is the first chance I've had to come back.'

Carol touches her arm. 'How hard for you. And you still grieving for your mum. How is she?'

'She's slowly getting stronger, but she's had a pretty tough time.'

'I'm glad she's on the mend. She's such a live wire, your Jessie. How long are you here for?'

'I'm not sure yet. I might be here awhile.'

'I expect there's a lot to do, clearing the house an' all.'

'I'm not selling it – at least, not yet.'

Carol looks puzzled, but Jo doesn't want to explain because she's not even sure how to. 'I'll catch up with you tomorrow. Can I pop round?'

As Jo makes her way to the shop she feels as if she's treading in her own ghostly footsteps. How much she has changed from that diffident teenager who used to live here. How much she has changed in the last week. While she's waiting in the queue to pay, she notices an advert for ballroom-dancing on a corkboard beside the cash desk. She feels a jolt of excitement. During those few minutes when she had danced for Jessie, she had been flooded with joy. Why did she stop doing something she loved so much? She takes a biro from her bag and writes the phone number on the back of her hand. The woman in front of her in queue is watching her. 'It's a good class,' she says. 'I go sometimes. It's very friendly.' And after the woman has paid, she smiles at Jo. 'I'll maybe see you there on Thursday. I'm Alison.'

As she walks back to the house, her idea of staying for just a few days melts away. Now she is here, she doesn't want to leave. She'll phone Rob later and tell him she might be here for a few weeks. She can feel herself unfolding as if she's been in a strait jacket for the last twenty-one years.

# 24

# Alice

***3 May 2018***

It is still dark, but the nurses are bustling about. There's the clatter of a trolley and the smell of toast. Alice watches the light change slowly and marvels at the pleasure that such small things can still give her.

She drifts in and out of consciousness, her life running before her like a reel of film that has been cut and spliced in multiple places. There is no order, no chronology. She knows it won't be long. But she has no fear of dying. She lost that fear long ago on a winter's day in 1942, when she transitioned from naive teenager to adult and learned she was on her own.

The nurses are kind to her. They know she was a matron. They treat their own well.

'Your granddaughter came, but we didn't like to wake you,' the nurse with the Scottish accent says.

Alice is disappointed.

'Shall I wake you next time?' the nurse says in her beautiful lilting voice.

Alice could listen to her all day.

'She brought a newspaper cutting. I left it on your locker.'

Alice wonders what colour Evie's hair was today. It was blue last time. Alice and Evie's mother don't get on, but Evie and Alice have always been close. By the time Evie came along, that hard block around her heart must have softened.

Evie's mother was a mistake, conceived in a passion at a time when Alice thought she was too old to get pregnant. She never told the father. She didn't need that complication, although Margaret – or 'Maggie', as she now calls herself – weaselled out of her who her father was when she was a teenager and tracked him down. It must have been a shock for him.

She thinks, I never gave her the love she needed. History repeating itself. I was too wrapped up in my career. I made sure she was well cared for, but that wasn't enough. Her name was a mistake too and I'm glad she's changed it. Poor Margaret, on a visit to meet her fiancé in London, had been killed in one of the last bombing raids in 1944. Arthur had survived, but never recovered from losing her. She was an angel, with her blonde curls and blue eyes, who was kindness personified. My daughter is none of those things. She has my temper and her father's brown eyes. I often wonder why I didn't have her adopted. Perhaps I thought she would give me the unconditional love I never had. But that's not true. I'm forgetting Dad.

'He trained as ambulance driver,' she says.

'Who did, Alice?' the nurse says.

'My dad,' she says. 'When he came back from the war. He was in the Western Desert Campaign.'

'Was he?' the nurse says. She's probably got no idea what that was.

Her dad said he couldn't believe the bomb damage when he disembarked in Liverpool. At least he made it home safely. She'd dreaded hearing more bad news. He'd written to her in Birmingham. By then he'd been in York in a mental hospital for two weeks, finally invalided out of the army. She'd never forget seeing him in the hospital. Nut-brown, wiry, not an ounce of fat on him, and his face lined and leathery from the sun. She'd forgotten how much Peter resembled him. It completely winded her.

He had held her while she cried: joy at seeing him and all the pent-up grief. He told her he'd written to her mum and sent a letter to Vivien, but there'd been no reply. He was not going back to Oxford. He said, 'You do a lot of thinking about what's important when your life is on the line.' He'd decided Alice was the only family he wanted to be near.

'Alice,' the nurse with the dark-brown eyes is speaking softly, 'we're going to give you a bed bath.' Alice has given so many, knows the routine. The nurse says, 'I expect things like this never change.'

How much has Evie told them? she wonders. Evie loves her stories of the past, especially the ones from during the war. Her mind reels back to a bed bath she gave a soldier a long time ago. The siren sounded and Sheila, the nurse who was helping, uttered, 'Couldn't they wait until we'd finished?' The poor soldier was only half-washed as they hurried his trolley towards the door. Alice grabbed the adjacent trolley with the soldier who'd lost both legs, and was halfway down the corridor with Sheila just in front of her when there was a sound so loud she thought her eardrums were going to burst. Afterwards she could hear nothing. She was covered in dust and there was a floor joist pinning her down. When she looked up, she could see the sky which was filled with stars. Then her hearing began to recover, and she heard the screaming. She looked for Sheila. She could see her head and part of her torso – the rest of her was gone.

Someone a long way off is calling her. 'Alice, we're going to turn you now.' The other nurse, the young one who doesn't look old enough to be out of school, says, 'She's crying. Did we hurt you?' Alice shakes her head.

'It was a long time ago. We thought the bombing had stopped. The Germans were on the run. It was like their last gasp.'

The nurse pulls the cover over her and plumps up her pillow.

The ward is filled with light. Its cleanliness always pleases her. She glances through the plate-glass window at the sky. It's pure blue, with tiny wisps of cloud. The sort of sky that lifts your heart. She recalls another sky, fragments of grey cloud between the yew trees.

'Man that is born of a woman, hath but a short time to live, and is full of misery. He cometh up, and is cut down, like a flower.' She watches from the edge of the churchyard as the coffin is lowered, the straps removed. Her mother is dry-eyed beside the grave, supported between Gran and Vivien. She looks like a deflated balloon. Thin, her hair completely grey. Alice had sat at the back of the church for the service. Margaret and her parents had accompanied her. It was her gran who'd told her when the burial would be, said it wasn't right that Alice hadn't been informed. She waited until everyone had gone before she placed her flowers on Peter's grave. She visited every year, always on his birthday, until her old body let her down. Two years after his death, she'd found her mum kneeling by the grave weeping. When she glanced up and saw her, Alice turned and walked away.

Frank didn't make it back either. She'd written to him when she moved to Birmingham, so he had her new address. He wrote twice, then his letters just stopped, and she assumed the worst. His few possessions were sent back to his parents, including Alice's letters, so they eventually tracked her down. They said that Frank had told them all about Alice and it gave them comfort to know he'd had a brief liaison in his short life. Alice had raged at the world. It didn't seem fair to lose so many. But she knew people who'd lost whole families.

'Where's my necklace?' Alice says.

'It's here.' The nurse takes her hand and moves it so her fingers can touch it. His parents knew he had bought it for her, he'd told them in one of his letters. When she went to see them, to offer her condolences, they had given her the necklace along with the letters she'd written to him. She tried to persuade them to keep it, they had so little left of him, but they said they had a treasure chest of memories.

She didn't understand then, but she does now. She'd asked Evie if she'd like it when she's gone. 'I would love to have it,' Evie said. And Alice believes her. She can read her face, just as she was able to read Peter's.

The Scottish nurse encourages her to drink some water. She holds a straw to her lips, and Alice sips obediently. She's a good nurse. She would have been glad if she'd been one of her team. 'I remember the first time I gave someone penicillin,' she says. 'I was proud that I played a small part in its development. But it rankles that Dr Heatley missed out on the Nobel Prize. Without him there wouldn't have been any penicillin. And as for that man Fleming, jumping on the bandwagon when the press got hold of the story … all the credit he got and yet his contribution was minor. Fleming discovered it but he abandoned it, couldn't do anything useful with it – a chance finding which he didn't pursue.'

'I didn't know that,' the nurse says. 'And yet everyone assumes it was Fleming.'

Alice scoffs. 'There was no brilliance in his discovery. It was Florey, Chain and Heatley that made it into a drug that could treat people, through sheer determination and ingenuity.'

The nurse has a quizzical look. 'Did you see the news-paper cutting?' she says. 'It's about penicillin. It's called the Penicillin Girls. A new exhibition in Oxford is celebrating their contribution to the development of penicillin.' She lifts it from the bedside table. 'Your granddaughter left it for you.'

'Can you read it to me?' Alice says. The article mentions Megan and Ruth, but not her. She was out of the picture by the time the fame came.

She's spinning back in time again, sloughing off the years and her old body.

'Can you read it to me?' the patient said.

Alice is about to go off duty and could easily tell her to ask the night staff, but she could see her distress. The patient was sitting up in bed with a letter in her hand. 'I know it's from my daughter by the pattern of her writing, but I find reading words difficult,' she said. 'I've never told her. It's stupid really. I'm embarrassed for her to know.'

Alice asked, 'How did you manage when she was a child?'

'Oh,' she said, 'I was very clever at hiding it.'

'You can get help. It's never too late.'

'I've tried,' she said, 'but it's no good. The words just dance around.'

There must have been a growing awareness of dyslexia then because Alice knew exactly what her problem was. But it was only because she mentioned that she'd hidden it from her daughter that she made the connection. She could never understand why Vivien had been clever enough to climb out of her working-class roots and become a teacher while her mother ended up working in a factory. Why she'd never read to her, why it was always her dad. Why it was Vivien who'd taught her to read, and why it was always Alice who wrote to her dad during the war. All those instances when she'd had a letter from school and her mum was always busy, so Alice had had to read it to her. She must have hated that Alice read so much.

She remembers learning to read and asking her mum what a word said. 'Not now, Alice, I'm busy,' was always the reply.' So she learned to wait until her dad was home. He was proud of her, always happy to help. Her mother must have been so ashamed. She'd watched Vivien succeed at school and must have been embarrassed that her sister was so much cleverer than her. No wonder she married when she was eighteen. She could at least beat Vivien at that. Was it shame that had made her so sour?

'Would you like tea, Alice?' the healthcare assistant says.

'Tea, yes that would be nice.'

The cup rattles in its saucer. Alice closes her eyes. Vivien pours out tea from a white china teapot into a matching white china cup. They are sitting in the corner of a Lyons tea house. 'It's good to see you, Alice,' she says. Alice doesn't reply, but stirs a lump of sugar into her tea. There's still rationing, so sugar is a luxury she rarely enjoys. Her aunt had written and asked to meet her. It's the first time since Peter's death that Alice has seen her. She doesn't know how she found out her address. She doubts her dad would have told her, having made it clear it was not to be shared. The only other person who knows is the vicar. She gives money to the church every month and asks that a small portion is used for flowers to be put regularly on Peter's grave. He must be the source, which might mean she has something important to say. She'd replied and said she would meet her, but would not discuss her mum.

Vivien looks very elegant in a New Look suit. She always liked nice clothes. Alice can't afford anything so expensive on a nurse's salary. When Alice arrives, late, her aunt stands up, clearly wanting to peck her on the cheek. Alice steps away and sits down. She has not forgiven her. Vivien's smile falls into a frown, but she says nothing, just returns to her seat, smoothing her skirt as she sits.

'I'm sorry for being late,' Alice says as Vivien pours the tea.

'Thank you for meeting me,' her aunt says. 'You look well.'

'Are you in London for long?'

'Just the weekend. I thought I would visit some of the galleries and perhaps the theatre. Do you ever go?'

'I often get free tickets from the doctors and grateful patients.' And so they talk about trivia. Vivien asks about her dad and Alice tells her he's getting married again.

She raises her eyebrows. 'He'll be wanting a divorce then.'

Alice is surprised. She thought that had happened years ago. But she keeps her face expressionless. She doesn't want this to lead to talk of her mum.

'Could he wait a few months?' Vivien says. 'She's dying, Alice.'

So this is what the meeting is all about. Vivien had lied when she'd agreed not to discuss Alice's mum. Alice finishes her tea. 'I'll ask him,' she says, picking up her handbag. 'Thanks for the tea. I have to get back to work.'

Vivien says. 'Can't you just see her one last time? She wants to apologise. And I do too. I know you think I let you down, but she threatened me. She said if I had anything more to do with you, she would tell the headmaster of my school that I was a lesbian and not fit to teach children.'

'How is Pat?' Alice says.

Vivien's eyes are round with surprise. 'You knew?' She frowns. 'Because of the photograph?'

'I saw you and Pat at her house. You need to make sure you close the curtains before you get passionate.'

Her aunt blushes. 'I was torn. I could see how hurt you were. How much you needed your family's support, but I couldn't risk my job. It's my life.'

Alice understands this. She wonders if she would have behaved in the same way. Her job is her life now too. She wouldn't give it up for anyone. Except for Peter. If he was still alive.

'I forgive you,' Alice says. 'But I can never forgive her. I'm amazed that you can. What a horrible way to behave to her own sister. What a cruel woman she is.'

'You're a cold fish, Alice Lawrence.'

*Who made me that way?* she wants to say, but doesn't. She should never have come. She won't make that mistake again.

'It changes you,' Alice says.

'What does, Gran?' Evie is sitting beside her. Her hair is purple today.

'War,' she says. 'And losing the most important person in your life.'

'Peter?' Evie says.

Alice nods. He's alive, while she's alive. Always living in her memory. Always sixteen years old, with the face of an angel. But it makes her sad that when she goes, he will fade too.

'He was a part of me, and I was a part of him,' Alice says. 'That's why he used to read my diary. He couldn't bear that

I had a life separate from his. It was just a phase, a part of growing up. But I was too young to understand.'

Evie rests her hand on Alice's hand.

'I've been thinking a lot about the diary,' Alice says. 'I regret not keeping it. Could you find out if that shop you gave my old clothes to came across it? I would like someone to read it to me one last time.'

'I'll phone the owner when I leave here,' Evie says.

'I couldn't save him. Two years later and it would have been a different outcome. And look at the way that gift has been squandered.'

'What gift?' the nurse says, straightening her blanket. Evie has gone.

'Penicillin,' Alice says. 'People have forgotten that all it took was a rose thorn to kill you. Poor PC Alexander. They dish it out like sweeties now. We knew about antimicrobial resistance when we first started treating people with penicillin.'

'There's a growing understanding now,' the nurse says.

'They need to educate the doctors, the people who expect it whenever they have a cold, the farmers who waste it on their animals.'

Later she's propped up in bed, listening to *Woman's Hour*. She still prefers the radio to the TV. The nurse says, 'There's someone to see you.'

'Evie?' Alice says.

'No. A mother and a daughter. They say they found your diary.'

A strange woman and a teenage girl are standing beside her bed. Alice can tell they are mother and daughter, the same green eyes, the same dark hair. The daughter towers above the mother. She can tell from their eyes and the way they carry themselves that they have travelled a difficult road recently. The daughter is dressed in high-waisted trousers and a rayon-crêpe blouse with puffed sleeves. As if she's stepped out of the 1940s. The mother has a kind face. She's wearing a dress which looks just like the one she made when she was seventeen. It looks better on her. For a moment Alice wonders if she has conjured them up from her distant past.

'I'm Jo,' the mother says, 'and this is Jessie. We've brought you the diary you wrote when you were a Penicillin Girl. I found it in one of your handbags. Your granddaughter told us you wanted it returned.' She's holding a battered exercise book in her hand.

The sight of it knocks Alice's breath away. There are such powerful memories inside the covers.

'When we read your entries, we felt as if we'd travelled back in time and experienced all your triumphs and all your sorrows. You helped us both overcome some difficulties in our lives.'

Alice wonders how her teenage words could possibly help anyone, but if they did, she's pleased.

'I hope you don't mind us visiting,' the daughter says. 'We really wanted to meet you.'

Alice looks at the daughter – such a pretty young woman – and holds out her hand. The daughter takes it and smiles. She has smooth soft skin not like the papery stuff on her old body. On her wrist is a bracelet of orange Bakelite beads. 'I would have loved to wear that when I was your age.'

'I want to thank you,' the daughter says. 'I had meningitis and antibiotics saved my life. I'm so sorry they couldn't save

Peter.' She keeps holding her hand and Alice finds it comforting. How odd that this complete stranger knows about Peter. She had thought it would be only Evie who would keep his memory alive. She rather likes that there are others who will remember him.

The daughter is talking again. 'Your diary helped me. I was very depressed when I came home. I was frightened.' She fingers the buttons on her blouse. 'I nearly died, and although I survived, I convinced myself there was another terrible disease waiting to strike me down.' She hesitates. 'When I read about Peter, I realised how lucky I am to live in a time where there are antibiotics.'

She has the look of a survivor. 'I'm glad,' Alice says. 'Don't make the same mistakes I made. Leave a little bit of your heart for forgiveness.'

'You never forgave them, your mother and aunt?' the daughter says.

*How strange* Alice thinks. *What did I write in that diary, such a long time ago?*

The sky is darkening. 'I left it too late …' But the visitors have gone. Did she imagine them? But as she turns her head, she sees her diary on the bedside table tied with a red ribbon. She will ask Evie to read it to her the next time she is here.

She's so tired and Peter is waiting.

'I won't be long,' she says.

# Author's Note

In 1928, Alexander Fleming stumbled across a mould that had antibacterial properties but, unable to isolate the active substance – penicillin – he abandoned work on it. In the 1940s Professor Howard Florey and his team of scientists success-fully extracted penicillin and turned it into a life-saving drug, through ingenuity and sheer determination. The 'Penicillin Girls' were the young women recruited by Professor Howard Florey to harvest penicillin from the mould, *penicillin notatum*. This was laborious work in the uncomfortably warm tem-peratures needed for the mould to thrive. Alice is a fictional Penicillin Girl, but her story is a blend of fact and fiction. I have tried to be historically accurate in the description of the scientists who developed penicillin and the timeline of events that led to its first use in patients. The interaction between Alice and the scientists is, of course, fictional.

# Acknowledgements

I am hugely grateful to Martine, Mick, Domenica and Lesley for their wisdom and inspiration; to Ruth, Lizzie, Hilary and Hillary for their encouragement in my early attempts at creative writing; to Laura, Polly, Beth, Jenny and Phillipa for their advice and feedback on early drafts of the novel.

I thank my editor Gale Winskill for her sage advice and Steve for all his support over the many years this novel has taken to come to fruition. Finally, I thank Dr Helen Umpleby for her invaluable guidance on the treatment of meningitis. All factual errors are mine.

Printed in Great Britain
by Amazon

45166981R00148